Children in Chancery

In the beginning: Robin (5), David (6), Wendy (3), and Felicity (4)
in the garden at the Red House, Aspley Guise, 1952

Children in Chancery

JOY BAKER

TO

DAVID, ROBIN, FELICITY, AND WENDY
because they did it
and to the Lord Chief Justice of England
because, in the end, he said they could.

This edition published 2025
by Living Book Press
Copyright © Joy Baker 1964
New material © Randall Hardy 2025, Juliet English 2025

ISBN: 978-1-76153-903-9 (hardcover)
         978-1-76153-904-6 (softcover)

First published in 1964.

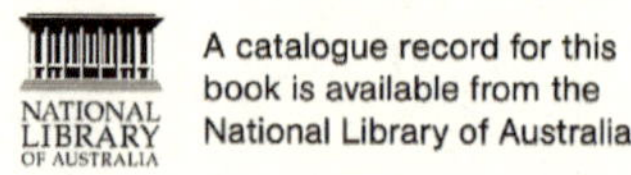
A catalogue record for this book is available from the National Library of Australia

FOREWORD

Randall Hardy - September 2025

<u>Joy Baker - a parent who resisted the State and won!</u>

When Joy Baker decided in 1952 that she would not send her children to school, she probably didn't realise that for most of the following decade she would be harassed by her local councils simply because she had decided to exercise her parental responsibility.

Sixteen years before her battles began, the Butler Act (as the 1944 Education Act is popularly known) had engraved into British law, through Section 36, the natural and historic "duty of parents" to ensure that their children received an education which was suitable to each and every one of them as individuals, whether in school *or otherwise*. It was into the space preserved by that Act that Joy walked, for the sake of her children. By so doing, her family became a direct challenge to the free state school system which was essentially in its infancy, having only been birthed in the late nineteenth century.

In Britain, the Elementary Education Act of 1870, also known as the Foster Act, is seen by many as a milestone marking the point in history where the British Government *assumed responsibility* for providing the nation's children with an education. At the time the majority failed to realise that this was the first legislative step towards shifting agency away from children and their families and handing it over to the State, and still today few understand how this shift has fundamentally changed the perceived purpose of education.

Britain has not been alone in steering this course. Across the Western world a narrative gained strength that ordinary parents were unable to provide their children with an education suitable to the State's objectives. Amanda Spielman for example, speaking as Ofsted's Chief Inspector at Wellington Festival of Education in 2019, stated that 'education' was not simply about equipping children for adult life, but that it was also about the "advancement of civilisation." She continued:

> "Education pioneers across the world knew this as they began to formalise State education systems. The founders of the common school movement in the United States in the nineteenth century wanted to mould fine upstanding citizens of the Republic, as much as they wanted to instil knowledge and a habit of reading and learning."

Across the world today most have unquestioningly accepted state-supervised schooling as the default means of education, despite past evidence that this was not the way to build a strong and stable society. At the end of the nineteenth century here in Britain wealthy families continued to employ 'tutors' to teach their children in their own homes. Boys in such families were commonly educated at home until the age of seven when they were sent to boarding schools, whilst girls usually stayed at home being taught the necessary skills of home management. The late Queen Elizabeth II for example was educated under her parents' supervision at home, and her studies included constitutional history and law. Her parents considered this to be the most *suitable* preparation for her future role as the British monarch. Today's heirs to the throne typically attend school, where they learn many things, of which only a limited number will equip them for royal service in adulthood.

Returning to the Butler Act, the evidence is that parental choice concerning the provision of education was insisted upon mainly by the upper classes, in order to ensure that their children were not herded into schools to receive a one-size-fits-all education.

Joy was born in June 1923 and left school at the age of fifteen, the year before the start of World War II. Later in this book you'll find this summary of her school days, "My eight years at school had been eight years of hell; and I left totally uneducated in all the things that mattered..." That experience more than anything else made her determined to "never condemn my own children to a similar waste of the happiest years of their lives."

She married Peter in the same year as the Butler Act received

Royal Assent. Coincidently, the marriage took place in the same month as the wartime Parliament debated the wording of Section 36 which, as noted above, contained the all-important wording affirming that it is the "duty of parents to secure the education of their children," and that they were able to fulfil that duty "either by regular attendance at school or otherwise."

During this debate on 21 March 1944, a small number of MPs objected to schooling being optional because it would create a "dual system," a split between children of "ordinary folk" and those of "the privileged." The wartime Government of the day however stood its ground, not because it was in the pocket of the wealthy, but because it recognised that otherwise it would be giving the State the complete oversight of every child's education that had enabled Hitler's regime to indoctrinate children by forcing them into schools which taught a single mandatory world-view. Then, as now, the German Basic Law (constitution) asserts that it is the State's duty to *supervise* the education which parents provide for their children; this is strikingly different to the current legal position in Britain.

It was the responsibility of James Ede, the Labour Parliamentary Secretary to the Board of Education, to make clear the then Government's convictions:

> "Let us realise that what the hon. Members are asking is a State monopoly of education. Surely we have seen enough in Europe during the last few years to indicate the danger of that... I do not believe, and the Government do not believe, that they have the right to prescribe the only form of education that shall be given in this country."

Thus was laid the foundation on which Joy would take her stand against those officials who opposed her exercising her responsibilities, and on which electively home educating families still need to stand today.

In my foreword to this republished edition of Joy's book I want to look to the future rather than to the past, but to do this it has been necessary to set her stand in the context of the development of the state education system through which she was living and raising her family. Joy had four children by the time she needed to resist the local authorities' [LA's] attempts to force the older ones into the school system. The family originally lived in Buckinghamshire then moved to Norfolk in 1954. The younger three were born in the late 1950s, whilst she was battling with Norfolk Council.

That her struggles with the authorities began just eight years after the Butler Act was passed is a sobering reminder that politicians and civil servants all have short memories, especially when they find what has gone before to be inconvenient. That is so very true today for even as I write, Labour's Children's Wellbeing and Schools Bill [CWS Bill] is currently being debated in the House of Lords. If the clauses seeking to establish Local Authority registers of Children Not in School [CNIS] are successful, which politically seems inevitable, then those reading this book will be presented with very different challenges to those against which Joy battled for many years. And yet in essence, the underlying issue will remain the same. Joy identified the rationale for her resistance thus:

> "No Act of Parliament is capable of deciding the upbringing and destiny of any individual child, and any Act which restricts the natural right of the parent to care for the child is in breach of a higher law than that of Parliament." [Chap. 18]

The 1944 Act, as explained above, made clear that parents retained their natural duty to provide their children with an education suitable to their needs, but Joy was faced with council officers who believed that parents like her were unable to deliver such an education. In this book she explains their approach as follows:

> "There had been considerable argument about this, as the [Norfolk] Education Committee insisted that the Justices had in fact given their decision on the grounds that the prosecution had failed to prove their case, as opposed to a finding that I had succeeded in proving mine; and in education proceedings, unlike any other legal actions, it is the defendant who has to prove his case."

We are all familiar with that phrase central to the British legal system, "innocent until proven guilty," but here was a local authority pressing for this mother to be held guilty until she could prove her innocence. The courts disagreed with this approach and supported Joy's argument that the LA needed to demonstrate a *failing on her part*, rather than proceeding on the basis of their own unmerited suspicion.

That remained the legal situation in England until the Department for Education [DfE] published revised Elective Home Education Guidance for Local Authorities in 2019. Paragraph 4.2 introduced a new interpretation of Section 436A of the Education Act 1996, which applied it to home educated children. The House of Lords had debated this clause in July 2006, and it is clear from the Hansard record at the time that uppermost in Peers' minds were children in hospitals, custodial care, psychiatric units or those who had been excluded from schools and the like, i.e. those who were known to the authorities but whose needs were being overlooked by them. Consequently the authorities were failing in their responsibilities to provide such children with a suitable education. (I should note at this point that whilst I am primarily discussing the situation in England, this argument has been taken up in Wales and similar ones are being put forward in other parts of the British Isles. Similarly, though originally drafted to apply to England, the CNIS clauses were extended to Wales after the CWS Bill was introduced.)

But now, with sleight of hand regarding the legal terminology, the DfE has turned the focus of s.436A to those children who are out of school through *parental choice*, then weaponised this by empowering LAs to demand that parents *prove* that the education they are providing is suitable not to the child but to the State - a reversal of the decision which Joy achieved through her years of struggle. Ironically, the guidance states:

> "Until a local authority *is satisfied* that a home-educated child is receiving a suitable full-time education, then a child being educated at home is potentially in scope of this duty. The department's children missing education statutory guidance for local authorities applies. However, this should not be taken as implying that it is the responsibility of parents

under s.436A to 'prove' that education at home is suitable. A proportionate approach needs to be taken." [emphasis mine]

Since the 2019 guidance came into force, there has been just one judicial review of how it is being implemented by a particular LA. Whilst that case failed, it is important to note that in his judgment Mr Justice Lane made clear that the case had "not challenged the lawfulness" of the Guidance. That said, the Government, along with many LAs, now assumes that it has now been established that it is necessary for parents to *demonstrate* to a council employee that the education they are providing to their child/children is suitable. At the same time the caveat in the above quotation regarding the need for a "proportionate approach" is not taken too seriously by many LAs. Some convey the impression that the DfE has commissioned them to get as many children as possible into school.

One thing which the CWS Bill will not have changed, if it has been enacted by the time you are reading this, is that ultimately it is the *courts* which will examine both the evidence of failure to provide an education suitable to the child as presented by the prosecution when a parent fails to comply with a School Attendance Order [SAO], as well as the evidence of provision offered by the parents. Local authority employees will *not* have superseded the courts.

That said, once the relevant provisions are enacted, the big change will be that LAs will be empowered to issue SAOs based not on a suggestion that a child is not being provided with an education suitable to their needs, but because parents failed to register the child as being home educated or to update any changes in their educational provision within the very tight time limits presently proposed. What the impact of this change will be is difficult to determine in advance, but it can be guaranteed that this will become the default policy position in many councils.

When placed alongside the shift in emphasis embedded in the 2019 Guidance, then the level of surveillance enabled by the Bill as it stands will be significantly greater than anything previously faced. Whilst there may be opportunity for a legal challenge to the relevant parts of the Act, or perhaps to the new statutory guidance which has to be published ahead of enactment, a favourable outcome cannot be guaranteed.

In 2010 when the clauses concerning the creation of home education registers were removed from Ed Balls' Children, Schools and Families Bill, it was obvious to those willing to face the facts that, given time, the same proposals would be reintroduced. Sadly, many home educators took their eyes off the political ball and were unprepared when the negative narrative around home education began to gain traction in 2015. Nor were they on guard in 2017 when Labour Peer, Lord Soley, introduced his Private Member's Bill with the same objectives. The lesson which must now be taken seriously is that if, for some unconnected reason the current Bill fails to become law, that will not be the end of the matter. The same proposals will be resurrected sooner or later.

Now therefore is the time for today's home educating families to learn important lessons from Joy Baker's resistance to the State's repeated attempts to force her children into school.

Joy sought to do her best by her children many years before the existence of emails and social media, both of which are commonplace today. She also did this at a time when there were no local or national support groups to advise her and guide her through the decade of battles she faced. She was not the only home education pioneer of that time, but the others were spread far and wide and were unlikely to be known to one another. It was some time later when home educating families began to connect, and initially that would more likely be via Royal Mail or telephone than in person. Whatever challenges those families faced then, for the most part they needed to stand on their own feet rather than leaning on others.

It is impossible to read this book without looking back in time, but I want to encourage readers to learn from Joy's commitment to her children and her determination to do what she believed was the best for them, and then to look to the future. Doing what you believe is best for your children is a privilege which should be protected for all parents, no matter how varied their convictions are. Joy knew it was her responsibility rather than the State's to prepare her children for adult life, and she was determined not to surrender this. That is why she stood firm, risking having the children taken from her and fighting for their return when they were.

In closing, I pose these questions to every home educating

parent who picks up this book some sixty or more years after Joy's final vindication in a hearing before the Lord Chief Justice on 17 July 1962. What if there were no home education support groups to stand with you? What if you were one of the few home educating families left? What if like Joy and her family you had to resist the State's desire to undermine your parental responsibilities without others to cheer you on? Would you stand firm until you were vindicated?

In the run-up to writing this foreword I have spoken on several occasions to parents, asking them to think through what type of home educator they are. The options I have set before them have been "conviction or convenience?" By the time you have read what follows, I'm sure you will know that Joy was true to her convictions. It seems to me that going forward, parents will be need to be convinced that parental responsibility is too important a matter to exchange for the option of a quiet life.

I close with Joy's own words:

> "The place for a child to be brought up and trained is in the home; instruction is only part of education and should be given to suit the individual and not forced on the mass. The Act does not require children to receive full-time *instruction*; and efficient full-time *education*, as here defined, can only be given in a child's home." [Chap. 8, emphasis original.]

Foreword for new edition of Children in Chancery by Joy Baker

Juliet English – September 2025
(Home educating parent and Learn Free Home Educators
Conference co-ordinator)

Moving to the UK from South Africa in 2007, Joy Baker was not someone I had heard of until we had lived here for some years. The brief snippets told to me about her sparked genuine curiosity! Who was this woman who educated her children at home in the 1950's and 1960's? What led her to challenge conventional norms? How did we come to know her story, and why does her story resonate still today?

I soon learned about her book, "Children in Chancery," which chronicles Joy's struggles with her local authority as she fought for the right to educate her children herself—a concept almost unheard of at the time. Joy's conviction was unwavering, as captured in her words: "The place for a child to be brought up and trained is in the home; instruction is only part of education and should be given to suit the individual and not forced on the mass." (Ch. 7)

It took perseverance and some expense to finally obtain a copy of her then out-of-print book, but the effort was rewarded by the insight it offered. What struck me most was Joy's eloquent defense of her beliefs about what children truly need to thrive. Through her family's experiences and the obstacles they faced from a local authority unable to grasp the idea of home education, it becomes clear how little has changed in the decades since. Misunderstanding, prejudice, and condescension from well-meaning officials remain familiar challenges to this day.

Joy's repeated confrontations with her local authority were never intended to set a precedent. She was simply a parent defending her rights against strangers who thought they knew better—and she refused to back down. Accounts describe Joy as determined and formidable, with a strong sense of justice—someone who would chase hunting parties off her land and stand up to poachers. It's no surprise she took her parental responsibilities so personally and so seriously. As she puts it: "It simply did not occur to me that the education and upbringing of my children, provided they did not run wild, were not illiterate, and conducted themselves as civilized members of society, could be anything to do with anyone but myself – still less that it could concern some department of the State." (Ch.1)

Over the years, as more people discovered Joy's book, its relevance to the ongoing conversation around home education grew. Many now see her story as marking the start of the "modern" home education movement. Joy became a symbol of ordinary parents standing up for the fundamental right to choose how the children they have birthed and raised should be educated.

Reading "Children in Chancery" left me wondering about the Baker children themselves. Where are they now? What lives have they led? My curiosity led to research, and thanks to social media, I was able to connect with a family member. It was a privilege to learn about Joy as a mother and grandmother, but also as a living, breathing person steadfast in her convictions. I was also able to share with them how her book continues to inspire others to "hold the line" when it comes to resisting state pressure and preserving educational freedom.

Some may be reassured to know that the Baker children have gone on to live happy, productive lives, achieving and contributing to society. Nevertheless, the years of harassment and negative portrayal by local authorities took their toll.

It is fitting that "Children in Chancery" is back in print at a time when government proposals threaten to tighten regulations on home education. Joy's story is a timely reminder of our responsibility as parents: to protect our children's childhoods, to nurture them in a caring environment, and to educate them in the ways that help them flourish. For many, school is a good and positive choice, but it should remain just that—a choice. Years of evidence now show that, not only does home education work, but it works well for most children. Some families come to home education not out of choice, but out of necessity for the wellbeing of their children, making the protection of educational choice more important than ever in the UK.

If you are now holding a copy of "Children in Chancery" in your hands, may you be inspired by the articulate voice of Joy Baker, reminding us that as parents, it is up to us to continue to define the clear boundaries between parent and state responsibility in respect of our children.

What does Chancery mean?
This is a question I had about the title of the book. This term is no longer in common use and appears to have a variety of applications. From what I've been able to glean, in the context of Joy Baker's book title, "chancery" may mean something similar to a child being a ward of the court.

A Note from the Author's Children

As adults, we look back with deep gratitude and admiration for the tremendous fight, determination, and courage our mother showed. With little or no help, she carried the burden single-handedly and never once wavered in her beliefs. We could not be more proud of her.

At the same time, we cannot help but feel deep anger and resentment toward the local education authorities for the stress and anxiety they caused, and most of all for the precious time they took from our mother during the most important years of our lives.

We extend our warmest wishes to all home educators for the future and hope that many will be encouraged and strengthened by her example.

Contents

ILLUSTRATIONS

Chancery

Under the law of Chancery, when a child becomes a ward of the court, the High Court takes control. Every major decision—where they live, how they're raised—requires court approval. They may remain in a parent's care, but the final say belongs to the Court.

I

The Law and I

IN THE YEAR 1944, two major events took place in my life, although I was not aware of it at the time. The present Education Act and my eldest son, David, have one thing in common—they were both conceived in the same year. Fortunately, perhaps for my peace of mind, I had no idea to what extent they were going to run foul of each other in the years ahead.

Six years earlier, at the age of fifteen, I had left school myself with the fixed determination that I would never condemn my own children to a similar waste of the happiest years of their lives. My eight years at school had been eight years of hell, and I left totally uneducated in all the things that mattered, with nothing to show for my schooling except an ineradicable horror of being in a crowd.

I had been a shy, nervous child, easily cast down by criticism or jeers, oversensitive to the opinions of others; my outlook and behavior must have been different from those of other children of my age, and to be 'different' in school is to be considered silly, to be made an outcast, to be the butt of everyone's tormenting. I could not mix happily with other children; from my earliest memories, I was shy and uncomfortable with others of my own age, who seemed to move in a world of which I had no knowledge, to find amusement in things that, for me, held no laughter, and to care nothing for the things that mattered to me.

I realized later that the burden of my being 'different' was only a desire to be myself, whereas most children seem to be imbued from the start of their school days with a desire to become part of an inseparable mass, in which being like everybody else is the highest aim; and that anyone wanting to be an individual in this mass needs to have a very thick skin and an overdeveloped ego, neither of which I possessed. This is, of course, why so many previously likable small children do tend to become truculent and bullying as soon as they start school.

All the fragile world of my childhood, with its idyllic background of an old-fashioned country garden, peopled for me with animals and birds and flowers and the endless fabric of my imagination, was suddenly exposed to what seemed to me a howling mob of strangers; and my daydreams, which were deeply rooted and very precious to me, seemed about as secure as the head of a French aristocrat on the way to the guillotine. Throughout every moment of my eight years of school, I felt myself to be under attack, surrounded by an unreal world of potential enemies and present hostility. To assume that any child could receive a proper education under such circumstances was patently absurd, and its main effect was, in fact, to leave me predisposed to be suspicious and defensive towards all interference by an artificial authority.

What I actually learned during those years was negligible. In all the endless hours sitting in grubby classrooms waiting for the miserable day to end, I succeeded only in falling into the pattern in which I was originally made, but painfully and against opposition. My ability in botany stemmed from my early interest in animals and growing things; out of the fascination I felt for words and my need for self-expression came my achievements in English. I remained virtually untouched by chemistry, foreign languages, and mathematics; neither history nor geography ever came to life for me until after I left school. I never learned to mix with others, and while I was at school, I never acquired sufficient confidence in myself to make life endurable. At the end of my school days, I was looking back on a hopeless patchwork of things half-learned, forgotten, and never understood. I spent the next five years finding confidence in myself again, consolidating the things I could do, and throwing out the things I could not—going back, in fact, to take up my own education from the point at which it had become mutilated at school.

In March 1944, I married Peter Shaw Baker, then editor of

Animal Pictorial, in Richmond, Surrey, whom I had met after being for many years a contributor to that magazine. By the time that my eldest son had reached 'school age,' my marriage had begun breaking up, on rocks that do not enter into this chronicle; so, during my ensuing resistance to the education authorities, I was for the most part entirely alone with the children, as a result of my husband's enforced absences from home, his unfortunate state of health, and our eventual complete separation. But although he took no active part in my seven years' struggle, my husband did, in fact, entirely agree with my views on our children's education, his personal experience of schooling having been as unhappy as my own.

At the time when I married and started my family, my memories and my opinion of school education were quite clear-cut and unequivocal. At worst, it was a system of child destruction, or at least destruction of individuality; at best, it was a waste of time.

My own school education had been instigated, with the best of intentions, by my parents, who felt, like so many other people without really knowing why, that children ought to go to school. But had my parents decided to educate me entirely at home—which they afterwards agreed would have been, in my case, a far better course—they would have been legally entitled to do so. Under the impression that we were a free country, and being too occupied with the birth of my first child to take much interest in the latest Education Act—which, in any case, I would have supposed would be reasonably interpreted—I had no idea of the extent to which the law had been changed. I assumed that I had the right, as my parents had had, to decide when, where, and how I educated my own children; and it would have seemed fantastic to me at that time that this now constituted a criminal offense.

My two elder sons, David and Robin, were aged six and five when, early in the year 1952, they first attracted the attention of the education authorities. This initial encounter was in the shape of a visit from the School Attendance Officer—now euphemistically termed the Welfare Officer—which I would have regarded as an unwarrantable intrusion if I had taken it seriously, but which appeared to me only an example of senseless officiousness, as I did not.

I was still unacquainted with the terms of the 1944 Education

Act; but I knew that, although education in some form was required by law during my own childhood, I was nevertheless kept at home until the age of seven and later kept away from school for a period of nearly a year without any government officials calling on my parents; and I was perfectly sure what kind of reception they would have gotten from my father if they had. It simply did not occur to me that the education and upbringing of my children, provided they did not run wild, were not illiterate, and conducted themselves as civilized members of society, could be anything to do with anyone but myself—still less that it could concern some department of the State. I still believed, indeed, that such a position would be the very reverse of all that this country stood for; and the Welfare Officer, on this and several subsequent visits, therefore received very short shrift.

At the end of July 1952, the Bedfordshire Director of Education wrote to 'respectfully draw my attention' to Section 36 of the Education Act, 'which lays the duty upon the parent of every child of compulsory school age to cause him to receive efficient full-time education suitable to his age, ability, and aptitude.'

'In this connection,' he concluded, 'and in view of the lack of information offered to my Welfare Officer when he recently called upon you, I am entitled to ask what arrangements are being made for the education of your two sons.'

To this, I replied that it was my intention to provide my sons with their education at home. I then received a further letter from the Director of Education.

'It is noticed,' he wrote, 'that it is your intention to provide tuition at home for your two sons. To give effect to the law of education, it is essential that efficient full-time education be provided, and the responsibility for its provision rests upon the parent. I must therefore request that a copy of the timetable and scheme of work which your sons will follow, together with the qualifications of the tutor, be submitted for the approval of the Local Education Authority.'

This appeared to me to be substantially ridiculous. If the responsibility rested on the parent—a statement with which I entirely agreed—then, provided there was no reason to suppose the parent was shiftless or irresponsible, there could be no occasion for interference by the State. Further, the request for 'timetable, scheme of work, and qualifications of tutor' with regard to children still in the nursery seemed to me utterly absurd. I was myself taught by my mother, who had no 'qualifications' whatever, until I was seven, and was then ahead of other children of my age when I started school. With what I felt was commendable restraint, I replied:

'I am in receipt of your letter of the 6th of August and would inform you that my two sons are receiving, and will continue to receive, efficient education suitable to their age, ability, and aptitude. If you have any reason to suppose this not to be the case, doubtless you will proceed as authorized.

'Before answering any further questions on the matter, I would be glad if you would forward me a copy of the Education Act of 1944, under which I understand your authority lies.'

To this, the Director of Education replied:

'I have received your letter dated the 7th of August 1952, and I would respectfully point out that the Local Education Authority must be satisfied that your children are being educated according to the law, and the onus of proof rests upon the parent.

'I do not supply copies of the Education Act, but a copy might be obtained at any of Her Majesty's Stationery Offices.'

This concluded the first stage of the battle. I still did not take it seriously; they were my children, and I did not see what it had to do with the State.

I had at this time no clear-cut idea of a personal system of education; I remembered only the misery of my own schooldays, and I would not risk my children suffering in the same way. It seemed to me that the whole school system was wrong; children should grow up and acquire basic learning in their own homes and then study individual subjects in which they showed an interest and aptitude at a later age when their minds were ready for concentrated mental work. They should not spend their most impressionable years getting physical cramp and mental indigestion in the unnatural surroundings of school.

I believed, too, that children could, in any case, absorb knowledge only when their minds were ready for it; and that they would reach out for knowledge as they were ready for it, without any need for enforced instruction in class. I had my first example of this when

David was four, and he stopped suddenly during a walk through the village to look at a 'W' carved on the wall of a building. 'What is that?' he demanded. 'I've seen things like it in books!'

But I did not feel that any of this would interest the Director of Education, so I did not reply to his letter of the 13th of August, and I heard nothing more for the next six months.

Meanwhile, David and Robin, with their two sisters—Felicity and Wendy, then aged four and three—were living the kind of life that I had been brought up to regard as right and proper for children of their age. They had a large, old-fashioned garden in which to play and, adjoining it, a field with a little wood at one end. I had let the grazing to a farmer from the next village, and on the field were four Jersey cows, a mare with foal, and several ponies. All four children played with the cows, sitting on their backs and feeding them with chestnut leaves; when the farmer came to look at the animals, he gave the children rides on the ponies, and they were playing in the field when, one evening in late spring, the foal was born. Felicity especially loved the horses; David spent most of his time with the cows.

They had a large nursery indoors and a varied assortment of toys and an even more varied assortment of what we called 'things'—the odd pieces of wood and metal, broken toys and items of furniture, and so on—that accumulate in any household, and which occupy children so much more effectively than ordinary toys; and I believed were much more effective than schoolroom teaching in developing their imagination, inventive powers, creative ability, and the practical application of ideas. With these, they would build a boat or an airplane one day, a farmyard or a house the next, and I never prompted or interfered with their play, preferring to watch their minds expanding, like opening buds, rather than trying to pull the petals out before they were ready to flower.

During this winter, I started teaching David to read, obtaining various school reading books for the purpose, but I soon found that the process was useless; he made no real progress, often being unable to remember words he had read five minutes before, and was soon distressed and bored. I found, too, that the words and phrases used in these learning-to-read books, being chosen in order to group together words with the same sounds, bore no relation to ordinary speech, and this caused the children nothing but confusion until I explained what the right word really was. In the end, I gave the children the books to play with and got instead the Pooh books by A. A. Milne and Kenneth Grahame's *The Wind in the Willows*, which I read to them every night; and I abandoned reading lessons altogether. David then frequently came to me wanting to know the meaning of a word he had picked out in one of the books, and I found that these words he remembered and understood.

It seemed obvious to me that David was simply not yet ready to read; neither he nor Robin had reached the point at which they felt any sustained interest in words or had acquired any real ability to concentrate. And in any case, although I myself had learned to read at the age of five, I do not think I gained any advantage from this whatever; in fact, it caused me a good deal of suffering, as throughout my childhood, I was always having nightmares from which I awoke in terror, unable to free my mind from some frightening or unhappy episode which I had read during the day. No one can tell, unfortunately, what is going to appear frightening to any particular child, and a great many children's books, although appearing quite innocuous to an adult mind, may have quite a different effect on the sensitive imagination of a child under ten. The more I considered the matter, the less could I see any advantage in learning to read not only until the child's mind was readily able to absorb the idea of reading but until it was able also to comfortably digest what had been read.

So David and Robin continued to grow up and develop in their own way; they investigated words and numbers in their own time and drew letters and figures for amusement on rainy days; they asked endless questions about everything they thought of and played with great energy and enthusiasm; and they never awoke crying in the night. None of which, apparently, met with the approval of the education authorities.

2

Into Battle

In march 1953, the Bedfordshire Director of Education opened a fresh offensive by sending me two copies of a printed notice, in respect of David and Robin, headed: 'notice to parent of failure of duty regarding education of child.'

'whereas [it continued] under the Education Act 1944, it is the duty of the parent of every child of compulsory school age to cause the child to receive efficient full-time education suitable to his (her) age, ability, and aptitude, either by regular attendance at school or otherwise;

'and whereas it appears to the Bedfordshire County Council, being the Local Education Authority for the area, that you are the parent of a child of compulsory school age living at Aspley Guise in the area of the Authority and are failing to perform the duty imposed on you as set out above;

'you are hereby required, within fourteen days from the service of this notice upon you, to satisfy the said Authority that the said child is receiving efficient full-time education suitable to his (her) age, ability, and aptitude, either by regular attendance at school or otherwise.'

To this, I replied: 'I am in receipt of your printed communications of the 20th of March referring to the education of my sons, David and Robin.

'I have already repeatedly informed you and your representatives, in response to numerous calls and communications, that it is not my intention to send my sons to school at the present time and that they are receiving efficient education suitable to their age, ability, and aptitude in their own home.

'I would be glad if you would inform me what reasons you have for stating that it 'appears to you' that this is not the case. Perhaps you would also be good enough to inform me how long it has been the practice of the education authorities to conduct what amounts to a deliberate persecution of the parents of young children in this way, without any grounds or foundation whatever? I would suggest that the money spent by the Council on enabling your representatives to travel round in cars for this purpose would be better used to improve the standard of education in the Council schools, which at present leaves much to be desired, judging by what I have seen of the results.'

In response to this, I received a lengthy letter from the Clerk of the Bedfordshire County Council, stating:

'The County Director of Education has consulted me about his correspondence with you about the education of your two children, Robin and David. Having read this correspondence carefully, it seems to me that there has been some misunderstanding, and I am therefore writing to you to try to clear it up.

'As you know, Parliament has stated quite clearly that it is the duty of the parent or guardian of every child between five and fifteen years of age to see that he is educated in a proper manner, whether in school or not (§36 Education Act, 1944). At the same time, Parliament has given the County Council the not always pleasant duty of seeing that parents fulfil this obligation (Ibid., §37).

'The County Council's task presents little difficulty when the parents send their children to recognized schools; it is only a question of ensuring regular attendance. But many parents prefer to educate their children at home by private tuition, and it is then the duty of the Council to satisfy themselves as to the adequacy of the tuition provided. Parents are usually able to do this either by inviting a visit from the Council representatives so that they may see the sort of education the children are receiving or by sending to the Council a copy of the timetable and the schedule of work, and specimen.

'May I emphasize that there is no suggestion that you or any other parents are wrong in deciding to educate your children otherwise than in school. It is only that the Council is put upon their inquiry when children do not attend school and have to ask parents to give full information about the adequacy of the education being provided. It is the inescapable duty of the Council to decide whether they consider it to be adequate or not, and this they cannot do if the parents give no details of the education that the children are receiving or merely reply that 'the education is adequate.'

'In the absence of detailed information, the Council is bound to assume that the education is inadequate and to take the steps which Parliament has prescribed for such cases. I enclose copies of Sections 36 and 37 of the Education Act, 1944, so that you may see what these steps are.

'I am hoping that this explanation will convince you that in writing to you to ask for information about the education you are giving your children, there has never been any intention to criticize or to interfere in any way beyond what is laid down in the Education Act, 1944. I hope also that you will agree that the simplest way to conclude the matter is either to permit a visit by one of the Officers of the County Council or, if this is distasteful to you, to send to Mr. Lucking (the Director of Education) here at the Shire Hall copies of your children's timetable, schedule of work, and specimens of their notebooks.'

What annoyed me most about this letter, as it had in the earlier correspondence, was the apparently automatic dismissal of any statement made by the parent regarding the child's education, as if this must necessarily be worthless. Basing my approach on the law prevailing in my own childhood, I appreciated that it might be the Authority's duty to inquire into the education being given to any child not attending a recognized school; but I was totally unable to accept the position where a straightforward assurance in answer to such an inquiry was discounted as being insufficient. I could not understand a law that gave to paid Government officials the right to disregard a reasonable statement made by someone whose word they had no reason to doubt—a statement concerning that person's own home and child. It seemed to me that this amounted to putting me on trial for a criminal offense without any evidence having to be produced that any offense had ever been committed.

I resented the unavoidable implication that my word was worthless and the arbitrary sweeping away of all the normal elemental rights and responsibilities of parenthood. In short, the correspondence got my back up, and the soothing phrases in which the Clerk of the Council's letter was couched did nothing to get it down again. Without, at that stage, having any idea of the full extent of what we were up against, I began to see education as an inexorable net closing in on David and Robin, drawing them into the maelstrom of misery which would distort and destroy their golden days—the shadow of which was already approaching Felicity and Wendy as they played unaware in the sun. My children were threatened, my defenses were up, and the ensuing battle only intensified the determination of my resistance.

I replied to the Clerk of the Council:

'I thank you for your letter of the 9th of April, referring to the matter of the education of my sons, Robin and David. I thank you also for sending me a copy of the relevant sections of the Education Act, 1944, which, as you will see from the previous correspondence in this matter, I first asked for (and was refused) nine months ago.

'I have perused the copy of this Act and your letter with care, but I am still unable to find any answer to the question in my letter to the Director of Education of March 21st—namely, *what reason* have the Education Committee for stating, in the notices served on me by them, that 'it appears' to them that my sons are not receiving adequate education?'

'The Education Act (Section 37, Para. I) only requires the local education authorities to serve such a notice upon a parent 'if it *appears to them* that the parent is failing to perform the duty imposed upon him by the foregoing section,' which (Section 36) provides that the child shall receive efficient education, 'at school or otherwise.'

'I have already informed you—not once, but repeatedly, both verbally and by letter—in response to your enquiries, that my sons are in fact receiving efficient education in their own home. May I then ask *why*, having been given this information, the Education

Committee should state that 'it appears to them' that such is not the case? May I ask them to state what grounds, if any, they have for stating that 'it appears to them' that my statements are incorrect?

'Your statement that 'in the absence of detailed information the Council are bound to assume that the education is inadequate' is obviously absurd—and it is not mentioned in the Act; nor can I find any provision under the Act for any such inspection or supervision of the work of a child at home as you now say you require. The Act requires the parent only to 'satisfy' the authorities that the child is receiving adequate education. What constitutes 'satisfaction' on this point is, apparently, left to the Education Committee to decide.

'What I wish to be informed of, therefore, is on what grounds the Committee have decided that, in this case, my statements in the matter are not sufficient to satisfy them—and what reasons they have for maintaining, in the face of my statements to the contrary, that 'it appears' that the children are not receiving adequate education at home.

'I was brought up in the belief (now rapidly diminishing) that this is a 'free' country, in which the State makes no unreasonable interference in the lives of its citizens. I claim, therefore, the right to bring up and educate my children according to my own methods, standards, and beliefs; and I regard your persistent demands as an unwarrantable intrusion into our lives. I was myself taught in my own home for a considerable period of my childhood, without any query, inspection, or investigation on the part of the local authorities.

'I have already informed you that my sons are receiving—and it is my intention that they should receive—efficient and suitable education in their home; and any School Attendance Order served on me in respect of them will be disregarded. If this makes me guilty of any 'offence,' I am quite prepared to deal with the consequences. Meanwhile, I would suggest that some lessons in courtesy would improve the education already received by your officers. I see no reason why my statements regarding my sons' education should fail to satisfy the Education Committee; and I am not prepared to amplify the statements I have already made until and unless you can inform me of your reasons for refusing to accept them.'

In response to this, I received, on April 16th, two more copies of the 'NOTICE TO PARENT OF FAILURE OF DUTY REGARDING EDUCATION OF CHILD.'

I wrote again to the Director of Education:

'I have been awaiting a reply to my letter of the 10th to the Clerk of the County Council—but I have received in this morning's post two further printed notices repeating the unfounded and (since it now appears obvious that you are quite unable to justify them) rather stupid assertions that 'it appears' to you that my sons are not receiving adequate education.

'If these are intended as an answer to my letters, it seems indeed strange that an education authority should be unable to reply to a plain and straightforward question in simple English, but must resort to the continual repetition of meaningless printed forms. I still await a reply to my letter of the 10th and wish to state clearly that until and unless I receive it, these and any other similar notices will be treated with the contempt which they—and their senders—merit.'

On April 21st, the Clerk of the County Council replied:

'I refer to your letter of the 10th April addressed to me and also to your letter of the 16th April addressed to the Director of Education. I confirm that the formal notices sent to you pursuant to Section 37 (I) of the Education Act, 1944, were in reply to your letter of the 10th April. The formal notices were not accompanied by any other letter because I had given a very full explanation of the position in my letter of the 9th April, and any further explanation could only be a repetition of that letter.

'I can only say that, in view of your apparent reluctance to give the Authority any information about the nature or efficiency of the education which you say you are providing, the Authority are bound to serve upon you notices under Sub-Section I of Section 37, and if you fail to satisfy the Authority within the fifteen days specified in the notice, the Authority may well decide to serve upon you School Attendance Orders requiring you to cause the children to become registered pupils at a school to be named in the Order. You would then have an opportunity of choosing which school you prefer, subject to the right of the Authority to appeal to the Minister if they do not agree with your choice.

'Although it is no part of the County Council's duty to provide you with copies of the Acts of Parliament, which, as you had previously been informed, are obtainable from Her Majesty's Stationery Office, I supplied you, as a matter of courtesy, with copies of Sections 36 and 37 of the Education Act, 1944. These are not the only sections relating to the question of compulsory attendance at schools, and I suggest that you should obtain for yourself a copy of the Act or consult your legal advisers. I would draw your attention to the provisions of Section 40 of the Act, which deals with matters relating to legal proceedings in the case of persons guilty of offences under Sub-Section 5 of Section 37.'

To this, I replied:

'I am in receipt of your letter of the 21st, from which it appears, in the midst of a good deal of verbiage and threats, that you are, in fact, unable or unwilling to answer the perfectly reasonable and pertinent questions put to you in my letter of April 10th.

'Such a state of affairs in a supposedly responsible authority needs no further comment from me to emphasize its absurdity. I have nothing to add to my letter of the 10th, to which I am still awaiting a reply. If you feel that it will be of any benefit to take such proceedings as you refer to against me—based on an entirely unfounded statement which you are quite unable to substantiate—by all means, do so. Any such proceedings will certainly form an interesting addition to my sons' education.'

The Clerk of the County Council replied to this:

'I hardly know how to reply to your letter of the 24th April, since if I am brief, you will doubtless regard me as rude, whilst if I take the trouble to explain the position to you in detail, you will describe it as verbiage.

'The position simply is that the County Council have got to be satisfied that your sons are being properly educated, and if you will not provide the necessary information, the Committee will have to consider instructing the School Attendance Officer to take the usual proceedings. I felt that it would be much more in your sons' interests that you should have a friendly discussion with someone who has the boys' welfare at heart than that we should incur the expense and unpleasantness of court proceedings, but if you are not willing to help, I fail to see how the Council can otherwise discharge their statutory responsibilities.'

To this, I replied:

'I am in receipt of your letter of the 25th and can only say that it seems to me very strange that you should apparently have so much difficulty in replying to the points raised in my letter of April 10th. I am already in possession of all the facts as stated by you in this and previous letters, and frankly, I can see no reason for so much useless repetition.

'You have already received my assurance that my sons are, in fact, receiving adequate education. I, on my part, have done all that seems to me reasonably necessary, or required by the Act (so far as you have had the courtesy to acquaint me with the text of this) to satisfy you in this matter. If you require anything further, I have asked only to be informed of your reasons for refusing to accept the statements I have made. If you are indeed forced, under the Act, to set aside assurances made by parents regarding their children's education, I would be obliged if you would quote the relevant passages requiring you to do so. If this is not the case, may I have your reasons for refusing to accept my statements as sufficient satisfaction on this point?

'I would add that I have at no time been approached with a view to any 'friendly discussion with someone who has the boys' welfare at heart.' The only representative of the Education Authority who has called to see me has been, on all occasions, most offensive.'

The Clerk of the County Council then wrote:

'In reply to your letter of the 28th April, I know that you are satisfied that your sons are being properly educated, but the point is that the County Council must be satisfied. When they know the facts, they might well share your view, but until they know how your sons are being educated, they are unable to form their own opinion. Since you decline to give this information, it does not seem that there is much point in continuing this correspondence.'

And I replied:

'I am in receipt of your letter of the 30th April, in which I notice you make no attempt to reply to my letter of the 28th.

'There seems to be nothing further I can do, therefore, except to refer you again to my letter of April 10th and leave it to you to decide whether it is better to give a direct answer to the points raised in this letter or to take these continually threatened proceedings against me.'

Shortly after this, two School Attendance Orders requiring David and Robin to attend the village school were served on me, and I tore them into small pieces and sent them back to the Education Authority.

At the beginning of June, I was summoned to appear in Woburn Magistrates' Court. There was no one with whom I could leave the four children at home, and obviously, I could not take them all with me to the court, which was four miles away. On the advice of my solicitor, Mr. E. T. Ray of Leighton Buzzard, I therefore wrote to the Justices' Clerk:

'With reference to the two summonses served on me under the Education Act 1944, in which I am charged with failing to comply with School Attendance Orders in respect of my sons, David and Robin, to be heard at the Town Hall, Woburn, on June 26th, 1953, I would be glad if you would put this letter before the Magistrates.

'I wish to be excused from attending the court in view of the difficulty of doing so with my four children and would therefore ask the Magistrates to deal with the case in my absence.

'I do not admit the truth of the information, and I plead not guilty. I am not sending my sons to school, and I do not intend to do so, as they are receiving efficient and suitable education in their own home.'

The result of this was that I was convicted, as anticipated, and fined £1 for each of the two children; but, as Mr. Ray had told me, my plea of not guilty gave me the right to appeal against the decision. Mr. Ray again advised me on the details of procedure, and I immediately gave formal notice of appeal.

3

Yet the Evening Listens

THERE WAS a delay of nearly three months before my appeal
was due to be heard; and in that time, a number of other changes
had taken place in our lives. We had moved from Aspley Guise,
so that the School Attendance Orders naming that village school
could no longer remain in force; and, as we had also moved out
of Bedfordshire, we were no longer in the area of the Bedfordshire
Education Authority. In these circumstances, I did not contest the
appeal, and it was therefore automatically dismissed.

In September 1953, we moved temporarily to Haddenham,
near Aylesbury, and then to St. Leonards, near Chesham, in Buckinghamshire. There, I received two letters, one from the Divisional
Education Officer at Amersham and one from the Chief Education
Officer at Aylesbury.

The Divisional Education Officer wrote on February 8th, 1954,
what was apparently a purely routine letter, asking why my children
did not appear to be attending school, pointing out that the law
required all children between the ages of five and fifteen to go to
school, and requesting an immediate reply so that this could be
considered by the Divisional Education Committee.

But by then, I had already heard from the Chief Education
Officer, who wrote on February 5th:

'I am directed by the Buckinghamshire Local Authority to state
that the Authority are of the opinion that your children, David,
Robin, and Felicity, are not receiving efficient full-time education
suitable to their age, ability, and aptitude, and that it is expedient
that the children should attend school.

'The Authority, therefore, propose to serve upon you, under the provisions of Section 37(2) of the Education Act, 1944, School Attendance Orders, which will require you to cause the children to become registered pupils at particular schools to be named in the Order. If you fail to comply with the Order, you will be guilty of an offence, and it will be the duty of the Authority to take proceedings against you.

'You have the right under Section 37 of the Act (which is set out in full for your convenience) to select the school which you want each of your children to attend. It is therefore open to you at any time up to fifteen days from the date of this letter to notify the Authority of the name of the schools which you want your children to attend.

'The Authority consider the following school suitable for your children:

St. Leonards C. of E. Primary School.

If you select this school, this will be the school named in the Order. If you would prefer some other school, you may indicate its name, but the Authority will then have to consider whether the school chosen by you is suitable, and also, in cases where this question arises, whether unreasonable expense would be involved. If they are not satisfied, they may decide to refer the matter to the Minister of Education, who has power to direct what school shall be named in the Order.

'If you do not choose any school, or do not reply to this letter within fifteen days of the date of despatch, the Authority will proceed to make an Order, inserting the name of St. Leonards C. of E. Primary School in the case of each child.'

A copy of Section 37 of the Education Act, 1944, was attached.

This could hardly have demonstrated more clearly the futility of the high-sounding phrases of the Education Act. The Education Committee apparently considered itself fitted to set aside the judgment of the parent and decide the 'ability and aptitude' of every child in its area; the school 'considered suitable' by the Authority being simply the school for that age group nearest to the child's home. The Authority made its decisions without any knowledge of the children concerned; I had already made my own observations of the product of the primary schools.

On February 20th, I replied:

'Reference your letter of February 5th, I am not sending my children to school, and it is not my intention to do so. I am, as you are already aware, educating the children at home.

'I object most strongly to state-imposed education, and I will not permit my children to be exposed to the compulsory religious teaching, bad manners, uncleanliness, and ignorance of all real knowledge which appears to constitute education at school. To subject them to this would be detrimental to their well-being, and I refuse to do so.

'Any School Attendance Order served on me will be ignored. If it is your duty to take proceedings against me for caring for my own children, do so and be damned to you.'

The Chief Education Officer replied to this with a request for details of the children's work and an approximate timetable. He referred to a visit which he said had been made by his assistant, Mrs. Davies, while we were at Haddenham, and suggested that Mrs. Davies might come to see me and discuss the question of the children's education, but if I wanted her to do this, I must make an appointment within fourteen days. The Committee must, he said, be fully satisfied that the children were receiving education suitable to their age, ability, and aptitude, before deciding not to press for their compulsory attendance at school.

To this, I replied on March 7th:

'I am in receipt of your letter of February 24th. You state that your assistant Mrs. Davies called on me at Haddenham; but if this is the case, she did not see me, and I was not aware that she had called.

'The education of my children is my own affair and not that of the State. I was always given to understand that it was to avoid state interference with the liberties of individuals that we fought the last war; it does not appear to have achieved that result.'

'I am fully aware of my duty and responsibility as a parent, and I am fulfilling these completely and in the best interests of the children. It appears to me that the well-being of the children is of infinitely more importance than any requirement of State officials. I dispute the right of any such official to interfere—and if some newspaper reports are correct, I am more than horrified at the results of their methods.

'If my statement that the children are being properly educated is not sufficient to satisfy you, I would be glad if you would explain why not. Is it now a ruling in this country that the word of an individual must necessarily be treated as worthless unless investigated by an official?

'I have nothing further to add to my letter of February 20th.'

I heard nothing more after this until, at the beginning of May, two representatives of the Education Authority, a man and a woman, called to see me, and a distinctly heated argument ensued. It was impossible for me now to regard the position calmly; my home and family were being attacked, and my feelings—and doubtless my attitude—were very much those of a wildcat facing a hunter attempting to capture her young.

I could not accept, in the first place, that any State authority had any rights whatever over my children—such a position was contrary to all my instincts and the tenets of my own upbringing. Their bland assumption of the right to hurt and destroy all I cared for infuriated me, and all the time I was talking to them I was conscious of a growing certainty that I was right—and a despairing conviction that I should never be able to prove it to a Government department. By the time they left, I realized that I was now involved in a private war.

The children were, of course, by this time becoming aware of what was going on and drawing their own conclusions. Listening to the news on the wireless that evening, David heard an account of the activities of Mau-Mau and asked me what 'terrorists' were. I explained that they were people who tried to impose their views on others by fear and force. David considered this for a little and then said, 'You mean like the Education Authorities?'

On May 7th, 1954, I wrote to the Chief Education Officer:

'Following the call here of your Mr. Bartlett and Mrs. Davies, I would like to confirm and enlarge on the substance of what I stated at that interview.

'I understand that you require proof of the education which my children are receiving in the form of 'book work,' which should be submitted to Mrs. Davies for her decision as to its suitability to their age, ability, and aptitude. May I therefore enquire what qualifications Mrs. Davies possesses which fit her to decide this? I do not refer to academic qualifications—although I would be interested to know these also—but the personal qualifications of insight and understanding which would enable her to judge the ability and aptitude of my children—or any children—of whom she has no knowledge whatever? Further, I would be glad if you could inform me why you are apparently unable to accept my assurance that my children are being educated, and why you cannot leave them to be educated in peace?

'I do not agree at all with the enforcing of a rigid timetable or the commencement of proper 'book work' at the age at which the State appears to consider it necessary. A child absorbs knowledge from the moment it is born—knowledge indisputably suited to its age, ability, and aptitude—and that process continues throughout life. But I believe a great deal of harm is done by forcing formal instruction on children too young to be able to concentrate on or absorb facts to order. I do not agree that any formal instruction should be imposed on a child until seven or eight years old—although, of course, the child will *learn* a great deal before this age. But so far as formal education is concerned, I agree with an authority writing in the *Daily Telegraph* recently who stated that up to that age children are 'better employed playing mothers and fathers' than attending school. My two elder children are learning to read—from the books of A. A. Milne. (I did try teaching them with books designed for the purpose, but the children pointed out so many absurdities in the text that I ceased to use them.) They are also learning to write, but this I do not want to take further until they are old enough to have a better mastery of the coordination between hand and eye, which does not develop until a later age and is not acquired by practice when young. I believe that too early teaching of writing is very largely responsible for the frequent establishment of an illegible adult hand. Their written work up to now is therefore limited to letters written on their own initiative to members of the family, and I have not kept school books as such. They are learning to spell accurately and to do mental arithmetic. They all listen to the school programmes on the wireless, the elder boy attending to every subject and giving me an account of it afterwards, the younger ones attending to the musical and English programmes. It is my intention to give my children the groundwork of their education during the years between eight and twelve—reading, writing, grammar and spelling, and arithmetic; and a general introduction to history, geography, botany, and biology. But I believe that comprehensive teaching of these latter subjects should be left until a much later age, when the mind is able to grasp them fully and see facts in clear perspective. The time spent in school in imparting quite useless instruction to minds that cannot possibly really understand it, and at best can only retain part for a limited period, appears to me an appalling waste of the most valuable period of all human life. No child's mind is trained by such a process, much less educated—it is merely battered at by it, and that, although it passes for such in schools, is not and never can be education. Mathematics and chemistry I would leave altogether until and unless a child shows some leaning towards them, and languages also, which, if learned at all, should be learned as a chosen study, not part of a general education. The boys will learn to work with their hands in the garden and workshop, and the girls in the house, as a matter of course. All team games I regard as an abomination and would not have my children participate in them. These are the lines on which I am educating my children.

'Your Mrs. Davies asked me if I had any aim or plan in the education of my children. May I quote a passage from the chapter on education in *Perseus in the Wind*, by Freya Stark:

… I would like to have learnt four things when the passing bell puts an end to schooling, and of these only one can be called intellectual. I would like to command happiness; to recognize beauty; to value death; to increase, to my capacity, enjoyment. Around the cardinal points, and inevitably attained by their attainment, I should place the conquest of fear, whose elimination must be the final aim of teachers. The rest of education deals with technical means for living and is of secondary importance, whatever economists may say. It is chiefly because they have reversed our order and made the technical intellect supreme that we are suffering in the world today.

'My aims are on these lines also. There are elemental things which I would teach my children, not included in the teaching of your schools—cleanliness, courtesy, and kindness, consideration for others, loyalty and gentleness, and the care of those weaker than themselves; strength and courage to stand up to fear and pain; a true understanding of animal life and the natural world. And I would give them, above all things, that which does not come from learning, that which is implicit in the peace of wood and field, in every springing blade of grass and the petal of every flower, in every sunrise and sunset, in the song of every wild bird—that which is beauty and happiness both, and more—that which is not knowledge but understanding of the meaning of life itself.

'May I quote again—from Keats's 'What the Thrush Said'—

'O fret not after knowledge—I have none,
And yet my song comes native with the warmth.
O fret not after knowledge—I have none,
And yet the evening listens.'

'I ask you, sir, does the evening listen to you?'

The only reply I received to this was the service of three School Attendance Orders, naming St. Leonards C. of E. Primary School, for David, Robin, and Felicity. These also I returned to the Education Committee—in pieces.

Before any further action could be taken against me, we had moved again to Norfolk and were staying temporarily with my parents in Brundall. Here, three summonses, sent on from Buckinghamshire, were duly served on me by the local constable, charging me with failing to send my children to St. Leonards Primary School. I was about to write a letter to the magistrates pointing out, apart from any other considerations, the difficulty of doing this from our present address and asking whether the Education Committee were proposing to provide daily transport, when I received a letter from the Clerk to the Justices stating that as we had moved out of the area, the summonses had been withdrawn, and it would not be necessary for me to attend the court.

There matters stood when, in July 1954, we moved to Yaxham and settled into our new, permanent home.

4

Courting Trouble

WE ARRIVED in Yaxham at the beginning of July, two weeks before the school holidays began, and within a few days, I received a visit from the local School Attendance Officer (or Welfare Officer). I informed him that I did not intend to send my children to school until the next term. The autumn term started in the middle of September, and on the following day, I received another visit from the School Attendance Officer.

By then, I had given the whole position a good deal of thought, and I was undecided whether it would be better to continue the children's education in accordance with my own ideas or to discard them as the outcome of my personal prejudice and to start our new life in a law-abiding manner by sending my children to school. The only drawback to this latter course was that I could not avoid the unshakable conviction that it was wrong; and when it came to the point of contemplating actually sending the children to school, I could not bring myself to put it into effect. But I had also to consider the feelings of my parents, now we were living only fifteen miles away, who, although they appreciated in retrospect the unhappiness I had suffered during my own schooldays, were worried about the possibility of my continually breaking the law.

I wondered whether it might be possible to find some small private school that would satisfy the requirements of the authorities without interfering too seriously with what I regarded as the more important aspects of education, but there was no such school near us. I made all the inquiries I could about the local village school, but unfortunately, nothing that I learned encouraged me to regard it as suitable for my children. The only possible alternative appeared to be the school in the next village, about which I knew very little but had heard spoken of as better than the local school. But I was still reluctant to take what was, to me, this retrograde step; although it seemed, if I was not to spend the rest of my life fighting the law, to be the only course.

I put most of this to the School Attendance Officer, hoping that it might be possible to reach a satisfactory and lawful solution; but he was not particularly helpful and appeared to take exception to my desire, considered wholly reasonable in my own childhood, not to send my children to a state school.

Meanwhile, my children, coming for the first time into a largely agricultural community, spent a great deal of their time watching and helping on the neighboring farms, David being particularly interested in the cows and Felicity in her element with the horses, which appeared to me to be of far more benefit to them mentally and physically than sitting cooped up in a small classroom; and I continued to put into practice my own educational methods at home.

Then I received my first visit from the Senior Welfare Officer, Mr. F. J. Earl—who could not have known, as he stood smiling on my doorstep, how many courts he was going to stand in during the years to come, facing me, not smiling quite so much, from the witness box.

Unfortunately, the more visits I received, the greater my objection to sending my children to school became. I had a long argument with Mr. Earl, but I was annoyed from the start by the attitude of bland self-assurance with which all these officials approached me, and I was particularly irritated by Mr. Earl's declaration that *he* had liked being at school and *his* child was very happy at school, to which I replied rather caustically that there were, after all, some biological grounds for supposing that my children would take after me and *not* after the School Attendance Officer.

Then, on October 12th, the Norfolk Education Authority served on me four copies of their 'NOTICE TO PARENT OF FAILURE OF DUTY REGARDING EDUCATION OF CHILD,' giving me twenty-one days in which to satisfy the authority that David, Robin, Felicity, and Wendy were receiving education suitable to their ages, ability, and aptitude. These I ignored, having learned from experience that a reply to them was a waste of time.

A month later, an event took place that shook our lives to their foundations and effectively wiped out any ideas I might have had of reasonable conciliation with the law.

I had to go to Aylesbury in connection with legal proceedings and could neither avoid personal attendance nor manage to get there and back in the same day. I therefore left the children in the care of my occasional domestic help, who had looked after them before when I went out during the day. I left on the morning of November 10th and returned from Norwich station by car at nine o'clock the following night. As soon as the car stopped, my domestic help ran out of the house, calling, 'Don't let the car go!' I asked the driver to wait and ran inside—to be told that on the previous night, the authorities had come and taken the children away.

A woman magistrate with several policemen, a policewoman, and an N.S.P.C.C. inspector had come to the house. Entry was gained through a window while the children were asleep in bed, and despite the protests of my domestic help, the children had been taken out of bed, dressed, and carried to the police car outside. But first, she said, the officials had told her that they would leave the children undisturbed *if she undertook to send them to school the next day.*

Obviously, she could not undertake to do anything of the kind, and the children had been removed to an unknown destination. They had also tried to persuade her not to wait in the house for my return; it was as well she ignored this, as otherwise, I would have been entirely helpless—not only would I have found the house empty and not known why, but I could not have gone far to seek help, as I found later that my bicycle, my only normal means of transport, had a puncture and a flat back tire.

As it was, half-frantic, I drove to the local policeman's house, but he refused to tell me where the children were and only suggested that I should ask the Inspector at Dereham police station. We drove there, and after a great deal of argument, we were accompanied by a policeman to the Dereham Children's Home. There, the matron refused to let me see the children, and when I cried and called them by name, she and the man in charge took hold of me and threw me out, barring the door.

The rest of the night was a confused horror of darkness and policemen—they kept arriving in cars and surrounded the Home. I knew that if I attempted to force entry or struck anyone, I could be immediately arrested and taken in custody to the police station (I was told afterward that they hoped I would do this, so they could get rid of me). I dismissed the car, and then, shivering with cold, lay down on the doorstep of the Home. As I was breaking no law, they could not remove me; I proposed to stay there until they let me take my children home.

Shortly after midnight, another police officer, Inspector Barnard, arrived. I did not know him, but he knew my father; he approached me with the first kindness I had met with that night and gave me his assurance that if I would agree to go home, the children would be returned to me the next day. I am afraid I seriously offended him by asking if he would put that in writing.

In the end, I agreed, and the Inspector brought me a cup of warm milk (which I hate, but drank because I didn't want to hurt his feelings any further) and took me home in his car. The children's empty beds lay heavily in the stillness and silence of the empty house.

The next morning, a police car called for me, and I was taken to Dereham police station, where, after being asked to sign a statement drafted for me by the N.S.P.C.C. Inspector, and refusing, I signed a statement I made myself. I was then driven to the Children's Home, and the children were brought out to the car.

I have never seen any children in so pathetic a state. Their faces were stiff with terror, the pupils of their eyes fixed and contracted, and the younger ones cried hysterically long after I got them home. It was obvious that everything they had been through was branded on their minds: after being comfortably bathed and put to bed, the horror of being awakened by policemen, made to dress, and taken by force from their home; the humiliation of being stripped of all their clothes in a strange house and being bathed and having their hair washed with carbolic soap. Felicity was even told that the next day, they would cut off her beautiful long golden hair. They said they had heard me calling them in the night, but then they were picked up and carried into a room on the other side of the house and given 'some sort of sweets,' and after that, they didn't remember anything more. Had this not, of course, been impossible in the Council's care, I would have assumed that they had been drugged.

For the next twenty-four hours, they alternated between fits of extreme excitement and near hysteria and periods of extreme exhaustion, when they would fall asleep without warning in chairs or on the floor. It was several days before they began to get back to normal again; and the Education Committee's next communication—a Notice dated November 11th, the day after the children were taken away—could not have arrived at a time when I was less likely to comply with it.

This Notice was headed:

'SCHOOL ATTENDANCE

'NOTICE UNDER SECTION 7(2) OF THE EDUCATION ACT, 1944, AS AMENDED BY SECTION 10 OF THE EDUCATION (MISCELLANEOUS PROVISIONS) ACT, 1953'

and its wording was identical with that of the letter I had received from the Chief Education Officer for Buckinghamshire in February, except that this Notice was signed by Dr. Lincoln Ralphs, Chief Education Officer for Norfolk, and the school 'considered suitable' for my children was Yaxham Voluntary Aided Primary School.

Accompanying this Notice was a letter from the Chief Education Officer, headed:

'SCHOOL ATTENDANCE

ISSUE OF STATUTORY NOTICE

'At their meeting on Wednesday, 3rd November 1954, the Committee authorized the issue of the enclosed Notice under Section 37(2) of the Education Act, 1944.

'I shall be glad if you will kindly let me have your reply within the fifteen days specified in the Notice, but in the meantime, I would advise you to ensure that your children receive education suitable to their age, ability, and aptitude so that further action on the part of the Committee will be unnecessary.'

To this, I replied on November 27th:

'Reference your letter of November 11th, I shall not be send-ing my children to the Yaxham Primary School as, having made enquiries regarding this school, I do not consider it suitable for my children. I would be glad if you would inform me how, having no knowledge whatever of the children concerned, you reached your conclusion that this school would be suitable? It was, until recently, my intention to send the three elder children to Mattishall School at the beginning of next term—the youngest child I do not intend, in any case, to send to school for another year. Following, however, the events of two weeks ago, when my children suffered extreme shock and terror at the hands of local police and authorities, I am necessarily giving fresh consideration to the position. I would draw your attention to the fact that the children were told that the police took them out of their beds in the middle of the night because they had not been attending school, and the woman who was in charge of them was informed that the children would be left in their home unmolested if she gave an undertaking that they would be sent to school the next day. You will doubtless appreciate that this outrage has had a serious effect on the minds of the children, and they are still suffering from its effects. I am, of course, taking up the matter in other quarters, but so far as the children's education is concerned, I can only inform you at present that they will not be attending any school for the remainder of this term, and that next term I shall either be sending the three elder children to Mattishall School or arranging for them to receive suitable education at home.'

In reply to this, the Chief Education Officer wrote on Decem-ber 10th:

'At their last meeting, the Committee were informed of your letter dated 27th November 1954, and that you proposed to send your children to Mattishall School at the beginning of next term. It was also reported that you had selected this school instead of Yaxham Voluntary Aided Primary School, which is the nearest appropriate school to your home. The Committee, therefore, decided that an application should be made to the Minister for a direction determining what school is to be named in the School Attendance Order.

'This letter is sent to you as a notice of the Committee's intention to refer the matter to the Minister in accordance with Section 37(3) of the Education Act, 1944.'

Two days later, I received a copy of the Chief Education Officer's letter to the Minister, headed:

1. Norfolk.

2. School Attendance.

This letter asked the Minister to give a direction determining the school to which my children should be sent and went on to give details of the action already taken by the Norfolk Education Committee. It continued:

'4. This application is made on the following grounds:

'(a) Yaxham Voluntary Aided Primary School is approximately one mile from where the children live. Garvestone County Primary School is approximately two miles from the home, and Mattishall County Primary School is approximately two and a half miles.

'(b) If Mattishall County Primary School is named in the School Attendance Order, it would appear that the Authority will be responsible for providing transport for the two children, Felicity and Wendy.

'(c) The Authority consider that unreasonable expense would thereby be incurred.

'5. For your information, it would appear that none of these children has yet attended school. Mrs. Baker was fined £1 in each of two cases for non-compliance with School Attendance Orders at Woburn Court, Bedfordshire, on 26th June 1953.

A copy of my letter of November 27th accompanied this. There was no mention, I noticed with interest, of the suitability of the schools in question; the only aspect considered was their distance from our home and the resulting possible expense.'

Ten days later, I received a letter from the Ministry of Education:

'I am directed by the Minister of Education to inform you that he has received from the Norfolk Local Education Authority an application under Section 37(3) of the Education Act, 1944, for a direction determining what school is to be named in the School Attendance Order proposed to be made by the Authority in respect of your children, David, Robin, Felicity, and Wendy Baker, who are all of statutory school age.

'It is understood that it is your wish that the Mattishall County Primary School shall be named in the order, but that the Authority propose to name the Yaxham Voluntary Aided Primary School.

'I am to enquire whether, before the Minister makes his decision in the matter, you wish to make any representations to him. I am to ask that your representations, if any, may be made as soon as possible. If no representations are received within ten days of the date of this letter, it will be assumed that you do not desire to make any and the matter will be determined.'

To this, I replied on January 10th, 1955:

'Reference your letter of December 24th, it appears that there has been some misunderstanding regarding the contents of my letter to the Norfolk Education Authority. In my letter, I informed the Authority that it was my intention to consider, in the light of the action taken against my children in the name of the Education Authority, whether to send them to Mattishall School this coming term or to educate them at home—with the exception of Wendy, who in any case I intended to educate at home for at least another year.

'I have now decided that it would be unwise to send any of the children to school, whether at Yaxham or Mattishall, for some time at any rate, in view of the very great shock and suffering that the authorities saw fit to inflict upon them. I shall not, therefore, be sending any of the children to school this term, either to Mattishall or Yaxham, and any School Attendance Order made by the Norfolk or any other authority will be ignored. I may say that I regard it as my duty to consider, above any other consideration, the health, happiness, and well-being of my children, irrespective of the impositions of any State-created 'authority' (which in any case I do not acknowledge), and I shall bring up and educate my children in accordance with my own ideas and beliefs, as my parents did, and their parents and their parents before them. I do not regard the education provided by the State as fit for any child who is to grow up an intelligent, sound, and individual adult, particularly when it comes to the children being forcibly removed from their home at night, by the police, in an attempt to enforce their attendance at a State school. I shall be obliged if you will so inform the Minister.'

A month later, I received from the Ministry of Education a copy of their reply to the Chief Education Officer:

'I am directed by the Minister of Education to refer to Dr. Ralph's letter of 11th December 1954 regarding the School Attendance Order which the Authority propose to serve in respect of the four children of Mrs. J. E. Baker and to say that a letter has been received from Mrs. Baker indicating that she is not disposed to take advantage of the opportunity offered by the proviso to Section 7(2) of the Education Act, 1944, to select the school to be named in the order.

'In these circumstances, it appears to the Minister that there is no question requiring his determination under Section 37(3) and that it is open to the Authority to take such action as they think fit in accordance with their powers under Section 37(2) of the Act.'

On March 9th, 1955, School Attendance Orders for each of the four children, naming Yaxham Voluntary Aided Primary School, were served on me by the Education Authority. These were accompanied by a letter from the Chief Education Officer:

'I have received a letter dated the 9th February 1955 from the Ministry of Education stating that you were not disposed to take advantage of the opportunity offered by the proviso to Section 37(2) of the Education Act, 1944, to select the school to be named in the School Attendance Orders. It is understood that a copy of this letter was sent to you.'

'The Committee, at their last meeting, were informed of the Minister's views and decided to authorize the issue of the enclosed School Attendance Orders upon you, requiring your four children, David, Robin, Felicity, and Wendy, to become registered pupils at Yaxham Voluntary Aided Primary School. They also decided that if you did not comply with the requirements of the Orders, legal proceedings should be taken against you. I trust, however, that the children will be admitted forthwith to Yaxham School so that it will not be necessary to take the matter before the Magistrates.'

To this, I replied on March 23rd:

'With reference to your letter of March 8th and enclosed School Attendance Orders, I have already stated that I shall not be sending any of my children to Yaxham School. I shall not, therefore, comply with the Orders made in respect of this school and return them to you herewith.

'I would refer you to my two earlier letters, to yourselves and to the Ministry of Education, the contents of which you have so far either misrepresented or ignored. My children are receiving, and will continue to receive, a proper education in their own home.

'Regarding the final paragraph of your letter, I can only say that I shall be exceedingly glad to have this whole matter ventilated in Court.'

The Chief Education Officer then wrote:

'Thank you for your letter of the 23rd March 1955.

'I note you state that your children are receiving a proper education in their own home, and I would ask, therefore, whether you are prepared for the Committee's Inspectors to visit to ascertain whether, in their opinion, the education given is suitable to the children's age, ability, and aptitude.

'If you are willing for the Inspectors to examine the children, will you kindly let me know on which days and times it will be convenient for them to call?'

As I received this letter immediately before the start of the school holidays, I replied to it on April 24th, at the beginning of the next term:

'With reference to your letter of March 26th, I am prepared to agree to your Inspector calling to examine my children, provided that you can give me satisfactory replies to the following queries: On what grounds have the Education Committee decided that Yaxham School is suitable for the four children in question, none of whom they have ever seen; and what qualifications will the Inspector possess that will enable him or her to assess the ability, aptitude, and educational needs of these children in a brief visit, more beneficially than can the parent who has studied the children throughout their lives; and provided that I may be permitted to visit Yaxham School, which the Committee consider suitable for my children (without prior notice having been given to those in charge), and inspect the children at work, the preparation of meals, and the lavatories.

'I await your reply with interest.'

The Chief Education Officer replied on April 28th:

'Thank you for your letter of 24th April 1955.

'In view of the delay in replying to my letter of 26th March 1955, instructions have already been given for the institution of legal proceedings against you for non-compliance with the School Attendance Orders, and I would, therefore, prefer to discuss the matters which you have raised following the court hearing.'

To this, I replied on May 1st:

'I am in receipt of your letter of April 28th, from which it appears that you are unable to answer the questions put to you in my letter of the 24th, and unwilling to agree to my seeing the conditions in Yaxham School.

'I would point out that the School Attendance Orders were served on me a matter of days before the end of the Easter term, and your subsequent request to inspect the children's schooling at home was made during the school holidays. I, therefore, delayed my reply until the start of the new term since it seemed to me obvious that you could not inspect the children at work, nor could I inspect the school, until the term began.

'I am interested to learn that you have, in fact, instituted proceedings for non-compliance with the School Attendance Orders during the holidays, when neither the School Attendance Orders, your request for an inspection, nor my request for an inspection of the school could possibly be complied with.

'It appears to me that this is a position which should indeed be put before the court.'

After I had written this, I was startled to hear from my mother that my father had just received a telephone call from Mr. Allwood, the Clerk to the Dereham magistrates, asking him to use his influence to make me send the children to school. If I did not, Mr. Allwood told my father, the children would be taken away from me.

I am sure that Mr. Allwood acted with the best of intentions, but I could not regard with any particular favour a warning given by the Clerk of the Court concerning the assumed result of a case not yet heard, for which the summonses had not yet even been served. I also objected to having pressure put on me through the medium of my parents' natural concern for the children's welfare.

I pointed out to my mother that the case had not come into court yet, still less been decided; and I could not agree to act on anyone else's opinions in so personal a matter. My mother replied that my father had told Mr. Allwood that he could not influence my decision in any way.

The following day, four summonses were served on me; and I took them to my solicitor, Mr. James Hipwell, who at first tried to persuade me not to contest the case.

In the end, he agreed. 'But you're only knocking your head against a brick wall,' he warned me.

'Well, I might dislodge a few bricks,' I said.

The summonses should have been heard on May 6th, but Mr. Hipwell asked for an adjournment for two weeks to give us time to prepare our case. He also suggested that he should follow up my request to inspect the local school, made in my letter of April 24th, and reiterate my willingness to have the children seen by the Committee's Inspectors if this request was complied with. As a result of his taking this up with the Education Authority, it was finally agreed that the Inspectors should visit my children on May 18th, and I should inspect both Yaxham and Mattishall schools on the following day.

The Inspectors arrived at ten o'clock in the morning—the Senior Inspector, Mr. Greenwood, and the Junior Inspector, Mr. Thompson. I was not permitted to be present during the examination. Mr. Thompson took the girls into the nursery, and Mr. Greenwood stayed with the boys in the dining room.

Although by now the children had got over the terror of their night in the hands of the authorities, they were still very frightened of being with strangers; and it was impossible to avoid their knowing the reason for the Inspectors' visit and feeling that it must be connected, as indeed it was, with their experiences of six months before. Felicity and Wendy were for some time tongue-tied with fear and shyness, although Mr. Thompson did make some effort to be friendly with them; but they were considerably hampered by the difficulty of understanding his pronounced Scottish accent—they had no accent themselves and, apart from Norfolk, had never heard anyone speak with an accent before.

Mr. Greenwood was a different proposition altogether. My first impression of him was that he had a grin like a crocodile, and his approach to David and Robin apparently produced very much the same effect.

Halfway through their examination, David came out, very white, and went into the lavatory. Like me, under nervous tension, he has always suffered from physical sickness and diarrhea. When he was able to return, Mr. Greenwood said that the time for the task he had been given was up—he had started to write a letter when he had to leave the room—and he was not allowed to complete it. Robin, who had suffered perhaps more acutely than any of them when they were taken from their home, spent most of the time too terrified to attempt to do anything and was finally sent out of the room in tears.

Mr. Greenwood and Mr. Thompson then left, and the inspection was over. In the afternoon, I took the children to the local cinema to see *The African Lion*, and, watching nature in the raw, they were able to forget the terrors of civilization. (This was, incidentally, only the second time they had been to a cinema in their lives; the first, six months previously, being also to a wildlife film, *Bear Country*. I do not agree with the indiscriminate film-going permitted to most children of the present generation, and none of my children ever go to a cinema unless there is something on that they particularly want to see.)

The next day—a cold, wet one—I set out to visit the two local schools. I went first to Yaxham, where I was shown into the infants' class—a handful of tinies, some of whom were under five, sitting in rows at little tables, staring at large A.B.C.s with lackluster eyes. They had very much the look of small captive animals, their initial fear dulled by repetition, all animation and feeling wiped from their faces—yet I am sure they were not like that at home.

I asked to see the lavatories—and met with the response, 'But they're outside, you know—and it's raining—you'll get so wet.'

'But these little children have to use them in all weathers?' I asked.

'Well, yes.'

So I went and looked—and the less said about that, the better.

Then I was taken into the main class—there were only two at Yaxham—which was painfully reminiscent of my own days at school. Educational methods and ideas may become more up-to-date, but somehow schools still smell the same.

I was shown the books the children were reading—the type of boys' and girls' adventure stories my brother and I had read at home occasionally, but not what I would have chosen as examples of good English or good literature.

I was shown exercise books containing essays and other written work by the children—and was appalled to find actual errors of fact, apparently taught and marked as correct by the teacher. 'Badgers live in forests,' one child wrote; but they don't necessarily—they live in woods, fields, even in large gardens. I have met one crossing a country road, many miles from a forest of any kind. Country children should learn nature study from personal experience and observation, and books by field naturalists, not by copying out meaningless sentences in class. 'Mobile means 'easily moved,'' another child had written. All right so far as it goes perhaps, but it doesn't go far enough; and what is that child going to make of hearing that someone has a 'mobile face'?

It is obvious that insufficient importance is placed in schools today on the proper and effective use of words, and from the start, I wanted my children to learn and understand all their different shades of meaning and use them with force and expression. Children normally do this naturally, until school teaching imposes rigid rules. It would not have passed in a school essay, but we all knew exactly what David meant when—not yet having met the word 'fusty'—he exclaimed at tea-time, 'This butter tastes like old sheds!'

I was also struck by the extreme uniformity of the children's handwriting. Without looking at the names on the covers, it was impossible to tell that the exercise books belonged to different children; and all were written in what in my childhood was known as 'an uneducated hand'—examples of which can be seen on the walls of almost every public building in the country.

I was then shown the kitchen, although it owed the dignity of this name to nothing more than the reception of ready-cooked meals delivered daily by the School Meals Service. That day's delivery had just arrived, in metal containers which looked more suitable for a prison than a school. I am of the old-fashioned opinion that children should have freshly cooked, attractively served meals, not warmed-up food carried around in a van.

I left Yaxham School unimpressed and arrived, half an hour later, at Mattishall School.

Mattishall was a larger school, with correspondingly larger classes. Again, I was first shown the infants' class. 'Some of them come as young as three and four years old,' the teacher told me. 'We like to get them as young as we can. By the time they are five, some of them are reading the newspapers.'

She did not specify *which* newspapers. Unfortunately, I am in entire agreement with the outlook ruling in my own childhood—I was not *allowed* to read the newspapers until I was long past that age. Certainly, in this generation, there is very little in the newspapers which makes suitable reading for a child of five.

In the next class, a boy was asked to read to me. The book on the desk in front of him was one containing stories alternated with pages of exercises and lists of words. Three times he started reading on the wrong page. At last, the teacher showed him the start of the story they had been reading, and he read it perfectly—also mechanically and without expression. It was obvious that he understood neither the layout of the book nor the meaning of the story he read.

As I was leaving, the children started laying the tables for their dinner—the same tables they had been using for schoolwork. A girl passed me holding a handful of spoons—by the bowls.

'Perhaps you could teach them to hold spoons and forks by the handles,' I suggested.

As for the lavatories, they were at the far end of the playground, and I was allowed to view them only from the distance of the schoolroom door.

The next day, I made my first appearance in Dereham Magistrates' Court.

5

'Keep us from the careless boots'

AT ELEVEN O'CLOCK in the morning on Friday, May 20th, 1955, my case came before the Dereham magistrates. Mr. Hipwell took me to the court in his car, with the four children, David, Robin, Felicity, and Wendy.

There were five men and one woman on the Bench. I afterwards learned that the Chairman, Major Wormald, was also chairman of the governors of Dereham High School for Girls, a governor of Dereham Secondary Modern School, and a school manager of the London Road and Toftwood schools, so perhaps he could hardly be described as an unbiased judge of the principle of home education.

Mr. Hipwell did not intend to call the children to give evidence but wanted them there so they could be seen by the magistrates if they wished to do so. We left the four of them in an anteroom in the care of a policewoman, and with Mr. Hipwell, I went into the court. Here, for the first time, I met Mr. Brighton, the Norfolk County Council's Assistant Solicitor, whose face was to become very familiar to me as the years passed by.

The proceedings were opened by Mr. Brighton, who read to the court the correspondence which had passed between myself and the Education Committee. Mr. Earl then went into the witness box and, in reply to Mr. Brighton, stated that he was Senior Welfare Officer of the Norfolk Education Committee. He had seen me at my home at the Rookery, Yaxham, on the 30th of September 1954 and made inquiries regarding the children's education. I had told him I did not intend to send the children to the ordinary school—he gathered that was Yaxham. The children were David, aged nine,

Robin, aged eight, Felicity, aged seven, and Wendy, aged six. I had said that I might send them to a private school the following term. He had asked if I had anyone teaching the children at home, and I had answered, 'No.'

Mr. Earl then produced duplicates of the School Attendance Orders served on me, and also a certificate signed by the head teacher of the Yaxham school certifying that the children's names were not entered on the register. This concluded his evidence, and he was then cross-examined by Mr. Hipwell.

In reply to Mr. Hipwell, Mr. Earl said that he had seen all the children in September 1954. They were healthy, bright, and intelligent children. He had seen Wendy only while he was talking to me. He would say that she was a bright and intelligent little girl. He had heard the correspondence read that morning. He remembered notices being served. The Authority's view was that I had failed to satisfy them regarding the children's education. They were justified in assuming that it was inadequate.

No one went to the Rookery after September 30th, he said, 'as Mrs. Baker had told me on the 30th that she did not want to see me or anyone like me.'

He agreed that in my letter of the 27th of November, I said that I would either be keeping the three older children at home or sending them to Mattishall. They thought that I might have selected Mattishall as the school. I had never said I wanted to send Wendy to school.

'Mrs. Baker did write asking to see the school,' he said, 'but we did not answer as these proceedings had been issued.'

The responsibility was upon the local School Welfare Officers, he said. They made inquiries to find out whether the child was attending school. This applied to every child in Norfolk. They had few instances where children were educated at home. They did not have many cases of children of seven or eight who were educated at home. He agreed that I was 'an intelligent person.' He did not think that a child could be educated 'in isolation.'

That concluded the examination of Mr. Earl. The next witness was Mr. Greenwood, Senior Inspector of Schools.

Examined by Mr. Brighton, Mr. Greenwood said he had visited

the children on the previous Wednesday. 'It was quite a delightful visit. Within a matter of minutes, the children had got over any shyness and were perfectly delightful.'

He said that he had examined the children. David could write in capital letters. Robin 'did not do anything for him at all.' Wendy could write a few capital letters, and Felicity could also write capital letters but could not write words. David was told to write a letter and 'after half an hour had written nine words.'

As far as reading was concerned, the two boys were a year to eighteen months behind what they should be. He would say that they were very keen about it. Wendy could recognize capital letters but could not recognize small letters, nor could she read words in a book. Felicity followed the story with her finger, but her finger was not in the place where she had got to; she was using her memory.

As far as arithmetic was concerned, Wendy 'seemed to have beginnings,' as did her sister, counting up to twenty or thirty. The boys could add and subtract, in the case of Robin, single figures, and David, double figures, but not division or multiplication. They knew no money, nor weights, nor measures. He had given David three examples in money. David could not turn 3s. 4d. into pennies, nor take 21d. from 8d., and he could not divide 2 into 72.

Cross-examined by Mr. Hipwell, Mr. Greenwood agreed that Wendy was six. She was a bright, intelligent, and happy little girl; a pleasant girl and of good intelligence. He agreed that if a parent or teacher was educating a child at home, you would expect the qualities he had just said. He would say I was not capable of educating Wendy. Wendy could not write down numbers. She should write down numbers at six. She should have beginnings of reading. Felicity was not very much advanced on Wendy. She was a charming girl and more than usually intelligent. Their intelligence was not having a chance of developing along these lines.

Robin and David did not appear to be very well on his visit. He would say they both had ambitions. Both of them were 'longing to go right ahead.'

This concluded Mr. Greenwood's evidence and cross-examination. I then went into the witness box to give evidence.

In reply to Mr. Hipwell, I told the court that I was a married woman living with my four children at the Rookery, Yaxham. The children were not at school. It was my contention that I was giving them a suitable education. I did not consider that a child should go to school until at least ten years old.

The children had been removed from their home in the night by uniformed police. This had an appreciable effect on them.

David's half-hour period of writing with Mr. Greenwood amounted to five minutes. He went to the lavatory, and when he came back, Mr. Greenwood removed the paper from him.

I taught the children to speak clearly, good manners, cleanliness, courtesy, consideration, and gentleness, which I considered more important than reading, writing, and arithmetic.

Cross-examined by Mr. Brighton, I said that I taught the children what they were ready to learn; I didn't force anything. I had told the children why Mr. Greenwood was coming. They were always told the truth.

Questioned by the Bench, I said, 'I want my children to develop as they are, and not as other people think they should be. I want them to grow up as individuals and not as part of a mass.'

The magistrates then retired, having decided that they did not wish to see the children. When they returned, the Chairman announced, 'We do not think the children are getting sufficient education at home.' I was fined £1 for each child.

I rejoined the children in the ante-room, where I found them very distressed at having been told by a policeman that if they didn't keep quiet, 'he would get a gun and shoot them.' They had been sitting there in a state of nervous tension for nearly two hours.

We left the court and returned home—to find the Press on our doorstep. *The Daily Sketch* and the *News Chronicle* came with photographers during the afternoon, and a reporter from the local paper, on behalf of the *Daily Mail*, arrived at half past nine that night and wanted to know the color of my eyes. The children were delighted by this contrast to their morning's experiences and cheerfully answered questions and posed for photographs. In reply to the inevitable question, I told the reporters firmly, 'I still shall not send them to school.'

My next concern was the lodging of an appeal against the magistrates' decision. I could not afford to be legally represented by counsel in the appeal court, but Mr. Hipwell prepared the Notices of Appeal for me, and I proposed to conduct the case myself.

The Notices of Appeal were sent—there had to be four of them, in duplicate, two for each child—and Mr. Hipwell obtained for me the Notes of Evidence from the magistrates' court. In due course, I was notified that the appeal would be heard on July 14th at the Shirehall in Norwich before the Norfolk Quarter Sessions Appeals Committee.

During the week before the hearing, I worked late at night preparing my case. Mr. Hipwell advised me on the necessary points of court procedure. More than anything, I was afraid of being so paralyzed with nervousness that I would be unable to say anything at all, but Mr. Hipwell assured me that I need not worry about this, as it happened on occasions to trained barristers. It occurred to me that if this was so, it was not surprising that it should also happen to children under ten years of age when facing an examination by the Schools Inspectors.

On the morning of July 14th, I arrived at the court—alone, as I had decided not to bring the children with me—to find reporters and photographers waiting for me outside the door. The day was excessively hot, and the small courtroom, although it had an efficient system of central heating, was unfortunately very inadequately provided with ventilation. This gave me perhaps an early advantage over the opposing barrister, Mr. Robert Ives, since he was hampered by a wig and gown—while I was wearing silk.

As I was conducting my own case, I was given permission to sit at the solicitors' table. As I took my place there, I wondered how I ought to refer to my opponent during the proceedings. I felt I could not use the accepted phrase 'my learned friend' and was not sure whether it would be in order to call him 'my educated enemy.'

My initial nervousness was exploded into anger by the opening remarks of Mr. Ives, who said that in the event of the appeals being dismissed, he had instructions to apply for an order that the children should be brought before a juvenile court. I rose at this to say that in the event of their dismissal, I would take my case to a higher court, and the Chairman of the Appeals Committee, Mr. A. Lombe Taylor, intervened to say reasonably that this point did not concern them at the present stage and could only be considered, if necessary, after the appeals had been heard.

Mr. Ives then proceeded to read to the court the correspondence between myself and the Education Committee. After this, he embarked on a lengthy address to the court, involving the quoting of numerous Acts of Parliament and passages from weighty legal volumes, most of which was beyond me. I sat back and, for some reason, felt the rest of my nervousness evaporate. Perhaps it isn't possible to be both nervous and bored.

At last, Mr. Ives concluded his preamble and called Mr. Earl, who gave very much the same evidence as he had in the magistrates' court. I was then asked if I wished to cross-examine, and I stood up and addressed Mr. Earl.

'These School Attendance Orders served on me state that the Education Authority have decided that Yaxham School is suitable for my four children. Can you tell me how, in view of the fact that your committee have never seen the children, they arrived at this decision?' Yaxham School is just over a mile from Mrs. Baker's home, and it is the school which children living in that area are normally expected to attend.

'It is not then really a decision that this school is the most suitable, but that it is the nearest school?'—It is the school considered suitable.

'The question of considering 'age, ability, and aptitude' is therefore pure nonsense? In fact, all the Authority care about is not that the children should receive suitable education, but that they should attend the nearest school?'—Yaxham School is regarded by the Education Authority as the proper school for children up to the age of eleven in that area. It is considered suitable for the ability and aptitude of these children.

'Although their actual individual ability and aptitude is not known to the Authority?'—It is considered suitable.

'You have stated in your evidence that I first mentioned educating my children at home in November 1954. But no attempt was made by the Authority to permit me to satisfy them regarding this until my solicitor insisted?'—That is correct.

'After the School Attendance Orders were served?'—Yes.

'In the magistrates' court, my solicitor put it to you that I was an educated woman. You did not agree but said that I was an intelligent person?'—Yes.

'I attended school for eight years. Are you saying that an intelligent person who has attended school for eight years may still not be educated?'—I have no knowledge of Mrs. Baker's education.

'You say you do not think a child can be educated in isolation. What do you call isolation?'—To be properly educated, a child needs to be with other children.

'Do you honestly consider that a child can be taught properly—let alone educated, which is a different thing altogether—in a large class?'—I think a great part of education for a child consists of it being in a class.

I sat down, and Mr. Earl retired. Mrs. Bird, headmistress of Yaxham Primary School, was then called to give evidence that my children had not been registered at the school. The court was then asked by Mr. Ives whether there was any objection to her leaving at that stage, as she had to get back to the school, and the Chairman of the Appeals Committee asked me if I objected.

I replied, 'No—I don't want her for anything,'—unintentionally raising a laugh which spread through the court.

Mr. Greenwood, the Senior Schools Inspector, was then called into the witness box. His evidence also was very much the same as he had given in the magistrates' court.

At one point, he stated that my children were only nervous with him because I had told them the reason for the Inspectors' visit. He showed to the court the sample of writing produced by David during his examination. In the five minutes allowed to him, my son had started writing a letter to me with the words, 'DEAR JOY, I LOVE YOU...'

Mr. Greenwood's evidence was not completed when the court adjourned for lunch. Over a cup of coffee in a quiet restaurant, I reconsidered my opening line of attack. When the court resumed, Mr. Greenwood's evidence was concluded, and I rose to cross-examine.

'You have stated that my children were nervous during their examination because I had told them the reason for your visit. Do you agree that I should have done this?'—No, it was not necessary.

'Then you are telling the court, on oath, Mr. Greenwood, that on some occasions you think it is better not to tell the truth?'

I never did get a straight answer to this question. After some spluttering and face-pulling, I understood Mr. Greenwood to say, 'That was different.'

'You have said that your visit to our home was 'quite delightful'?'—Yes.

'Do you find it delightful to see a child crumple into tears at your approach?'—I think it was a pity.

'You have said they were shy. Did you realize that they were not shy but very frightened?'—No, I don't think they were.

'Did you find it delightful to see a child suffering acute discomfort from nervous sickness and diarrhoea?'—I don't think he was.

'You asked the boys to write 'about anything.' Is this what they are asked to do in school? Are not pupils in schools usually given a choice of subject? Is it not the normal reaction of the mind of a child or an adult to go completely blank if asked without warning to write or say 'something'?'—I don't think so.

'When you showed Robin a book you had brought with you, did you not realize that he was fascinated by the pictures, not 'longing to read the book'?'—I don't think so.

'You say that Felicity read from a story, but because she did not follow with her finger the same words she was reading, she was not reading?'—She did not appear to be.

'You mean you thought she might not be?'—I don't think she was.

'It was not you, but your assistant, who conducted the examination of the girls?'—Yes.

'Your assistant is a Scot?'—Maybe.

'He has, in fact, a marked Scottish accent?'—No, I don't think so.

'Did you appreciate that none of the children could understand properly what he said?'—I think they did.

'You said in evidence to the magistrates that the children were a year to eighteen months behind what they should be?'—In reading, yes.

'How do you assess what they should be?'—They are below the standard for their age.

'The standard for children in schools?'—Yes.

'Are there not children both above and below this standard in schools?'—There may be.

'There are then children of the same age as mine at the same standard in schools?'—These children are below the standard for their age.

'You say that my children are bright, intelligent, happy, healthy, charming, and delightful?'—Yes.

'Don't you think that this may be the result of my method of education?'—No.

'Would you not consider these qualities as desirable, if not more desirable, than anything they could acquire at school?'—No.

'You say the boys were 'longing to go right ahead.' Is this a good or a bad thing?'—They should have the opportunity to go ahead.

'The purpose of your examination was not to decide their future opportunities, but to assess the efficiency of their present education?'—Yes.

'And you found them bright, intelligent, and ready to go ahead. Should not the first five years' education achieve precisely this?'—They are not receiving efficient education.

'What do you mean when you say Wendy and Felicity 'seemed to have beginnings' in arithmetic? Did they, or did they not?'—They seemed to have.

'You say that Wendy could not write down numbers. But you were handed specimens of Wendy's work, including numbers she had written?'—I was told she had written them. I did not see her do so.

'You say that a child of six should be further forward than Wendy?'—Yes.

'It is not enough at that age for a child to be bright, healthy, intelligent, and happy, to be starting to learn figures and letters, and taking an interest in books and the real world around her, plus a vivid imagination?'—No.

'I appreciate that I cannot put questions to the Committee, but I would like to ask them to consider in their minds what standard they had reached at the tender age of six. You don't agree, Mr. Greenwood, that for a little girl of six, the words often quoted in my childhood could apply—'Be good, sweet maid, and let who will be clever'?'—No.

There was a good deal more of this cross-examination, which established mainly that Mr. Greenwood would never give a straight-forward answer to a question if it was possible to give an evasive one. By the time that I finally sat down, I was becoming angry, the court was becoming restive, and the smug expression on Mr. Greenwood's face was wearing noticeably thin.

Mr. Ives then called the second Schools Inspector, Mr. Thompson, who described himself as an 'educational psychologist.' When I questioned Mr. Greenwood about his assistant's Scottish accent, I did not know that Mr. Thompson was being called to give evidence himself. I was delighted when, in reply to the first question put to him by Mr. Ives concerning his qualifications, Mr. Thompson replied in a broad Scottish accent, 'Edinburr-rgh Univairr-sity!' He must have been surprised at the chuckle that ran through the court at this, and again when his reply to the second question put to him by Mr. Ives was also, 'Edinburr-rgh Univairr-sity!'

The rest of his evidence was factual and fair, and when he was offered to me for cross-examination, I said, 'No questions.' This concluded the case for the Education Authority, and I rose again to present my case, took the oath, and started to address the court:

'I am not sending my children to school because I am educating them at home. I have my own views on education, and I believe schools do a great deal of harm. I maintain that it is wrong to separate upbringing and scholastic instruction and that education should be the combining of both in the secure surroundings of the child's home. I regard education as a preparation for life rather than sessions of formal instruction, which are often incomprehensible to the minds of the children and given in surroundings inevitably uncongenial and frequently repellent to the sensitive child.

'No two of my four children are alike, and each requires and receives an individual approach, which would be impossible in any school, where the tendency is to stamp out individuality.

'I do not agree that formal instruction should start at five unless the mind of the child is obviously ready for it. I maintain that seven is the earliest age that any normal child should be required to start taking lessons as such, and I understand that this view is supported by experts. I believe it is correct that our present Queen started lessons at that age. I would be interested to know whether the Education Authorities regard her as having been inadequately educated.

'At seven, I have started teaching my children reading, writing, and elementary arithmetic and awakening an interest in drawing, nature study, and music, as and when they showed an interest in these things. Also, as part of their education, they have from an early age been taught and encouraged to carry out various aspects of housework and other domestic duties.

'The elder boy listens to all the instructional programmes on the wireless and is, in this way, receiving tuition in history, geography, natural history, and, at his own wish, other more advanced subjects. I have intentionally withheld any more extensive instruction in history and, to a certain extent, in geography because I believe these to be subjects which, if they are to be properly understood and seen in true perspective rather than as a series of disconnected episodes and facts, can be absorbed only by a more mature mind. It is my intention, therefore, that the children's study of geography should be intensified between the ages of ten and fifteen and that they should read history as a whole when they are capable of understanding it between the ages of fifteen and twenty. In my experience, the mind of a child finds it easier to comprehend the functions of the natural world and the nature of the universe than the complicated political events which constitute a great deal of history.

'The children have not been required to practise handwriting to any great extent, as I believe it is only in later years, between ten and fifteen, that a child acquires fully the necessary coordination between hand and eye required to write well; and I am anxious that my children should acquire a good individual hand and not learn at an early age the uniform 'uneducated' hand common to the majority of their contemporaries attending the State schools. In view of this, the greater part of the children's instruction and work has been oral.'

At this point, I put before the Appeals Committee an example of each of the children's handwriting. Each of them had copied out part of a poem, the 'Wild Flowers' Prayer,' which was therefore silently studied by all the magistrates:

> 'Keep us from the careless boots
> Trampling on our tender shoots,
> And from those who take for granted
> Every flower can be transplanted.'

I then resumed:

'The children are taught to speak correctly, proper table manners, personal cleanliness, and the qualities of courtesy, gentleness, and consideration for others, which I regard as more important than routine school subjects.

'Considerable periods, particularly during the afternoons, are devoted to practical outdoor occupations—gardening, nature study, and farm work—combining practical instruction with physical exercise, which takes the place of physical training and organized games, to both of which I am opposed.

'The children are taken to see art galleries, museums, and other places of educational interest, and films of educational value from time to time, and they listen to orchestral concerts. They have been taught elementary first aid. We also have discussions when questions raised by the children are answered and discussed, and others arising from them are dealt with.

'The primary purpose of education during the early years—when a child is not capable of absorbing any quantity of dry facts—is to awaken and interest the mind so that it is readily receptive to the facts that it can and will absorb without any difficulty in later years. All the education given to a child up to the age of seven or eight in school could be assimilated by any intelligent adult in a matter of a few weeks.

'No one is expected or advised by health experts to force food down a child's throat because it has reached an age when a text-book says it should have that type or quantity of food. In feeding a child, you judge what is required by its consumption of what is given to it and its apparent need for more. Why, then, should the mind be forcibly fed? A child's mind and body grow and develop without referring to textbooks or consulting education authorities. It is as senseless to put a child day after day in a classroom and give it instruction, nine-tenths of which its mind is not ready to receive, and call the result education, as it would be to seat a child at a table and surround it with plates of food which it could not digest, and maintain that it was properly fed.

'I have never known any child at school who had any real interest in what it was being taught or any real desire to learn. My children have been given the instruction for which they were ready. Because I have, to a great extent, let them come to me to seek knowledge rather than having it forced upon them, they now have minds wide open and alert, undimmed by school teaching, capable of absorbing within the next few years all the education that their contemporaries have wasted the last five years of their lives struggling to acquire. As a child's mind grows, its ability to absorb knowledge obviously grows with it. This ability can be stultified by too much teaching too early. The mind needs space to grow.

'A flower opens in its own time. If interfering hands force open the bud before it is ready, the flower is deformed and spoiled. A child's mind opens as a flower does under the warmth and light of the minds which influence it. Those who are responsible for the influencing and educating of a child should be those who also love it. I have given my children the warmth and light of natural educa-tion combined with the love of their mother in the security of their own home, and I want to protect them from the interfering fingers of the Education Authorities, who would try to pull the bud apart because some official has decreed it should open on a date before that which God and nature have made it to do.

'You cannot set arbitrary standards as to the ages at which children should know or do anything. When my children were still babies, I was informed by countless friends, relatives, and doctors that they should cut their teeth at such and such an age, that they should be dry and clean, that they should walk or talk at the age prescribed for these achievements. In point of fact, none of my children did any of these things when they were supposed to. I had three in nappies long past the age when I was told they should have been trained, but also, once they were past the nappy stage, I never had one accident or lapse back, while proud mothers of children who were clean and dry at a year old often find their children are neither a year or so later. David and Robin did not talk until they were four, but at that age, they started to do so with the clarity and range of words that you would expect in a child of seven or eight.

'My children have been slow to develop in almost every way, but they have developed well. They have learned gradually, but they have learned thoroughly. Everything they have been taught is alive knowledge, not dead teacher's words in their minds. They are ready and eager to go on learning, whereas too many children in school have lost interest in learning because they associate it with the dullness and boredom of school instruction and have ceased to regard the assimilation of knowledge as a perennially exciting part of life. I maintain that for a child up to ten, an alive mind seeking and absorbing knowledge of its own free will is a far greater educational achievement than a bored mind stuffed with uninteresting facts that are never related to daily life at all.

'It is my contention that the whole school system is an unnatural one, particularly for girls, and tends to undermine seriously the value of home life. It is totally unnatural for young children to be enclosed by the same four walls and to sit in rows at desks for seven hours a day. Any school is by its nature an institution, which means that children at their most sensitive time of life are made to divide their time between home life and institution life, the one frequently conflicting with the other, with the inevitable resulting conflict in the child's mind. Education should be one with upbringing. It should take place uninterruptedly in the child's home, and the instruction given to a child under ten should come from one source only, from the parent who understands it. I have in no sense isolated my children. They mix with, play with, and work with the other children in the village, but they are not forced to sit in rows with them, being talked at by someone who does not care for them as individual human beings at all.

'I find that my children gravitate to the company of others some years older than themselves, with whom they get on well and appear to hold their own in work, play, and conversation to the enjoyment of all concerned, despite the 'disadvantage' that my children are supposed to be under due to not attending school, and despite their being, in the opinion of Mr. Greenwood, a year or so below the standard for their age.

'Mr. Greenwood has done all that he could not only to prove what the children could not do but to distort the facts of what took place. He has stated there was little difference in the standards reached between the two boys and between the two girls. I can only say that this proves in the strongest possible way how little Mr. Greenwood was able to ascertain in his brief inspection of the children. I have studied them for their whole lives and based my teaching on the precise sort of children they are.

'No two children could be more dissimilar than my two boys. David, the elder, has a great desire for knowledge and will pursue any subject in which he is being instructed until either the subject or his mind is exhausted. He has a great sense of personal responsibility and suffers greatly if he feels himself in any way inferior to what is expected of him. He also suffers from physical sickness and diarrhoea on occasions of great nervous stress. The inspection by Mr. Greenwood was such an occasion. Mr. Greenwood has suggested in his evidence that David's absence from the room during his inspection was not genuine. I can only assure the court from my personal knowledge that it was. David had been suffering from acute discomfort and was trying to work under those conditions. In the end, he had no alternative but to leave the room. I have every reason to understand this—it is only in comparatively recent years that I have ceased suffering in the same way myself.

'Mr. Greenwood gave David a book to read, and having allowed him to read a passage silently, questioned him on it. The boy made it obvious that he had understood what he had read. Mr. Greenwood has suggested that he had previously known the contents of the book and could not read it. But this particular book was one which David had never seen before, nor had had read to him. It was not a child's book but a book on animal life written for adults by the naturalist Oliver G. Pike. Like most people, when David is nervous, he finds it easier to read silently than to read aloud. David reads the newspaper—by this, I mean the *Eastern Daily Press*, not the picture papers—and discusses the news with me.

'Robin is far less mature than David. He lacks the power of concentration and has a nervous temperament. He is not capable of understanding subjects which David can grasp without difficulty. But he is neater with his hands and has artistic ability which David has not. He is behind David in reading and has not the same feeling for words that David has, but he is progressing contentedly in his own time.

'Mr. Greenwood said that the boys knew no weights or measures. It is true that they have never done sums in these, but they are both acquainted with them in a practical form. Both can use scales and rulers and take measurements and find weights. They are well acquainted with bigger weights from practical experience on the farms. They have not done money sums on paper, but they do handle money when they go shopping for me and are able to reckon up the correct change. David could, in fact, do all the sums which Mr. Greenwood says he could not work out on paper—in his head. I have taught them these things in the way that they affect normal life; the knowledge of how to translate this into paperwork should come at a later stage, when the mind can more easily grasp technicalities.

'I believe that mathematical ability is the least natural and rarest and seldom in any case develops at an early age. Children in general—and anyway, my children—have practical and not mathematical minds. Having that kind of mind myself also, and having been taught mathematics for eight years without any of it having any effect whatsoever, I do maintain that while you can teach a child the nature of God and the universe and achieve understanding, you cannot get the average child to learn arithmetic, out of the practical sphere, other than parrot-wise—which is forgotten as soon as the mind finds something interesting instead. Knowledge drummed into a child throughout the course of a school term, so that by the end of the term the child appears to have a grasp of the subject, does not constitute education unless the child has an equally good grasp of the subject several years later; by which time, in fact, it has probably been forgotten or pushed out by other subjects which have been drummed into the mind in the same way. Most school instruction is of this quality, so that while children appear to know, and at the time do know, all they have been taught, it has not actually penetrated their understanding, only their immediate memory, and had no lasting value whatever.

' Mr. Earl has been kind enough to say that I am an intelligent woman—and I was an intelligent child. When I was twelve or thirteen, my class worked for a whole term on one particular kind of sum—I think it was simple interest—and at the end of the term, I came out top of my class in this and other subjects. But I have not now the slightest idea of how to do this sum, and I am not even sure what kind of sum it was.

'There was, at the same time, in my class a girl of thirteen who, up to that age, had been the admitted dunce of the school and was regarded as unteachable. But at thirteen, she developed a sudden flair for mathematics and, within a year, was taking the highest awards in every mathematical subject. I do not believe that development of this kind is brought about by education, and I think it would take place without any education at all. The development of the mind is unpredictable, and to attempt to lay down by law the age at which a child is ready to receive any kind of instruction is an absurdity.

'The aim of education should be to help and encourage the mind to develop in its natural way. I have a brother who is a distinguished scientist and mathematician—but he has never been able to spell. I was the reverse. Yet at school, we both received the same instruction, half of which was useless to him and the other half meaningless to me. Not until we left school were we able to stop chafing our minds on the incomprehensible and give them freely to the things that we understood. Half my time in class was spent trying to understand things which meant nothing to me. Is

Felicity (10), Martin (1), David (12), Wendy (9), and Robin (11) with their mother and three-month-old April at Heath Farm House, Thuxton, after their appeal to Quarter Session s in May 1958

(*b*) Hugh (3) – photograph by David (13)

(*a*) Wendy (10) at Hunstanton, 1959 – photograph by Felicity (11)

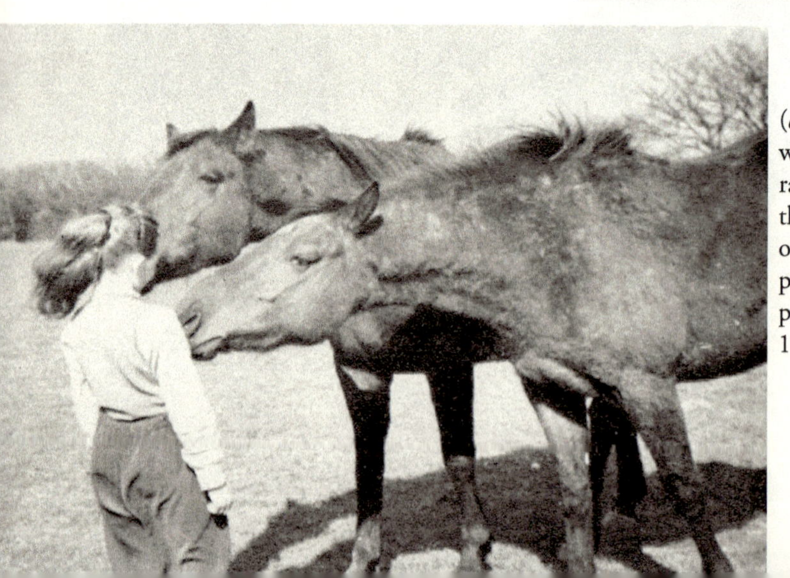

(*c*) Felicity (11) with young racehorses thirteen-year old David's prize-winning photograph 1959

that education? I have learned more—even about the subjects in which I have no ability—since I left school and was free to seek knowledge as I needed and was ready for it.

'The Education Authority requires children to receive 'education suitable to their age, ability, and aptitude,' but in practice, neither ability nor aptitude is taken into consideration, since children are directed to the school intended for children of their age nearest to their home. Since no two children are alike, and age is no guide in determining a child's mental development, this means that schools cannot attempt to give an education suited to the needs of any individual child.

'Mr. Greenwood has said that because Wendy is six, she should have reached a certain standard of education. If Mr. Greenwood knew Wendy, he would perhaps appreciate that this is pure non-sense. Wendy is a child of unusual character who is developing extremely slowly. Her mind is quite unready to receive any formal teaching, but she has made a start and can write letters and figures; she can count up to thirty; she can add. She has resisted learning to read, preferring to invent a story in her own imagination, and I do not think there is any reason why this should be regarded as backwardness. It is obvious to anyone knowing her intelligence that she will read when her mind is ready to do so. At present, it is not, and any attempt to force her further on would result in real distress. Following Mr. Greenwood's inspection, I found Wendy lying awake, crying in the night, sobbing that she *couldn't* do ABC.' Only when I had reassured her that it didn't matter in the least did she regain the happiness and gaiety that Mr. Greenwood found so delightful.

'When I was six, I was sent for a time to a kindergarten in the village where I lived. A little girl of the same age sitting next to me got into trouble with the teacher one day because she could not write the figure 3. The teacher stood over her, becoming increasingly angry as the child protested, sobbing, that she could not write a 3, while the teacher insisted that she could and must. In the end, the child wet her knickers from fright and had to be taken home. Does anyone suppose that this child, the daughter of a doctor and by now a married woman, has been in any way worse off in later years because she could not write a 3 at the age of six?

'Felicity is some way in advance of Wendy—and, incidentally, she learned her ABC only a few months ago as a result of ten minutes' tuition from David, and I see no reason to be perturbed if Wendy does the same thing next year. Felicity can count, can write letters and figures, and also words and sentences. She also is slow in reading, preferring to invent stories of her own, but is beginning to recognize words and will before long start reading seriously. At present, the three younger children all find more interest in living things than paper, and I consider this is as it should be. The right time is between ten and fifteen to develop study on a more intellectual plane.

'Mr. Greenwood says that Wendy should be able to write numbers and could not do so. This is untrue, as she can and does, if rather shakily, and a specimen of what she had done was handed to Mr. Greenwood. I do not know what she was asked to do by Mr. Greenwood or Mr. Thompson, as I was not permitted to remain in the room while she was being examined, but I should not find it surprising if a very frightened child of six was unable under these circumstances to do what she was asked.

'Mr. Greenwood's statement that the children were not frightened and got over their shyness within a few minutes is quite untrue. The children were not shy, but they were all very frightened, and perhaps having seen Mr. Greenwood's general attitude in the witness box, you can understand this. It is impossible to get any idea of a child's ability while it is in such a state of tension and fear, and it is on Mr. Greenwood's findings during this brief period that the Education Authority's case is based.

'I have recently inspected both Yaxham and Mattishall schools— and I would like to point out that the suggestion that I might send my children to Mattishall was originally made to me by Mr. Earl, but in any case, having inspected it, the question of my making an application to send the children there does not arise.

'It is Yaxham School that the authorities have chosen as suitable for my children. On my inspection, I found it to be quite unsuitable in every way. I object to the condition of the lavatories and to the kitchen accommodation, and I consider the meals cooked hours before in Dereham and brought in tin containers to the school totally unpalatable—children need fresh food properly cooked and served, not kept warm for hours in a van.

'In the infants' class, where Felicity and Wendy would be, I saw a pathetic group of small children who looked painfully obviously in need of home surroundings, instead of bare boards and bare wooden desks. I commented on this and was told they had 'plenty of toys to play with.' If this is the case, why get them to school to play? Their expressions were those of bewilderment and boredom—expressions such as I have never seen and will never put on Felicity's and Wendy's faces. It is the aliveness and eagerness that Mr. Greenwood has commented on in my children which are stamped out by the merciless dust storm of school that the law demands must overwhelm the defenseless minds of children from the age of five.

'I was dissatisfied with the standard of instruction given at Yaxham School. I am afraid that my boys would find the proceedings in the senior class rather childish after their education at home. They would doubtless learn to write essays about various characters in literature without really understanding what they were writing about, make cardboard models, and apparently read such books as *Biggles Flies Again*, which I was shown at Yaxham School, and which in my childhood I read in my brother's weekly paper but was not encouraged to regard as education. I was shown some of the children's exercise books in which there were actual errors of fact, marked by the teacher as correct. From what I saw of Yaxham School, it is apparent to me that I am giving my children a far better education than they could receive at it.

'My aim in the education of my children is to develop their minds and give them the knowledge for which they are ready, as they are ready for it—not to stuff their minds with an assortment of facts, nine-tenths of which are unnecessary and meaningless and have no bearing on their growth into adult life. It is my aim to help my children to grow from happy childhood into contented adults. If the boys have ambitions to enter into the more learned professions, I shall see that a suitable education is given to them at the appropriate time, but if they would be happier as farm laborers, I would rather see them contented laborers than harassed business-men. As for the girls, I can hope for nothing better than that they should be contented wives and mothers, and I am doing my best to guide them into happy womanhood.

'Mr. Greenwood has said that the children are of good intelligence and would therefore do well at school. I disagree. The greater the intelligence of the child, the greater the damage school education is likely to inflict. It is more often the dull child who gets through school days cheerfully, learning what it can and ignoring what it can't; it is the intelligent child who learns too fast, who tries too hard, who worries too much, who has nightmares or wakes crying in fear of having done something wrongly or being unable to do something it has been told is important the next day. The teacher with a large class cannot possibly satisfy and content the sensitive, individual, and intelligent child.

'It is my aim to produce individuals of sound mind and strong character, not to hand over the individual creations of my own mind and body to be welded with other children into a state-organized mass. It is not that I regard my children as being different from others, but I do regard them as my children, and not the property of the state. The Education Authorities have expressed their concern for the welfare of my children if they are kept away from school; but Mr. Greenwood has assured us that they are happy, healthy, intelligent, and delightful in every way, and has produced no evidence to show that they will not continue to be so under my sole care. The only danger to their welfare apparently exists in the fact that Wendy may know her ABC at seven instead of six, and David can read at ten instead of at eight. I think they will survive this.

'I am not saying that my children could not advance faster in learning—I am saying that it would not benefit them to do so, that they are learning at a natural rate, not a forced one; and that they are being, not retarded to their detriment as Mr. Greenwood believes, but encouraged to develop in a natural way which will bring them in the end ahead of their contemporaries in the things that matter most.'

I sat down and got up again immediately as Mr. Ives rose to cross-examine me.

'Mrs. Baker,' he said, 'do you believe in educational psychology?'

I wasn't sure about this, so I asked, 'What is educational psychology?'

Mr. Ives looked disconcerted and said he didn't know.

Trying to be helpful, I asked, 'Isn't Mr. Thompson an educational psychologist?'

Mr. Ives looked relieved and said yes, he was.

'Then I don't!' I said, and another chuckle ran round the court.

'Mrs. Baker,' said Mr. Ives, 'at what age did you leave school?'

'I left at fifteen,' I said, 'and it was only then that I started learning.'

'Don't you think,' he asked, 'that anyone does a job better if they are trained for it?'

I was tired by then, and I did not realize that he was referring to my lack of qualifications as a teacher.

'You mean that I would have conducted this case better if I had been trained as a barrister?' I said.

To my amazement, Mr. Ives laid down his papers and sat down laughing.

'No,' he said, 'I don't think you would!'

So I stood up for the last time to make my final address to the court.

'You have heard my statement and the evidence for the prosecution, and you may perhaps appreciate the contrast between the strength of the forces I am defending my children against, and I, who am myself defendant, sole witness for the defense, solicitor and counsel for the defense, and mother of the children concerned, for whom I care more than anything in the world.

'I am not saying that I know what is best for these children on any sentimental grounds, but because I know and understand them, and I ask you to consider, in the light of what you have heard today, whether that knowledge and understanding does not weigh more heavily than the opinion of the Schools Inspector, Mr. Greenwood, who saw the children for two hours only, when they were, as a result of his visit, in a state of nervous tension and fear.

'I ask you to consider whether Mr. Greenwood could possibly fairly assess the children's ability in that time and under those circumstances, and I would stress that it is on Mr. Greenwood's finding during this brief period that the whole case for the Education Authority is based.

'Can this court maintain that two complete strangers could understand the whole of four children's minds in the space of two hours, and that the children's education is better based on the result of this inspection than on a lifetime's study and care?

'I submit that these proceedings are in the main a matter of a difference of opinion as to what 'suitable education' for these children should consist of. No amount of argument can decide which view is right—mine or the Education Authority's. But I am not seeking to force my view on anyone else's children—it is the Education Authority who seek to force theirs on mine. Is not the whole point of this case whether, under the present Act, the individual parent has or has not the right to decide on the most suitable education for her own child?

'I believe that health, happiness, expanding intelligence, and an eager mind are far more important than book-learning up to the age of ten, and as important after it. It has been the aim of my education to produce healthy bodies and alert, intelligent minds in happy, contented children—rather than exercise books filled with imperfectly absorbed and largely useless facts. I think it has been established that I have succeeded in this.

'The Education Authority has stressed that these proceedings have been taken against me for the children's own welfare, but I would point out that the Education Authority can neither know nor care anything about these individual children, whereas I, who am asking only to be allowed to continue to devote my life to their welfare, do know and *do* care. Does this court maintain that the Authority's view must be right and that of the individual must be wrong?

'I submit that the Act allows some freedom to the individual and that the education I am giving my children is education suitable to their age, ability, and aptitude within the meaning of the

Act; and I claim the right to hold and act on my own views in the matter of the education of my own children.

'It has been established by Mr. Greenwood's own evidence that my methods have been in no way detrimental to my children. I submit that what the Education Authority thinks my methods may bring about in later life is not evidence.

'I therefore ask you to allow my appeal and take the claws of the Education Authority out of my children, so they may continue to live and learn in peace.'

I sat down for the last time, gathered up my papers, and waited while the Appeals Committee discussed the problem of where they should retire to consider their decision, there being no magistrates' room attached to that court. In the end, they decided to stay where they were, and everyone else left the court and waited on the landing outside.

Standing there, surrounded on all sides by my enemies, I felt outnumbered and rather hopeless. It had been a very long day, and I had been on my feet for nearly three hours. It seemed a long time before the door opened again and we all went back into the court.

When we were settled again, the Chairman began to speak. 'We have considered the evidence before us, and we are not satisfied—'

My heart sank.

'That the Education Committee—'

Suddenly, my heart stood still.

'We are not satisfied that the Education Committee has complied with the full requirements of the Education Act. The Committee should have made their inquiries into the education being given to these children before the School Attendance Orders were made, but these inquiries were not made until after the making of the orders.

'Mrs. Baker has argued her case with great ability. We do not propose to express an opinion as to the education which these children are receiving. The appeals will be allowed and the Attendance Orders discharged.'

I stood up and said breathlessly, 'Thank you very much.'

'You do appreciate, Mrs. Baker, that this is a technical point,' said the Chairman.

'I don't mind what it is, so long as I can keep my children!' I said.

As I left the court, I found myself facing Mr. Greenwood, who was wearing a rather stupefied expression. 'Well, Mrs. Baker—' he began.

'Goodbye, Mr. Greenwood!' I said, and it was my turn to smile this time. Then I ran out of the court to catch my bus home and tell the children, 'We *won*!'

Since everyone had been convinced that I had lost my case early in the day, there had been no reporters in the court when the decision was given. They started to arrive soon after I got home, and my last memory of that day is of the four children in their nightclothes being 'interviewed' by the *Daily Mirror* on their way to bed. I felt that in view of the shock and strain they had previously undergone, a little out-of-the-ordinary excitement constituted a very reasonable reward.

The next day, we got all the newspapers and sat and looked at the headlines—from the *Daily Telegraph's* 'Mother of Four Wins Appeal' to the *Daily Mirror's* 'Victory for the 'Teach 'em at Home' Mum.' Even more satisfying were the Notices which were sent to me shortly afterwards, headed 'Summary Jurisdiction (Appeals) Act, 1933. Decision of Quarter Sessions,' and which concluded: 'IT WAS ORDERED—That the Appeals be allowed and that the conviction be quashed and that the School Attendance Orders cease to be in force.'

It did appear that we were now going to be allowed to live in peace.

6

The Unhappiest Days of My Life

Dᴜʀɪɴɢ the first few weeks after the appeal, our lives were anything but peaceful, since we were constantly receiving visits from newspapers and magazines of all kinds and nationalities; and I found to my astonishment that I had become, if only briefly, a figure of international interest. The children began to get tired of being called in to pose for photographs, and I began to accept giving interviews to reporters in the middle of whatever I happened to be doing about the house as part of my everyday life.

It was on one of these occasions that Robin and Felicity made their first entry into the serious domestic work of our home, when, in the middle of clearing away tea one evening, I was interrupted by a reporter from the *Sunday Graphic*. Knowing from experience that this could mean several hours' delay in the children's bedtime, I called Robin and asked him if he and Felicity would do the washing up.

'All by ourselves? May we *really*?' he said delightedly—and he and Felicity made one rush for the kitchen. When I joined them some time later, I found that they had washed up not only the tea things but everything else within reach, and what they couldn't wash in the sink, they were rubbing over with the dishcloth. The kitchen was shining, and they were both nearly bursting with excitement and pride in their work.

The climax in our press publicity came when I received a telephone call from the London office of an Australian magazine, requesting an interview and pictures. We spent a whole afternoon talking to their reporter and being photographed in the house, in

71

the garden, and on the neighbouring farm, and felt that, in distance at any rate, publicity about us could go no farther than Australia.

During all my interviews, one question invariably cropped up: what was it about my own schooldays which had caused such strenuous opposition to schools and influenced so tremendously my present ideas on education? I found it difficult to answer this question in a few words; looking back into my childhood, there did not seem to be a time when school was not an unrelieved nightmare. Yet I can remember a time when I wanted to go to school. I was six and had already been taught to read and write by my mother; although I am bound to say that my handwriting has always been almost completely illegible, and the only noticeable result of my learning to read at this age was that my mother had then to deal with my continually waking at night, upset by something I had read. Desks, pens, pencils, and paper fascinated me, and I imagined school as a place where I would be able to handle these things in quiet, studious surroundings and feel that I was 'grown up.'

My first school was a small private class, with only two other pupils. I cannot remember doing any lessons there except painting purple pansies (which I was never able to do properly) or playing any games with the other children, although one of them did once decide to play a game with me which consisted of locking me in the lavatory. This school came to an end after a few months owing to the ill health of the teacher, without having, so far as I can see, either damaged or benefited me in any way; and after a little time, I was sent with a number of other local children to a kindergarten started by an elderly lady in the village.

There, I first encountered fear—it would not be an exaggeration to say terror. I had no reason to be afraid myself, for my grasp of education must have been already considerably in advance of that which I was supposed to be receiving; but I very soon found out that I could not bear to see another child crying, and the difficulties encountered by the other pupils often reduced me also to tears. I remember particularly my misery when the small girl behind me, the daughter of our doctor, sat sobbing as she was scolded and snapped at by the teacher because she could not write a figure 3.

As a result of this, although I cannot remember ever being

found fault with myself, I was in a continual state of dread that I might be. On one occasion, during a reading lesson, I was told by the teacher to go and help a rather backward small boy to 'build up his words.' I could have understood being asked to help him to read, but I had not the slightest idea what 'build up his words' meant—I visualized them being piled one on top of the other. Terrified, I sat beside him and told him what the words were, looking around apprehensively every few minutes in case the teacher noticed and said I was doing the wrong thing. This might be said to have been my first attempt at teaching—and I still hold the view I instinctively had then, that we would both have been better occupied picking primroses.

All this was bad enough, but soon a new agony was added to my life. The teacher, a religious woman, used to read to us every morning from the Bible, starting on the first day of the term with Genesis, Chapter 1, Verse 1. She read on from there, breaking off each day's reading at a moment of suspense, like a newspaper serial. The effect on my six-year-old mind was catastrophic. When she reached the point at which Eve ate the apple, I went home and broke down completely—I imagined the apple to be poisoned and could not face going back and hearing what happened next.

This, after some correspondence between my parents and the teacher, which left her convinced that I came from a regrettably irreligious home, ended my attendance at that school. It had not benefited me educationally, but left its mark in other ways. For many years after my introduction to the Bible, I was difficult over food—and to this day, I have never been able to eat a raw apple.

My next school was another small private class in the village, with only three other pupils. Here, I learned to sing Onward, Christian Soldiers and All Things Bright and Beautiful—or, rather, I learned that I could not sing. I did the work in class without difficulty, and when it concerned the use of words or natural history, I rather enjoyed it; but I dreaded the mid-morning playtime, being quite unable to join in with, or think of anything to say to, other girls of my age. When I was seven, I was taken away from there and sent as a day pupil to my first big school.

I remember very clearly the first hour of my first day. I was shown where to put my coat and hat and then told to 'go with the others'—into a big hall packed with pushing, shouting, giggling children of all ages from five to fourteen. I had no idea what was going to happen, where I was supposed to go, or what I should do. After what seemed like hours, a bell rang, and I was pushed along with everyone else into another large room, where after much scuffling and shuffling, we all stood in lines and sang a hymn.

Then everyone disappeared, and as they all went in different directions, I didn't know which ones to follow, so I stayed where I was. A teacher appeared from the other end of the room and shepherded me into a chair, and I found myself being shown the ABC. A few minutes later, another teacher came and retrieved me—the class in that room was the kindergarten, and as I could read and write, I should have been in Class I. I was taken out of the schoolhouse to a long wooden building in the grounds, known as the Annexe, which housed Classes I, 2, and 3. There, I was shown my desk, and my school life began.

This was the beginning of a nightmare eight years long. Many people agree that their first day at school was misery, but say that this unhappiness doesn't last. My first-day misery lasted the whole of my school life. I never became part of my surroundings; I never even learned my way about; from first to last, I was a stranger in a strange land.

No one at school ever showed me anything or explained anything to me as an individual. Always I was told to 'go with the others'— without being informed where it was we were to go. I never knew when or why I had to go to a different room and was continually being humiliated by arriving in the wrong places. I had been at school for several weeks before I learned the whereabouts of the lavatories; I was too shy to ask, and as time went on, I dared not reveal that I did not know—I heard another child asking after being at school only a few days and being scornfully told that she should have found out before. Eventually, I found them accidentally—and wished I hadn't. There were only two, used by over fifty children. Consequently, they were never properly flushed—the cistern never had time to fill up—and, judging by their condition, were never cleaned either. When my mother came to the school for the annual sports, I hoped she would see them and make a complaint. But she was conducted upstairs to a private lavatory, out of bounds to day pupils at the school.

I liked lessons when I understood them; but they also were explained to the whole class, and those who failed to understand at first were left to flounder. I dreaded the subjects I couldn't do, in particular any form of mathematics, because no one seemed to appreciate that there were things my mind was just not capable of learning. (Those subjects I have remained incapable of learning to this day, but I have never found them in the least necessary.)

The same thing applied to many of the other children, but it did not appear to worry them. It worried me. I remember being told by one teacher that I was 'feeble' because I could not follow a lesson in French. I sat in tears for the rest of the lesson; but I have never learned or needed French, and 'feeble' is an adjective that has not been applied to me since I left school.

I was a fastidious child and acutely sensitive to the cleanliness of my surroundings, and I suffered quite appallingly at school as a result. We had drawing and scripture lessons in the school dining room, and a mess of dropped food left on the table in front of me could make the lesson a prolonged misery. Normally, I went home to dinner, but on days when I stayed, I could never eat anything and sat staring at the ceiling, trying desperately not to cry, being scolded by the teachers and laughed at by the other children until the end of the meal.

Lessons that I liked were spoiled for me by the lack of seriousness of the other children, few of whom liked lessons of any kind, so it was impossible to work quietly; and playtime was wretched because I could never join in with the other children—I didn't know how—and in a playground full of children, there was nothing for me to do. I longed to be able to be alone, finding the absolute lack of privacy a continual torment and frustration. I was scolded for not joining in with the others, but shyness and a complete absence of any common ground with them made it impossible for me to do so. Once, when I did attempt to join in a game that was in progress, I was promptly annihilated by a girl of my own age, from my own village, who turned on me, saying, 'Who asked you to play?'

I never enjoyed team games, although I might perhaps have become more proficient at hockey if I had ever been allowed to take any place other than back, which usually involved my standing for an hour or so at one end of the field, wondering whether the game would become more interesting if I were given an active part in it and told beforehand what I was expected to do.

For many years, I wished I could be 'like the others,' as I was always being told I ought to be; I dreamed of being popular; but the more I tried, the more I was laughed at, told I was silly, and left apart. School seemed to me increasingly like a trap, a cage; and all the time I was there, I was homesick for the fields and country-side I had grown up with, for my garden and my animals, and all the things I loved and understood. On the night before each new term, I used to lie awake, longing for something to happen—a serious epidemic or the school burning down—that would make it impossible for me to go the next day.

One morning, I tripped and fell in the school playground and hit my chin on the hard concrete. It knocked me out, and as I slowly regained consciousness, I heard the familiar sounds of the other children playing around me—and for a little while, I believed that I had died and was awakening in hell.

This was the sort of suffering to which I was determined that I would never subject my own children—a suffering all the worse because I could not describe it or explain it in words, and for which I received not sympathy but derision.

As I grew older, I went on being unhappy. I was better able to assess and understand my own unhappiness; I even wrote essays, which gained high marks for English and black looks for frankness, about my outlook and ideals, my impressions of my surroundings, and my idea of the ideal school. My 'being different' from the other girls resolved itself into my lack of interest in their current 'crazes'—enthusing over dance-band leaders and film stars being the chief of these—and a growing interest in a number of subjects ranging from theology to photography, which, to the other girls of my age, apparently didn't exist. I accepted the fact that to 'fit in' at school meant becoming a carbon copy of everyone else, but I had an increasing conviction that there was nothing about everyone else to make this a desirable achievement.

From this time on, I kept apart from the rest of the girls by my own choice and only really lived when I was out of school. At home, I cultivated half an acre of garden, spent hours out with my camera, started writing articles on nature study and gardening—some of which were published—and for companionship, was quite content to be with my cat, the birth of whose kittens taught me more that was of subsequent value to me than any of the lessons I sat through in school.

I ceased trying to absorb subjects I could not comprehend, but my marks in those I could—botany, English literature, and composition—were so high that several times in the end-of-term exams, I came out at the top of my form. Towards the end of my school days, my headmistress suggested that I should drop the subjects that I was good at and concentrate on those I couldn't do, with the object of taking the School Certificate. She lectured me about this for several hours and reduced me to tears, but I didn't take the School Certificate, and I have never found myself at any disadvantage as a result.

During the whole of my school days, I only once got into trouble with the school authorities. I was thirteen, and I had to make a daily six-mile bus journey between school and home. School ended at four o'clock, and there were two buses serving two different routes used by the pupils at the end of the school day, one leaving shortly after four o'clock and the other at five o'clock. Mine was the second one.

It was the practice at the school to send all the children for both buses down to the bus stop in the charge of one of the teachers at the time required for the earlier bus.

It occurred to me that this was a pointless waste of time for those catching the later bus, and I therefore made a practice of returning to the classroom, then empty and quiet, after school and doing my homework, going down to the bus stop shortly before my bus was due. After I had been doing this for several weeks, I was called into the headmaster's study and lectured very severely for not going down to the bus with all the others. My plea that this was not the time that my bus went and that I was using the time to do homework was brushed aside. The important thing was that I must go with the others. I left the room in tears, the more upset because I could not understand what wrong I had done.

Two years after this, I left school and was, of course, immediately required to start making my own decisions—having up to then been sternly reprimanded for doing so. Most people have to live their lives as individuals—and human beings should be individuals—yet we insist on inflicting on our children an education suitable only for members of a herd. No training is of any value for the developing child that does not leave full room for the encouragement of the child's expanding independence, initiative, and individuality; and this cannot be achieved through the mass discipline and crowd influence of school life.

By the time I left school, therefore, I had already a fixed determination that my own children would never be put through this type of schooling; and it soon became obvious to me that the only education of any value which I had received between the ages of five and fifteen took place when I was not in school. It appeared to me then that school education was, from every point of view, a waste of time, very often an obstacle to real learning, and invariably detrimental to the development of the child's character.

This was the basis of my views on education, which gained practical impetus with the birth of my first son seven years later and came to a head when I stood up and faced the magistrates in the Quarter Sessions Appeals Court.

7

Doing What Comes Naturally

W HEN all the ripples arising from my victory in the appeal court had subsided and our waters were calm again, I was able to survey my changed position and take stock. I felt rather as one might after stepping onto a stationary vehicle to appreciate the view and being suddenly whirled away without warning over a rough and stony track, to come to a halt again a very long way from the starting point.

I had begun by assuming that, as the mother of my children, I had the right to bring them up according to my own views, including the choosing of their education; and I found myself abruptly in a brave new world where education was no longer a thing of value to be prized, but a trapper's net closing inexorably over my defenseless young. It was not that I found fault with the provision of free education, but I could not accept compulsory mass education, enforced by laws which made acting on individual views a criminal offense.

My own experience had shown me very pointedly that school could be, and often was, virtually valueless as a means of learning, disastrous as a preparation for social life, and wholly destructive to any development of individual character; and that it could impose a very long period of very real suffering on a sensitive child. That this should be compulsory and unavoidable was, to me, as terrible a thing as any of the horrors experienced under a dictatorship; that it could be the accepted law in my own country was something that, for a long time, I simply could not believe.

But now I had won the right to educate my children in accordance with my own views, even though my victory was, in fact, an insecure one, liable to be overthrown by renewed action on the part of the Education Authorities. I had to decide just how to proceed—with the Welfare Officer prowling in the background and the possibility of future proceedings hanging over my head. Would it be better to compromise and try to arrange for each child, from the age of ten, some more orthodox form of education?

I might have considered this if any suitable form of individual education had been readily available. But I could not afford to employ a tutor, nor to send my children to a private school of my own choice—even if such a school could be found to exist. And I now had the opportunity, if only temporarily, to put my theories into practice; if not with the approval, at least without the imme-diate opposition, of the authorities. To do so was to take upon myself the entire responsibility for my children's education. Yet was this really so fantastic? My parents had, after all, been in the same position. They had chosen to send me to school, although they knew I was unhappy there and longed to be able to stay at home, because they believed it was the right thing to do; when they could equally have kept me at home had they wished, since I already complied with the requirements of the Education Act then in force, as a result of my mother's teaching, by the time I started school. This decision made an appalling mess of my early life and has left its mark up to the present day. Yet I could not blame them for doing, as my parents, what they believed was best. In the same position, should I discard what I believed in with all my heart and do what I believed was wrong? Should I let my chil-dren suffer in order to obey a man-made law? I found it difficult to feel conscious of the validity of a law that had only been made a few years previously—a law that laid down that what was legal behavior for my parents was illegal for me. It is easy to accept the fundamental laws, but government regulations do not move the mind to any feeling of right and wrong. I believed that to do what was right for my children could not be wrong in the eyes of God, and I could see no further than that. I had been granted a victory which everyone had told me was impossible; it was up to me to make the best possible use of it.

So I determined to continue on my own educational course and let my children continue to develop in their own way. At least none of them showed any sign of wanting to go to school, although they played out of school hours with the local schoolchildren. They seldom suffered from shyness with other children because of, and not despite, their being able to meet or avoid them as and when they wished and not being forced to mix with them indiscriminately all day at school.

Wendy was shy by nature. One afternoon, she abruptly left the farm next door where they were playing, with the explanation: 'I am coming home to play. There's a girl there who *looks at me*.' She played at home until the lure of horses and harvest wagons drew her back and overcame her fear. School would have annihilated Wendy. But I knew very well how she felt; she grew out of this phase in a few months, but I was still suffering from it several years after I left school.

Granted that I had no teaching qualifications, as Mr. Ives had pointed out in court, but that did not mean that I could not teach in my own way. My mother had no teaching qualifications either, and she gave me all my basic (and subsequently useful) education. All further knowledge that I needed, I had acquired myself, as I needed it. This seemed to me to be by far the most reasonable method, and the least wasteful in time and effort, of obtaining an education. The only drawback in my case was that I had also had eight useless and detrimental years in school. And so far as this orthodox school education was concerned, I myself had in fact finally complied with the requirements of the present law; I had been through the treadmill of school until I was fifteen and must therefore be considered, legally, 'educated.' Anything of value that I had learned in my years of schooling, I could pass on to my own children. Those subjects which I had failed to learn, I could not teach them; but then, if I, not having learned these subjects, was still considered legally educated as a result of having been at school when I didn't learn them, surely my children could be considered no less educated through having not learned them while *not* at school?

In my case, the things I couldn't learn were those for which

I had never had any need or use in my future life. But if any of my children showed an aptitude for any subjects which I couldn't teach them, then I would have to try to obtain individual tuition for them in those subjects. Meanwhile, they were happy, healthy, intelligent children, with a good deal of practical common sense combined with highly imaginative minds. I knew their individual personalities better than anyone else and could give them the understanding and encouragement which they would certainly never get at school. And if I did find I had made a mistake any-where in the course of their education, I could take steps to put it right, which a school would never do. Once in the vicious sausage machine of compulsory education, they would be churned through it to the end, without hope of reprieve, until they were turned out educated into a semblance of all the other sausages at the age of fifteen—when I would be permitted to take them over again and try to cope with the results. Looking at some of the results already apparent in children of school-leaving age, I shuddered. I do not think it is a coincidence that the rise in juvenile delinquency has followed the introduction of the present Education Act. And if they avoided the sausage effect, they would be battered misfits—like me—individuals made to believe that individuality is a thing to be ashamed of. I would keep my children with me and let them grow up not part of the Government system of child mass production but proudly marked 'Home Made.'

The children themselves were perfectly happy about this. They never found time hanging on their hands—as so many schoolchil-dren, out of school, seemed to do—and their days were filled to the brim with helping on the farms, playing in the nursery and the garden, asking questions about everything under the sun, and growing both in stature and in understanding.

None of them, of course, had any knowledge of team games, which I regarded as an abomination, but being a family of four, they were in no sense isolated and worked and played both indi-vidually and in cooperation with one another. At this time, David was taking a great interest in Dr. Fuchs's crossing of the Antarctic; I learned more about this from David, who never missed an item on it in the papers or on the news, than he learned from me. The

Robin (11) with Hugh (2), Wendy (9), Martin (1), Mrs. Baker, David (12)
and Felicity (10) with three-month-old April at Thuxton in May 1958

Two photographs of Wendy (11)
by David (14)

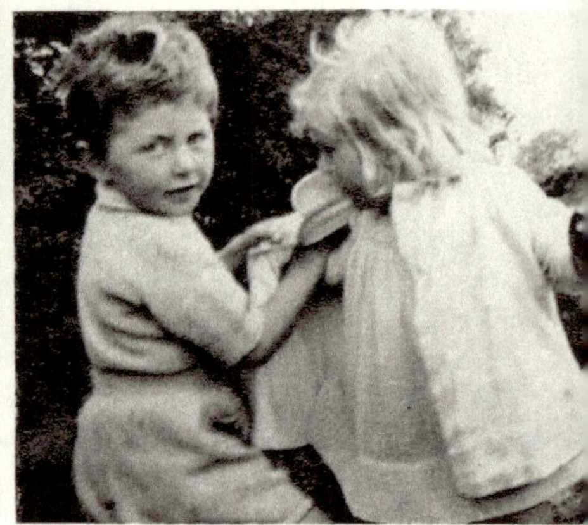

'The Kiss' – a picture sequence by eleven-year-old
Wendy featuring Martin (3) and April (2)

Theron became a household word; and one afternoon, I went into the nursery to discover that it had become something more. David had built a 'model' of the Theron with the nursery chairs, table, and cushions (these were always available to the children for games of this kind and had in the past been haystacks, mountains, houses, boats, and, more recently, a convincing binder), and he invited me to see how it worked. He was standing at the 'wheel' at one end of the structure. Felicity and Wendy watched with me from the 'shore'—Robin was not in sight. David consulted and set some 'instruments,' settled himself at the wheel, and pulled a lever. Immediately, from the interior of the ship, came a realistic sound of engines running. The lever was attached to a string which led down under the cushions and chairs; there, Robin was crouching, with the string tied to his finger, and as soon as it was pulled, he started making engine noises until it was pulled again for him to stop. This was David's invention, and the realism with which it was carried out made us all feel something of the excitement of setting out for the unknown.

So many times, when we were being besieged by reporters, I was asked, 'But how do you give them lessons?' and I replied, 'I don't; I let them learn. They ask questions, and I answer them. I teach them as babies should be fed—on demand.' Their mental scope was therefore unlimited, their imaginative range unrestricted by the boundaries that would have been imposed by school but never hampered by a lack of facts to work on, since their world was spread out in front of them for them to explore into, and they were told anything and everything they wanted to know. So our lives continued through calm waters, and I even began to forget about the Education Authorities.

Six months after my victorious appeal, a number of things happened.

In February 1956, my third son, Hugh, was born—prematurely—in the Norfolk and Norwich Hospital; and in March, we left the Rookery, Yaxham, and moved to Heath Farm House in Thuxton—the house on the hill.

In May, I received a brief and civil note from Dr. Lincoln Ralphs, Chief Education Officer for Norfolk, asking if I wished for any assistance with David's education. I replied with equal civility that I did not need any help.

In June, we had a visit from a slightly subdued Mr. Earl, asking whether David was at school and what plans I had for the children's education. I told him that I did not wish to discuss it with him, and I did not accept his authority to question me about my children.

Later that month, shortly after his eleventh birthday, David had measles; and as soon as he had recovered, all the rest of us had it as well. David, who had never been a very domesticated boy, took charge of the household and everyone in it, called the doctor, did the shopping, prepared what meals we were able to eat, including baby Hugh's feeds, brought the baby to me to change and feed, and fetched our medicines from the doctor's surgery. For over a week, he was on his feet from six in the morning until ten at night; and at the end of that time, I knew he had passed a most unorthodox but searching test.

Felicity had been helping me to bath and change Hugh from the day I brought him back from hospital; we bathed, dressed, and fed him together from then on, and by the time he was six months old, she was able to look after him entirely herself. It was not surprising that he was a very contented baby; he had three 'mothers' and never had to be handled by strangers. Felicity and Wendy were then eight and seven years old; they had put aside their dolls when Hugh was born and were learning instead, with a real live baby, the basic principles of housewifery and baby care.

During this summer, Felicity found herself for the first time in close contact with horses. There were many in the fields around us—ponies and racehorses as well as cart horses—and she and Wendy spent all their free time with them, riding and playing on the backs of the cart horses, while Robin sometimes joined them and sometimes went out with friends of his own, and David helped with the cows on the nearest farm. Soon, Felicity was riding the white pony bareback, cantering with complete assurance around the big field.

By now, the two boys did all our errands and shopping, both in the village and in Dereham, five miles away. Robin started taking an interest in cooking and was soon helping me to prepare most of our meals. And throughout all these activities, all the children were continually becoming aware of fresh fields of interest around them, asking questions, embarking on discussions, and—now they were growing older—arguing about such a wide variety of subjects that I, for my part, was exercising my mind far more energetically than I had ever been encouraged to do in school.

People have suggested that by my method of education, the children's learning must be limited, but in fact, the reverse is the case. Learning at school is limited not only to the subjects on the curriculum but to the particular subject being taught at any one time—you cannot, in class, start a discussion on theology in the middle of a history lesson, however relevant in its way the introduction of such a discussion may be—whereas we could and did discuss any subject as, when, and where any of the children were interested in it.

In October that year, we had another visit from Mr. Earl. I told him that I was still educating the children at home.

In November, we left Thuxton to spend the winter at Sibton, in Suffolk. During the five months we were there, I received one visit from the local School Attendance Officer. His interview with me did not make much progress because, when he realized who I was, he broke off the conversation abruptly and returned in some haste to his car.

In January 1957, my fourth son, Martin, was born; and for the five days that I was in hospital, Felicity looked after Hugh single-handed, did his washing, saw to the airing of his clothes, and took him into her own room if he cried in the night.

At the beginning of April, we moved back to Heath Farm House, Thuxton; and before the end of the month, we were again visited by Mr. Earl, asking if there was any change in my educational methods and views. I assured him that there was no change.

On David's twelfth birthday, he asked for a camera; and within a few weeks, he was producing with it results that were outstandingly good. (Some of these early photographs were among those illustrating my book *The House on the Hill*.) Three months later, he won a prize with a photograph of Wendy and Robin in a photographic competition intended for the adult readers of Parents magazine.

Robin was now developing a marked ability in cooking and was able to cook and serve all our family meals. He had also become interested in gardening, and under my guidance, set to work to make a garden out of the overgrown patch of nettles and thistles which surrounded our house when we moved in. By the end of the summer, we had two lawns and a number of flower beds, and Robin was supplying us with home-grown lettuces as well as a profusion of flowers.

Felicity was now riding one of the racehorses as well as the pony, despite warnings that this particular horse was vicious and dangerous to go near, let alone ride. She cantered around the field on his bare back, totally unafraid, and seeing them together, no one could doubt the very real understanding that existed between them. It was apparent that she possessed a natural skill in handling horses.

And Wendy was spending her time growing up—interested in everything, slowly spreading her petals wider like a flower in the sun before deciding in exactly what direction she wanted to grow.

Meanwhile, in May, I received from the Norfolk Education Committee four new 'Notices to Parent of Failure of Duty Regarding Education of Child.' Accompanying these was a letter from the Chief Education Officer, offering me the services of the Committee's Inspectors to satisfy them regarding the children's education, which I was required to do within sixteen days.

I replied on June 2nd:

'I am in receipt of your Notices regarding my four children, David, Robin, Felicity, and Wendy, and your letter dated May 16th.

'I hereby notify you that the four children are still receiving, at home, efficient full-time education suitable to their age, ability, and aptitude. They are not, of course, receiving the type of education given in the State schools, as I think you are aware that I do not regard such education as being anything but detrimental to any intelligent child.

'Regarding your suggestion that your Committee's Inspectors should call on me in order to satisfy the Committee that my children are receiving adequate education, I do not feel that this would serve any useful purpose, judging by my previous experience of the methods employed by your Inspectors. Your Inspectors are no doubt qualified to judge the educational standards of children subjected to school instruction, but as they appear to have no interest in or knowledge of any other method of education, it would seem to be somewhat irrational to seek their judgment on it.'

'I would point out that while the Act requires children to receive 'efficient full-time education,' it does not define the word 'education.' The dictionary definition of education is 'the bringing-up, as of a child; the training that goes to cultivate the power and form of character; instruction.'

'The place for a child to be brought up and trained is in the home; instruction is only part of education and should be given to suit the individual and not forced on the mass. The Act does not require children to receive full-time *instruction*, and efficient full-time *education*, as here defined, can only be given in a child's home.

'I have already outlined my educational methods at some length in the court proceedings instituted by you two years ago; I have not changed either my views or my methods since then. If you require me to describe fully the system of education which my children are receiving, I will certainly do so, but this will involve compiling a lengthy exposition, and I cannot undertake this in the sixteen days as required. You will no doubt appreciate that educating my family is a full-time job in itself. Perhaps, therefore, you will inform me if you consider this necessary.'

In reply to this, I received a further letter from Dr. Lincoln Ralphs, which was, in fact, apart from the additional last paragraph, a School Attendance Notice under Section 37(2) of the Education Act, 1944; identical, except for the name of the school, with that sent to me on November 11th, 1954. The Authority now considered East Dereham Secondary Modern Boys' School suitable for David and Garvestone County Primary School for Robin, Felicity, and Wendy, and the letter concluded:

'6. Without prejudice to the terms of this letter, I am to inform you that the services of the Authority's Inspectors are still available to assist you in satisfying the Authority that the children are receiving suitable education.'

In other words, the verbiage as before. It could not reasonably be described as an answer to any particular letter.

I replied to this on June 29th:

'I am in receipt of your letter of the 17th.

'I would be interested to know on what grounds you now state that the Authority are not satisfied that my children, David, Robin, Felicity, and Wendy, are receiving efficient full-time education suitable to their age, ability, and aptitude. I would refer you to my letter of May 16th, in which I offered to supply you with full details of the children's education if you considered it necessary; this, apparently, you prefer to ignore. I would be glad, therefore, if you would inform me how the Authority purports to judge the children's education?

'I would point out to you that your arbitrary decision—taken as always without any knowledge of the children concerned—that it is 'expedient' that they should attend school, overlooks entirely the harmful effect of breaking the pattern of a child's education halfway through. These children's education has followed a definite pattern planned from birth to maturity, open to adjustment whenever and however needed to follow the child's changing and expanding needs, and totally different from the so-called 'education'—in reality only forced mass instruction under conditions of part-time imprisonment—inflicted on children in schools. I think even your School Inspectors would have to admit that the effect of a complete change in the method of education halfway through a child's formative years could not be anything but detrimental to his or her development.

'Regarding your statement that the East Dereham Secondary School would be suitable for David and the Garvestone Primary School for Robin, Felicity, and Wendy, I would be glad to know for what reasons you consider these schools would be suitable for the children. I personally do not consider them suitable, and unlike yourselves, I have personal knowledge of both the children and the schools. I am not, however, interested in selecting any other school, as I do not propose to change the children's present method of education.

'Regarding the final paragraph of your letter, I have already dealt with this point fully in my letter of May 16th and have as yet received no intelligent reply.'

On July 19th, four new School Attendance Orders were served on me, accompanied by another letter from Dr. Lincoln Ralphs.

'After careful consideration,' Dr. Ralphs informed me, 'the Committee decided to authorize the issue of the enclosed Attendance Orders in respect of your children, David, Robin, Felicity, and Wendy.'

He continued: 'In your letter of 29th June 1957, you asked how the Authority purports to judge the children's education. I would, therefore, explain that the Authority is usually guided in assessing whether a child's education is suitable to his or her age, ability, and aptitude by the reports of their Inspectors made after an examination of the child. As you know, in my letters of 16th May and 17th June 1957, the services of the Authority's Inspectors were made available to assist you in satisfying the Authority that the children were receiving suitable education.

'In reply to the other question regarding the suitability of the schools to be named in the School Attendance Orders, East Dereham Secondary Modern Boys' School provides secondary education for children of the same age as your son David, and Garvestone School provides primary education for children of the same age as Robin, Felicity, and Wendy.'

As in all their previous letters, the actual questions I had asked were carefully ignored; the only relevant point was the service of the School Attendance Orders. These I ignored in my turn, and in November 1957, I was again summoned to appear before Dereham Magistrates' Court.

8

The Camel's Hump

On november 8th, 1957, I set out again for the magistrates' court, armed with another carefully prepared brief, to conduct my own case before the Dereham Bench. I was now expecting my seventh baby and was rather noticeably six months pregnant, but there did not seem to be any point in bringing this to the attention of the court. I had no illusions as to what was ahead of me; it could not be supposed that any sort of affection existed between myself and these particular magistrates.

At the start of the proceedings, I asked to be allowed to conduct my case from the solicitors' table, as I had in the appeal court, in order to facilitate my handling of the various papers and documents I needed for reference; but this request was refused by Mrs. F. Wayne, the Chairman of the Bench. I was, however, permitted to sit there during the hearing of the evidence for the prosecution. I took my place and laid out my papers opposite Mr. Brighton, the Council's Assistant Solicitor, and Mr. Earl, the Welfare Officer.

Mr. Brighton opened the case for the Education Authority. He informed the court that the proceedings were brought under the Education Act of 1944 and explained that children had to attend school unless it could be proved that someone was giving them efficient full-time education suitable to their age, ability, and aptitude. There had been exchanged this year, he said, a series of letters between Mrs. Baker on the one side and the Chief Education Officer on the other—and he read these letters, with the Notices and Attendance Orders which had accompanied them, in full to the court.

He then called Mr. Earl, who gave evidence that he had called to see me on the 5th of June, 1956. 'I told Mrs. Baker I had come to see whether her son David was attending school or whether she had made other arrangements. She said, 'I don't intend to discuss my plans with anyone."

Mr. Earl continued: 'I went to see Mrs. Baker again on the 13th of October, 1956. She said the children were not attending school.

'Mrs. Baker then left Norfolk and returned during April 1957, and I went to see her on the 1st of May. I reminded her that I had been to see her on the 13th of October and asked her if the position was the same. She told me there was no change. I reminded her of a statement made by her that she intended to seek a school for David. She stated that she had said if he was ready for it.

'I reported to the Education Authority, and as a result, the first statutory Notice was served.'

Mr. Earl then produced a copy of the Notice, a Post Office receipt for its delivery, and my letter in reply. He also produced a copy of the Notice dated 17th of June and my reply, copies of the School Attendance Orders with their accompanying letter and Post Office receipt, and the rest of the correspondence between myself and the Chief Education Officer. Finally, he produced certificates from the head teachers of East Dereham and Garvestone schools showing that the children had not attended these schools.

Questioned by the Bench, he said that David was twelve, Robin eleven, Felicity nine, and Wendy eight.

This concluded the evidence for the prosecution, and I stood up to cross-examine Mr. Earl.

'You state that these children are not receiving full-time education suitable to their age, ability, and aptitude?—I am here to state that the Education Authority have not been satisfied that your children are receiving proper education.'

'What knowledge have you of the education being given to these children?—The Authority wished to find out the nature of the education the children were receiving, but you would not permit the Inspector to examine the children, and they therefore have no information.'

'You are aware that in my letter of June 2nd, I notified the

Authority that I was continuing to educate the children at home in accordance with the methods I had already described at some length to the Quarter Sessions appeal court and offered to give full details of this education to the Authority if they considered it necessary?—I agree that you did state to the court the nature of the education you were giving to the children.'

'And it is correct that when I described this method of education to the appeal court, I won the case?—Your appeal was allowed on a technical point.'

'It is correct that the Authority ignored my letter but stated that they were not satisfied that the children were receiving efficient education?—You replied to the Authority sixteen days after the Notice was served on you. That was the time the Authority had given you to satisfy them. The matter was considered by the Committee, and it was decided to issue the second statutory Notice.'

'They did not wish to have any further details of the children's education?—If you had made certain statements to the Authority or given them any evidence within the sixteen days allowed to you, the Authority might have taken a different course.'

'They were not prepared to allow any further time for me to satisfy them?—If you had provided the additional evidence, the Authority might have accepted it.'

'But in fact, they did not inform me of this but proceeded to issue the statutory Notice?—They decided to go ahead.'

'Your Notices state that the Authority has decided that Dereham Secondary Modern Boys' School is suitable for David and Robin?—Yes.'

'If this school is considered suitable by the Authority, it must follow that they consider these boys' education to be up to the standard of other boys of their age at that school?—The only facts the Authority knew were the ages of the children, and Dereham Secondary Modern School is for children of the age of David and Robin.'

'Then age is the only factor taken into consideration by the Authority when deciding what school is suitable for a child?—Once the children had been admitted to school and an assessment made of their ability, arrangements might then have to be reviewed.'

'But the Authority had, in fact, been offered details of these children's education and had not wished to receive them?—The Authority proceeded with these cases because they lacked knowledge as to the children's education.'

'Knowledge which they had been offered but did not wish to have?—They took what they considered to be the proper course.'

'Without any knowledge of whether these children would, in fact, receive suitable education at the schools named?—The schools operate under the Norfolk Education Committee.'

'Do you not think that the effect of a complete change in the method of education halfway through a child's formative years would be detrimental rather than helpful to its educational development?—I am not an expert in educational methods. I could not say whether it would or not.'

'It is now over two years since I won my appeal in the previous case?—Yes.'

'Following my successful appeal, were the Authority satisfied that the children were receiving a proper education?—The Authority were mainly concerned because you had stated that you would seek a school for David.'

'I informed you when you visited me that I was continuing to educate my children at home. If the Authority was not satisfied about their education, why was no action taken earlier?—After I visited you on the 13th of October, the facts were reported to the Committee. The Authority were on the point of taking action in November 1956 but were prevented because you had left the county.'

'But the Authority took no action between July 1955 and November 1956?—No.

'Why did the Authority wait so long before taking action?'

Mr. Earl hesitated. 'I saw you on the 1st May, and it was considered at the Authority's meeting on the 8th May,' he began. Here the Clerk of the Court, Mr. L. H. Allwood, intervened. 'Come now, Mr. Earl, that won't wash!' he said. 'What Mrs. Baker is asking is, why was no action taken by the Authority between July 1955 and November 1956?' Mr. Earl appeared confused. He replied: 'I don't know. I—no, I don't know.'

I resumed. 'In fact, Mr. Earl, having left the matter for this length of time, the Authority suddenly decided to bring these proceedings without having any actual reason for doing so?—The Authority has a duty placed upon it to see that the children are receiving education according to the Act.

'But they left it for one year and four months without taking any action?—Yes.

This concluded my cross-examination, and Mr. Earl was then re-examined by Mr. Brighton for the Education Authority.

'Mr. Earl, was not the reason that the Authority took no action after Mrs. Baker's appeal because she had said it was her intention to seek a school for her son David?—Yes, I believe so.

'The Authority felt that he was the important one?—Yes, they regarded his case as being the most urgent.

'They wanted to give Mrs. Baker the opportunity of getting him to school before taking any further action?—Yes.

Mr. Brighton sat down, and Mr. Earl returned to his seat at the table. The Clerk of the Court then asked me if I wished to give evidence. I affirmed that I did and was curtly requested by Mrs. Wayne to go into the witness box. Throughout the rest of the hearing, I had to stand, in considerable physical discomfort, balancing papers and documents on the narrow edge of the box.

This angered me from the start; perhaps also, as a result of my pregnancy, I was rather liable to react sharply to this kind of attitude. I went into the witness box, put down my papers, took the Testament in my right hand, and before the Clerk could get across the court to me to administer the oath, rapped it out in the manner of seasoned policemen when giving evidence: 'I-swear-by-Almighty-God-that-the-evidence-I-shall-give-to-the-court-shall-be-the-truth-the-whole-truth-and-nothing-but-the-truth.'

There was a dead silence following this, and in it, I picked up my brief and started to present my case.

'I think it is already clear that I am not sending my children to school because I do not believe in school education and am educating them myself at home. I maintain that it is wrong to separate upbringing and instruction, and that education should be the combining of both in the secure and natural surroundings of the child's home. It is now two years since this view was upheld by the decision of the Quarter Sessions Appeals Committee in Norwich, during which time no action has been taken against me by the Education Authorities, other than a number of visits by Mr. Earl for the apparent purpose of ascertaining whether my views remained unchanged.

'In May this year, I received formal Notices from the Education Authority calling upon me to satisfy them that the children were receiving efficient education and offering the services of their Inspectors to examine the children. I replied as you have already heard.

'In their reply of the 17th of June, the Education Authority ignored my offer to give details of the education being given to my children but stated that they were not satisfied with it. They further stated that they considered East Dereham Secondary Modern Boys' School and Garvestone County Primary School suitable to the children's age, ability, and aptitude—although they had, of course, no information concerning the children's individual ability and aptitude. They again stated, in their final paragraph, 'the service of the Authority's Inspectors are still available to assist you in satisfying the Authority that the children are receiving suitable education.' I replied again as you have heard.

'Regarding the question of the Authority's Inspectors, I had, of course, refused the Authority's offer of their services on this occasion for the reasons given in the letter which Mr. Brighton read to the court. I would point out also that when proceedings were taken against me two years ago, I did agree to the children being examined by the school Inspectors, and although this Bench decided the case against me, I subsequently won it on appeal. It does appear to me, therefore, that despite the importance the Authority appears to place on it, the services of their Inspectors would be of little value either to them or me.

'Mr. Earl has told the court that I said I intended to send David to school. But what I said after the hearing of my appeal was that I should consider the question of finding a suitable school for David. After consideration, I decided to continue his education, with the other children, at home.

'You have been told that the Authority regarded David as the 'most urgent case' and that they 'wanted to give me the opportunity of sending him to school' before taking any further action. I find it difficult to understand why they regarded David, at ten, as being so much more urgent than Robin, at nine; and it appears to me very strange that they give this urgency as the reason why they waited for nearly eighteen months 'to give me the opportunity' of sending this one child to school.

'It appears to me far more likely that they took no action over this period because they had no grounds for assuming that the children were not all being properly educated. And having decided, after nearly two years, to bring fresh proceedings against me, their main reason for doing so appears to be that I could not draw up a detailed statement regarding my children's education within a fixed period of sixteen days. The mere fact that it could not be described within a limited time would not, I should have thought, necessarily mean that the education was inefficient.

'My whole purpose in keeping my children away from school is to avoid their having school education. 'Compulsory education' is in itself a contradiction in terms. At school, you can sit children in rows at desks and tell them things, and you may instruct a proportion of them more or less adequately in a number of quite useless subjects, but this is not education. If we all had now only the learning we received in school, we should be entirely unequipped to face adult life. Yet children are kept at school until well into adolescence and then, for the most part, pushed out without warning into an adult world for which they have no preparation whatever. The time at which education starts is when we are born—and there is no 'leaving age.' We are all still being educated—we absorb knowledge and understanding as we live. So do children—except during the unfortunate period of their lives when they are shut up in school.

'The Education Act provides that children shall receive efficient full-time education, but it does not define what 'education' consists of. Is education enforced instruction in certain fixed subjects, decided by a Government department, given at fixed times to all children regardless of individual development? Or is it full-time encouragement and help in the development of a sound and healthy body and an active and enquiring mind, and the acquiring of permanent knowledge and understanding of those subjects within the range, capability, and interest of each individual child, at the times when that child is ready and able to most beneficially absorb them? The former is school; the latter is my system of education.'

'My eldest son David has pointed out that if we had been negroes living in Arkansas, he and my other children would recently have been *prevented* from attending school by force. He was also interested in one comment on the situation: 'School attendance at bayonet point is not compatible with the American way of life.' Apparently, school attendance under threat of legal action is now compatible with the British way of life.

'You may say that the Education Act is a comparatively trivial regulation. But it is not a trivial matter when it is the taking of our children's minds out of their parents' care and putting them into that of strangers governed by an arbitrary authority, under threats of fines, imprisonment, or the bodily removal of the children permanently from their homes. This is not education—it is dictatorship.

'I believe in education by natural development and instruction given 'on demand' and not by the calendar and clock. And it works. That I have proved already—but I cannot prove final results unless I can continue and complete the children's education. I have proved that without any formal instruction whatever, beyond a few hours' assistance in the early stages, a child will learn to read—up to the point of reading the more literary daily newspapers and technical books and magazines. I have proved that less than an hour's instruction is needed to teach a child the alphabet—at the right age—against weeks of teaching too young. A child can absorb any knowledge without difficulty if it is given when the mind is ready for it. And no two children are ready at the same age. Why put children at desks at five years old and younger and struggle to teach them what will come to them with only the slightest help and instruction a few years later on? Sometimes I have wondered if one of my children or another was backward in some subject and should be pushed with it. But when I have tried, it has been obvious that the response was not there; and perhaps a few months, perhaps years later, the child has itself sought instruction in that subject and absorbed it readily. This is impossible in school—but it is true education.

'Subjects covered by my method of education have included most of those taught in school—but not at the same age or in the same way. For that reason alone, it must be obvious that no school inspector could give a fair picture of their actual development; and also that to send them to school now would be extremely damaging to their mental development.

'David is up to adult standard in reading; Robin can read most things but is still acquiring the more difficult words. Felicity and Wendy are still in the process of learning. They are taking longer than the boys did, but I do not see in this any cause for alarm. They have the whole of their childhood to learn to read in, and while they are not reading, they are learning other things.

'On this point of learning to read young, I have very definite views. I myself learned to read at a very early age—but not to stand up to what I had read. As a result, my childhood was filled with sleepless nights and horrors which I can still remember, arising from something I had read. I do not believe that any young children are sufficiently developed mentally to read even the most innocuous-seeming children's stories without the risk of unpredictable results. It is impossible in a normal household to keep reading matter from a child, and it is impossible to tell in any case what things will upset what child until it is too late. It is far more sensible to let the child learn to read at a later age when the mind has developed sufficiently to withstand and deal with the subject matter absorbed indiscriminately into it.

'I would also point out that a number of children leave school unable to read, despite the fact that their education has presumably satisfied the Education Authorities. David has recently got to know a tractor driver in our locality who left Dereham School ten years ago. He cannot read; David has been thoughtfully reading a book on tractor management to him. It does not follow that because a child sits in school for ten long years, he will even be instructed, let alone educated. He will merely have satisfied the Education Act.

'Handwriting is another subject on which I hold strong, if unorthodox, views. I believe that this is commonly taught a great deal too young, before the child has any mastery of the necessary coordination of hand and eye. There is a dreadful similarity in the handwritings of schoolchildren—of which we can see examples on every available wall and poster in every town and village—but which hardly constitutes any advertisement for school education. It is a revealing fact that an adult who writes in the handwriting taught at school is commonly referred to as having an 'uneducated' hand.

'Writing also involves the question of manual dexterity, and this varies very greatly with the individual child. David's hands are those of a manual worker, although his mind is that of a barrister in the making. He has an extensive vocabulary and an acutely active mind—but his hands are just not suited to the deft manipulation of a pen. They are, however, hands that can tackle any mechanical job and tend any living thing with steadiness and skill. Writing, therefore, is for him a laborious task and one I will not discourage him by pressing. A good deal was made two years ago by Mr. Greenwood of David's inability to write an essay—but a year ago, given access to a typewriter, he started writing stories about a family of rabbits. His difficulty lay in lack of manual ability, not mental. Which is the more important: the ability to use the mind unhindered by discouragement, or the ability to write a clear if meaningless hand? If it is suggested that this difficulty would have been overcome by school instruction, I can bring an immediate example to prove this is incorrect. I was taught and had to exercise handwriting from an early age at school. My writing was so bad that frequently I had essays returned because my teachers were unable to read them. My brother, who is now a brilliant scientist, has never been able to write a legible hand. When he writes letters, he prints the address on the envelope in capitals; and he also was taught at school. The great majority of adults cannot or do not produce a legible or attractive handwriting. But a handwriting that at school—or in the case of my children, not at school—is termed backward, becomes, as soon as the child is past school, an accepted thing. It is no reflection on a person's education to say that their handwriting is appalling—if it were, we must regard the great majority of our doctors as uneducated.

'I believe that if people were not taught to write at all until they reached adult life, they could learn without difficulty a good hand. But in practice, you can't stop children from learning to write. Therefore, all my children can write; David, as I have said, laboriously, Robin neatly and with enjoyment, and the girls still unsteadily in capitals. They will be taught good handwriting at a later age.

'Despite this approach to handwriting, they have all a very good idea of spelling, which they have acquired, like most things, without any set lessons at all. Here again, I become aware of the futility of school education. My brother, the scientist, who had a school and university education, still put an 'h' in 'sugar' and 'sure.'

'This approach to handwriting has one other result, educationally beneficial. Instead of taking notes of things they wish to remember or facts in which they are interested, they have to retain these things in their minds. This has greatly developed their capacity for committing facts to permanent memory. You can write down facts given by a teacher without fully understanding them,—but you must understand them in order to retain them in your mind.

'I do not believe there is any point in teaching any subjects to children in which they have no interest and for which they have no aptitude. In my experience, the mind merely discards such subjects as soon as it reaches adult status, and the time spent trying to instill such knowledge into it is therefore wasted. If such instruction is intended to train the mind without bothering about the ultimate result, there are plenty of other subjects on which the mind can be trained. None of my children has so far shown any mathematical ability, and I can see no reason why they should be made to study these subjects unless and until it develops. When I left school at fifteen, my standard in mathematics must have been, despite everybody's efforts, about that of a child of ten. It still is. But I have never felt the need of what I am supposed to have missed. None of my children has received formal instruction in written arithmetic, other than David and Robin periodically at their own request, but they are all capable of adding, subtracting, multiplying, and dividing mentally. David has, for the past year or more, done the greater part of the household shopping, in the course of which he has learned the practical use of figures where quantities, weights, and money are concerned. He has been entrusted with amounts of up to £10, and I have never yet found an error in his calculations. Further, he has on a number of occasions accurately queried incorrect change or prices offered. Robin is now following in the same lines with equal success. Both David and Robin do frequently ask to be set sums for their own entertainment. They have never learned the multiplication tables by heart but can give the answer to the multiplication of most figures in the tables after brief consideration.

'I have never been able to see any useful purpose in history as taught in schools. History is an adult subject, largely quite unsuitable for children and quite beyond their understanding. It concerns the behavior of adult people, and most children find the behavior of the adults about them quite incomprehensible enough. It is absurd to suppose that they can understand the behavior of centuries of mankind. My children have been given a general idea of the history of this country and the beginning of human life on the earth. But my purpose is to teach them—or rather to let them read—history as a subject in full when they are old enough to see the whole in perspective and understand it—and that is not until well after school leaving age.

'Geography can be understood at a younger age since it is the result of natural phenomena. I believe geography to be a necessary part of a child's education, but I don't believe you can make a class of children sit down and be told, 'Now this term we are going to do Africa'—or whatever it may be. David had, in response to his own requests, a globe of the world two years ago as a Christmas present and has treasured it ever since. He has studied it in detail in a general way and asked questions about everything that interested him—which means that he asked a great many questions. As any country or area comes into the news, he finds it on the globe and looks it up in his atlas. His interest draws the attention of the younger children, and they all therefore absorb all the information we can collect about it. In this way, he has learned a more accurate knowledge of the globe than I, school-taught, have ever possessed. Does he know the same things which are taught in school? Probably not—he knows it from the angle in which it will enter into his adult life. His great interest is in the Antarctic, and he reads everything available about the present Antarctic expedition.

'Natural history all the children have absorbed as a matter of course throughout their lives. Living in the country, they have always taken a direct interest in the plant and animal life around them, and David and Robin have read all the nature books that I possess and many others since bought for them. They can identify birds and their eggs—without ever having wanted to collect them—and they understand, from practical observation and what to them is leisure-time reading, all the facts which I absorbed throughout hours of botany lessons in school.

'The ages of David and Robin give rise to the question of the eleven-plus exam. My personal opinion, like that of many others, is that this so-called system of assessing a child's intelligence is an absurdity. Nevertheless, when David was given an encyclopedia for his last birthday and found a section devoted to specimens of eleven-plus tests, he tackled them with enthusiasm. I did not impose a time limit, which I believe does nothing but panic the child's mind and handicap the sensitive more than the dull. He did all the tests within reasonable time; he had no difficulty in answering any of the questions—except one—and all his answers were correct. The one question he could not answer, I failed to answer also. We looked up the answer finally, but having seen it, were still no further forward. I do not know whether this result indicates that his intelligence is high or mine is low, but perhaps the court can judge. I would, in this connection, remind you that selection for the grammar schools is made on the results of the eleven-plus exam, which is supposed to be a test of intelligence, not knowledge—but without any reason to dispute David's or Robin's intelligence, the Education Authority has stated that they regard Dereham Secondary Modern Boys' School as suitable for them—that is, the school they would have been sent to had they been attending a primary school and failed the eleven-plus.

'I have been talking about school subjects, but education covers, and my children learn, a great deal more. I don't know exactly what schools aim to turn out; the only reasonable answer seems to be schoolteachers. I am bringing up and educating my children to become men and women healthy in mind and body, to become good husbands and wives, good fathers and mothers—and I maintain that this is the most important achievement of all. They are being educated in family life as no family broken by school attendance can be; they are being prepared ultimately to take the responsibilities of adults while enjoying the freedom which should be the right of every child; and they are developing their own individual interests, not in the scanty hours permitted after homework, but as part of their whole education.'

At this point, Mrs. Wayne intervened to ask, in a rather bored voice, whether I had much more to say. I replied firmly that I had a good deal to say yet, and Mrs. Wayne glanced at the clock and announced: 'We will adjourn for lunch, then. The court will resume at two.'

I didn't really want any lunch, but I was glad to be able to sit down; Mr. Richard Bales of the *Daily Sketch*, who had been interested in the case from the beginning, took me out to a restaurant near the court. At two o'clock, I was back in the witness box, ready to continue my evidence.

'I now propose to deal briefly with each of the children individually.

'David, who is now twelve, is a child of many divergent interests. His main interest is in farming, and to this, he brings capable hands, a strong body, and an active mind. He spends all the time he can learning the work of the farms around us and will work from dawn to dusk. But he is also interested in law and is still undecided whether he wants to be a farmer or a barrister. He has the equipment for either, and his present education is training both his mind and his body so that when he reaches the age at which he can make a mature decision, he will be in a position to take up either the labour of the one or the studies of the other with vigour and ability. He has recently taken up photography and, in the course of only three months, has shown an outstanding ability. He entered three of his photographs in a recent competition in Parents magazine, and in competition with all their readers, he was among the first ten prizewinners. I consider this a far more effective test of both his education and ability than any school exam.

'Robin, at eleven, is an entirely different character, lacking David's power of concentration and width of interest, but he has a manual neatness that David lacks. He has unusual domestic ability and is an excellent cook. He is a keen gardener, as well as sharing David's interest in farming, especially where the care of animals is concerned. His main educational needs at present are not academic, but the development of his individual tastes and sense of responsibility—the reverse of which would be encouraged in school.

'Felicity, at nine, is a happy child and also a woman in miniature, which is surely what a growing girl should be. She will learn scholastic subjects if these are associated with practical things. Her main interests are in babies and horses. She can ride a galloping horse bareback, although she has never had a riding lesson in her life. She can care for a child of a year old entirely and single-handed; she can dress, feed, bathe, and put nappies on a baby from a few weeks old with a great deal more skill than I, who had only a school education, could bring to my first child. She started to learn to read through the necessity of reading the names of the baby foods when she took charge of her year-old brother—without any other adult aid—when I had to go into hospital for the birth of my last baby. She has since taken charge of both children, one six months old and the other eighteen months, during my absence for three days. She is learning to cook, she can turn out a room with a domestic efficiency which I never had a chance to acquire, and she still believes in fairies. I do not understand why any sane person should want to turn her into that awkward, giggling, school-uniformed monstrosity—a schoolgirl.

'Wendy, at eight, is the problem of my family. She is immature without being backward in intelligence in any degree. She is unteachable, but, given the right circumstances, quick to learn. She is aggressive and yet nervous to the point of paralyzing shyness when faced with anything of which she is afraid, and she is afraid of anything with which she is not allowed and helped to become acquainted gradually and in her own time. She is slow in learning to read, but she can make up stories of incredible length and imaginative quality. She is impatient of dry facts but has a love of poetry even when she cannot comprehend the meaning of the words. She is a child who is developing so slowly, and who is so easily brought to a state of panic by any attempt to enforce knowledge on her, that of all my children, I believe that attendance at school under compulsory conditions would be, for her, most seriously disastrous. Her mind is a sensitive and wholly unawakened thing, and on the security or lack of it with which she is surrounded now, I believe her whole adult life will depend. There is nothing any intelligent parent can do for such a child other than to offer what instruction the mind is ready for and leave the rest to the progress of the child's natural development.

'Wendy was most seriously affected by the school inspectors' visit two years ago. At that time, she did not know and had utterly failed to learn her ABC. After the inspection, I was awakened night after night by her desperate cries with only one theme—'I try and *try*, but I can't do ABC.' My job was not to instruct her but to tell her it didn't matter—that it didn't matter in the least if she never learned ABC—and only after I had managed to instill that into her mind did she relax again and get back to normal. A year later, she came to me and said she thought she could learn ABC now. In less than an hour, she did. For the rest of the day, we all got quite tired of hearing the alphabet—she was still saying it when I bathed her and put her to bed. She is now learning to read, and personally, I don't think it matters if this takes her another five years, provided I don't have her damp with tears, crying in bed every night.'

'Many mothers have this experience with their children at school—and they are powerless to help them. Yet why, after all, should children have to learn these things between five and fifteen? Why should it be now a criminal offence to acknowledge the fact that some children learn later than others? Why should not education in any subject start *after* fifteen years of age if it is obvious that this will be more beneficial to the child?

'All my children have been taught good manners as part of their education. I do not know if any members of the Bench ever have occasion to travel on the 4:16 train from Dereham to Norwich during the school term. I avoid doing so when I can because of the appalling behaviour of the boys and girls from the Dereham Secondary Modern Schools. I might add that the behaviour of the children from the Grammar School at Swaffham is, if anything, worse. Shouting, running up and down the train, trying to push each other out of windows, grabbing each other's caps and hair—is this what they learn in school? Such behaviour is not natural to children—and mine would never behave in this way. David had his cap snatched off by one boy some months ago because he was sitting quietly, bringing back the week's shopping. Which child showed the better education?

'Not long ago my children had a visit from a boy who goes to Garvestone Primary School. He came uninvited, and his idea of seeking and accepting our hospitality was to pick our apples and throw them at my two girls. He hit Wendy in the stomach, making a red mark on the skin. Then he ran away, leaving her in tears. I don't think he can have learnt such behaviour at home—he was the vicar's son. I don't want my boys to acquire this sort of 'schoolboy' behaviour.

'I believe the importance placed on school instruction is a plain absurdity. There are many different ways in which children can be prepared for adult life and a great many different kinds of adult life for which different children need preparation. A schoolteacher knows nothing of the child's mind and heart, little of its background, and less of its probable future. To bring up and educate a child you should have studied it and its development from birth onwards; you need also to love it with all your heart. Only a parent can do this. Instruction is something that takes place in the course of education, not education itself.

'If too much is made of the learning of set school subjects, the child's mind quickly becomes bored. It is much more interesting to look out of the window. I believe it is the child who looks out of the window—the apparently inattentive child—who may be the real scholar. There may be something being done in a field outside the window of real interest to the boy who is going to be a farmer—but he is supposed to be paying attention to English grammar or singing hymns. There may be a whole spring morning unfolding before the eyes of the young poet—but he is supposed to be doing sums. The future mother may be watching a baby crying in a pram and wanting to comfort it—but she ought to be learning dates in history. Yet what these children are interested in is what they need to study—what they, despite what their teacher says, are going to need to know as soon as they escape from the hampering shell of school.

'Children will reach for their own educational needs if they are allowed to do it. They may do it when they are five or fifteen, it doesn't matter—it only matters that they should be given them when they are ready. My children are behind the accepted standards in some subjects because I do not believe in teaching those subjects at an early age, or because their minds are not yet ready to learn them. But if these children had reached the same standards while attending school, the Education Act and the Education Authority would be satisfied.

'The Authority can give their definition of education in three words—'children in school.' Whether the child learns anything, benefits, or suffers, doesn't matter to them. If I have a child at school who is ill with unhappiness, I am not allowed to keep that child away—that is a criminal offence. Could I sue the Education Authority, if my children did attend their schools, on the grounds that they were not giving the children a proper education? That, according to the Act, is my responsibility—but when I take the responsibility in full, personally, that is a criminal offence.

'It has been clearly stated by the Education Authorities that the purpose of modern education is to produce scientists and technologists. Are parents and the children themselves then to be allowed no choice? If I want to produce farmers, writers, or just happy wives and mothers in my children—and I did, after all, produce the children in the first place—does the State deny me the right? If children are to be sent to school to be turned into scientists or technologists by force, this is not education, it is vivisection—vivisection of our living young.

'The system of compulsory education by age takes no account, not only of the varying mental development of different children, but of their physical and emotional development, particularly during adolescence. My eldest son, who is physically as tough as he well could be, is entering into that period of pre-adolescence acknowledged by child-care experts, but not apparently by the

Education Authority. Alternating with reasoned adult behaviour, he has periods of depression which he cannot explain, often accompanied by extreme exhaustion. This is not due to either physical or mental overwork but simply to the demands on his system, both physical and emotional, made by growing up. We cannot order the development of our children to fit a compulsory educational system; so the child at school is expected to carry on normally during these times, with the fear of being laughed at or punished if he fails, since another younger child may experience no such difficulties and make the elder appear lazy or a fool. They are expected, on top of a day's schoolwork, to do homework; and yet I have seen my son, after no extra effort or exertion, lying asleep at the tea table, while his younger brother, having done the same things, is full of energy. And a few years ago, it was the younger boy who fell asleep in the middle of the evening from sheer child-tiredness, at which time the elder boy appeared incapable of being tired at all. The time for fullest mental activity is after the child has completed the physical transition from childhood to young man—or womanhood, and this is the time when intellectual education should be intensified. But according to the Education Authority, this comes after 'school-leaving age.'

'It seems a strange fact that this modern insistence on education should coincide so precisely with the enormous prevalence of the comic paper—that the age of universal literacy should go hand in hand with the universal absorption of, not books, but strip cartoons. The average schoolchild, almost without exception, reads these shocking pieces of print. But the literature demanded by my supposedly uneducated children is *Mother and Baby, Parents Magazine, Riding, Amateur Photographer, Popular Gardening, The Farmer and Stock-breeder,* and *The Eastern Daily Press.*

'I do not want my children's minds filled and interfered with by schoolteachers. The Education Authority made it plain at the hearing of my appeal that their intention was to try to take my children away from me entirely—to put them into an institution—because they are being educated according to my views and not according to the rules of the State. Hitler could go no further. I will resist this to the furthermost point. These are my children, and no human being has the true right to take them from me. Yet I have to fight in court for the right to keep my own children, to justify a course of action which has resulted—and not even the Education Authority denies this—in happy, healthy, alert, intelligent children, who compare favourably with any child in school.

'What constitutes an educated person? I should know, because I am always being described as an 'educated woman'—although I left school at fifteen, several years short of School Certificate standard in most subjects, after attending as little as possible while I was supposed to be there. But what most people mean by 'well-educated' is that I speak properly. All my children have been taught to speak well—a great deal better than their counterparts at school.

'I would like to quote from an article in Parents magazine, concerning an old classics master from Merchant Taylors', who was asked to itemize the marks of an educated man or woman. He put forward six factors:

'First, the correct use of the mother tongue;

'Secondly, continuing intellectual growth;

'Thirdly, good manners;

'Fourthly, good taste;

'Fifthly, the inculcation of the power to do;

'Lastly, the power to reflect.'

'None of these factors is learned in school, but all are included in my system of education.

'In the same article, the author states: 'The purpose of education is not to learn facts but to exercise faculties. Too many people imagine that a teacher's job is to cram the child's head with knowledge. The very word education means the precise opposite. Education is the art of drawing out the potential talents which are already there.'

'I recently saw a quotation from a speech by Mr. Khrushchev: 'We must abolish the cult of the individual once and for all.' It would seem that this is also the view of the Education Authority.

'I would like to read to you now the following comment on my views, published two years ago in the *Daily Sketch*, headed:

'Shout for Joy'

'All praise to Mrs. Joy Baker, of Norfolk. She has won the right to educate her children at home instead of sending them to school.

'Yes, I'm on the subject of education again; there are few subjects, in my view, more important.

'I am all for the individual in these matters. The State is there to safeguard standards in education, not to impose a mould.

'There is no legal obligation on a parent to send children to school. The Education Act simply requires that the child should have a full-time education.

'Most parents can meet that requirement only by sending their children to school. Mrs. Baker appears to have the time and the ability to teach them fully herself.'

'This was written by Lord Hailsham—until recently Minister of Education.

'It has been suggested that I am incompetent to teach my children because I am untrained as a teacher. As the fact that I have nearly thirteen years' experience as a parent and teacher to these children apparently doesn't count, I would like to remind you that there are other people totally untrained for a job carrying great human responsibility—country magistrates.

'The law concerning going to school is imposed by man. The law of natural development was made by God. I prefer to follow the higher authority.'

I collected my papers, wishing there was somewhere I could sit down, if only for a few moments, and then turned to face Mr. Brighton's cross-examination.

It was an anticlimax. I was tired out, and Mr. Brighton appeared at a loss for something suitable to ask. In reply to his first questions, I said that I did not teach my children unless they wanted to learn. If a child showed no aptitude for a subject, it could learn something else.

I agreed that the Chairman of the Appeals Committee said that I won on a technicality, but he gave me the right to decide about my children's education. I did not think they would have allowed my appeal if they had been opposed to my views.

I would try to impress a subject on a child if I thought it was necessary. My children responded to the teaching I gave them. They would acquire, in the course of everyday life, the same knowledge as children who went to school.

'Mrs. Baker,' continued Mr. Brighton, 'have any of your children ever been to school?'

I said they had not.

'Have you any friends who are schoolteachers?'

'No,' I said. 'It is hardly likely, is it?'

'What knowledge have you of the schools today?'

'I inspected two of the local schools quite recently, and I was not impressed by them.'

'Do you think that you are better able to teach your children than people who have years of teaching experience?'

'No one has experience of teaching my children,' I said, 'and I have had experience of the State school system.'

'How many other children have you below school age?'

'Two, so far,' I said.

'Do you agree with the eleven-plus exam?'

'No,' I said. 'I think it is idiotic.'

This concluded Mr. Brighton's rather desultory questioning, and I turned again to the Bench to give my final address.

'You have heard my statement and the evidence for the prosecution. I submit that these proceedings are not a matter of law but a matter of opinion as to what suitable education for these children should consist of. No amount of argument can decide which view is right—mine or the Education Authority's. But I am not seeking to force my view on anyone else's children—it is the Education Authority who seek to force theirs on mine. Is not the whole point of this case whether, under the present Act, the individual parents have or have not the right to decide on the most suitable education for their own child?

'I submit that the Act allows some freedom to the individual, and that the education I am giving to my children is efficient full-time education suitable to their ages, abilities, and aptitudes within the meaning of the Act; and I claim the right to hold and act on my own views in this matter of the education of my own children.

'I therefore ask you to dismiss these summonses and allow me to bring up and educate my children in peace.'

Rather wearily, I stepped down from the witness box and walked back to a seat in the body of the court. The magistrates turned and filed out through the doorway behind the bench.

They seemed to be gone for a very long time. I grew restless, wondering what this portended. It did not seriously occur to me that I might have succeeded; I had watched their faces whilst I was talking and seen their expressions as they left the court.

At last, the door opened again, and we all rose to our feet as the little procession returned. When everyone was seated again, Mrs. Wayne addressed me.

'We have considered what you have said, and before making a decision, we would like to see your older children and ask them a few questions. We have only your word to go on, and we would like to see the children so that we can judge for ourselves. If you agree to this, the hearing will be adjourned until next Friday in order that the children may be brought to the court.'

I said I agreed. Inwardly, it seemed to me that this proposal to give an examination in court was imposing an unreasonable strain on children of nine and twelve years old.

The case was then adjourned, and I went home to prepare David and Felicity for their coming ordeal. There had been no other course which I could take; to refuse the examination was to lose without justification; but I knew very well the weight that this would place on David's young shoulders. David had always had a very highly developed sense of personal responsibility, and, as the eldest, he would feel that our success or failure depended on him. It was a heavy responsibility for a boy of twelve.

He faced up to it, as I knew he would, with determination and courage, while I tried to reassure him that magistrates were unpredictable anyway, and no real importance could, under these conditions, be attached to failure. He looked at me steadily and said, 'But it would be important if we won?' The night before the resumed hearing he lay awake for a long time. He looked very small and defenceless when I finally went up to his room and found him asleep.

On the morning of Friday, November 15th, David, Felicity, and I set out for the magistrates' court. I assumed that, as I had explained the children's individual interests to the magistrates, their 'examination' would cover those particular subjects, which formed an important part of their education. David therefore took with him some of his photographs, and Felicity carried in her arms nine-month-old baby Martin, with all the equipment she needed to change and dress him, so that she could demonstrate her ability in handling a child. With Martin, warm and cuddly in her arms, the coming interview with the magistrates seemed less frightening. David carried himself with a calm, alert confidence, which revealed nothing of the inner turmoil I knew he was experiencing. So the four of us arrived at the court.

We were met at the entrance by several policemen and a bevy of reporters; the news of this unusual 'exam' had brought representatives of all the national newspapers to hear the result of the case. Once we were in the building, the children had no time to feel afraid; we were surrounded by reporters even while we waited in the little anteroom outside the courtroom, and their interest and friendliness put David and Felicity at ease. Martin was delighted by so much attention and smiled happily at everyone.

After some time one of the policemen came in and called us. David had chosen to go alone to face the magistrates. Proudly, with his head held high, he went through the courtroom, accompanied by two uniformed policemen, to the magistrates' room beyond.

Felicity, Martin, and I waited. Felicity looked apprehensive. Martin laughed and played with her long copper hair.

After half an hour David returned. 'He has some written work to do,' a court official informed us; Mrs. Wayne had given him a grocery bill to add up. David was shut alone in the little anteroom, while Felicity and I, with Martin still in her arms, were taken by the policemen through the court. Martin was astonished by this but remained placid; Felicity was by now very frightened.

We were taken into the magistrates' room and sat down facing the three men and two women magistrates. Felicity clung to Martin—apart from my presence, the only thing left to her that she understood. If they would only let her start by looking after him, I thought, she would gain confidence for whatever else they wanted her to do.

But the magistrates had other ideas.

'Give the baby to Mummy, dear,' Mrs. Wayne said acidly. 'Now, what do you want to be when you grow up?'

Felicity at that time cherished a dream of marrying a man who had a lot of horses and having a lot of babies. Too shy to tell five complete strangers this, she sat silent, in tears.

'You needn't be afraid,' said Mrs. Wayne brightly. 'We're quite ordinary people, you know.'

Hardly ordinary, I thought, when she is brought before you by two policemen and you have the power to send her mother to prison.

There was an interruption. David knocked at the door and came in, holding his arithmetic exercise. 'Please could you tell me what this figure is meant to be?' he asked the Chairman. 'I can't make out your handwriting!'

Mrs. Wayne took the grocery list and deciphered the item in question. David thanked her and went back to finish his task.

'Where is he doing his written work?' one of the magistrates asked. 'Has he been put somewhere private?'

'He's in the little anteroom,' replied Mrs. Wayne.

'I don't know if that's very private,' I interposed. 'When we were there, it was seething with reporters!'

This remark caused a minor panic among the members of the Bench. I got a black look from Mrs. Wayne, and a policeman was hastily dispatched to find out where David was working. He returned a few minutes later to report that David was alone in the anteroom and another policeman was guarding the door.

One of the magistrates then produced a book with coloured pictures of wild animals, remarking to the others, 'I pinched this from the library.' Felicity looked startled; she didn't know magistrates pinched things.

'Now, can you tell us what animal this is?' In a small, precise voice, Felicity named all the animals correctly.

'What day is it?' barked a fat man at the end of the table, who hadn't spoken before. Felicity looked surprised at a magistrate not knowing this but told him politely that it was Friday. ('He should have known,' she commented afterwards, 'because the court always sits on a Friday!')

After this, we were told we could go, and we joined David, who had finished his grocery bill, in the anteroom. We were immediately surrounded again by reporters, wanting to know what had happened during the 'exams.'

I also wanted to know what David's examination had been like. Had the magistrates let him talk at all about farming, Antarctica, photography?

'They didn't ask me anything about farming—or the Antarctic,' he told us, 'and they didn't seem very interested in my photographs. They asked me who was captain of England's cricket team, and I told them Peter May. They showed me some coins and asked me to name the kings' heads on them. I knew those too. They asked a lot of questions about sport. When I answered the questions, Mrs. Wayne kept saying, 'Jolly good!' But she didn't tell me whether I added her grocery bill up right.

'I wrote my name and address, and read part of an article in the *Reader's Digest*. And they asked me one question about camels, and they got the answer wrong. They asked me what did a camel have in its hump, and I said it stored fat, and they said no, it was water. And then I got them to look it up in a book, and they found I was right!'

The door opened, and a policeman called me into the court to hear the magistrates' decision. By now the reporters had all gathered around David, so I left him holding a press conference. (The children were not allowed to come into the court to hear the decision; this would have been against the law.)

Mrs. Wayne addressed me: 'From what you have said and from what we have observed ourselves, we do not consider you have discharged the onus upon you to prove you are causing the children to receive efficient full-time education suitable to their ages, abilities, and aptitudes, otherwise than at school.'

I was fined £2—ten shillings for each child. As soon as the Chairman had finished speaking, I stood up and stated, 'I wish to inform the court that it is my intention to appeal against this decision, and formal notices of appeal will be lodged in due course.'

I then returned to the ante-room to find Felicity changing an unperturbed Martin, and David still being interviewed by the Press. When we left the court, we found a group of photographers waiting for us outside the door, and for several minutes we were held up on the pavement while cameras were aimed at us and flashbulbs went off in all directions. Martin chuckled delightedly, and David regarded the cameras with a technical interest. It was a bewildering and exciting experience; and I had the additional satisfaction of knowing that nothing could have annoyed the magistrates more. At last, we got away and returned home.

The next day, David and I went to Norwich and had the even more exciting experience of seeing our pictures on the front page of the *News Chronicle*, and the headlines shouting: 'Boy Puts J.P.s Right About Camels,' and 'Home-School David Stumps J.P.s Over the Camel's Hump.'

David had indeed flung his stone squarely at this magisterial Goliath. From the temporary setback of failure, he had plucked the flower of personal victory.

9

David in the Witness-Box

MY APPEAL to Quarter Sessions should have been heard during the following January, but the birth of my baby was expected in February, and my doctor certified that it would be unwise for me to undergo the strain of another appearance in court before the baby was born. While the appeal was pending, no further action could be taken by the Education Authorities; so we had, therefore, a few months' respite, during which I could have my baby in peace.

On February 8th, 1958, my third daughter, April, was born at the house on the hill. Before I was on my feet again, I was conscious of the renewed threat hanging over us, awaiting the outcome of the appeal. My doctor did not consider I was fit enough to undertake this until three months after April was born, and the date was finally fixed for May 16th.

My solicitor, Mr. Hipwell, had advised me to apply to the Justices for legal aid for the appeal. 'Point out to them,' he said, 'in your application, that you won your last appeal, which you conducted yourself, *on a point of law*.' I accordingly did this and was granted legal aid.

On the evening before the hearing, David and I went to Norwich to meet our counsel, Mr. William Howard, in the lounge of the Royal Hotel. Mr. Howard proposed to call David to give evidence in court. He questioned him briefly on a variety of subjects and then handed him a copy of a glossy motoring journal that lay on the table. David read the passage he indicated, clearly and without hesitation. Mr. Howard looked thoughtful. 'That's the thing that impresses me most,' he said.

On the following morning, accompanied by David, Robin, Felicity, and Wendy, I set off for the Shirehall. Mr. Howard wanted to have the other three children there, although they would not be called to give evidence, in case the Justices wanted to see them. I had also to take April with me, as I was still feeding her and would not be able to get back from the court in time.

Mr. Richard Bales, of the *Daily Sketch*, had arranged to call for us and take us to the court in his car. It was a cold, blustery day with sleet in the wind, and April cried protestingly as I carried her down the field, sheltered as far as possible under my coat. She was very good in the car, but when we reached the court, I found that the journey had been too much for her, and her nappies, securely pinned up when we started out, had worked loose. I stood in the entrance to the Shirehall with a very messy baby in my arms and a seriously damaged jacket and skirt.

My greeting to Mr. Howard, who met us in the hall, was necessarily brief. A court official showed us into a waiting room, where I laid April down in her carrycot, which we had brought with us, and told Felicity to change and clean her as quickly as possible; then I fled down the passage to do what I could to my own costume before I had to stand up in it in court. Fortunately, the damage was mostly covered by my coat, and what still showed would not be visible when I stood in the witness box.

When I returned to the children, I found April clean again and smelling of baby powder, though rather fretful. It was apparent that she did not like courts and had every intention of saying so. But it was now getting late, and I had little time to comfort her. I left her in Felicity's arms and went into court.

The case was to be heard by Lord Evershed, Master of the Rolls, sitting as Chairman of the Quarter Sessions Appeals Committee. At the start of the hearing, I sat at the side of the courtroom, facing a high window that framed an incongruous view of long grass and swaying white cow parsley; the Shirehall being built against the side of the hill on which Norwich Castle stands. I sat and watched the grass rippling in the wind as Mr. H. Cassel, Counsel for the County Council, made his preliminary remarks, after which Mr. Earl gave formal evidence of his visits to me, the service of the School

Attendance Orders, and the non-attendance of the children at the designated schools. Then Mr. Howard called me to give evidence.

I told the court my name and address and the ages of my seven children—David, twelve; Robin, eleven; Felicity, ten; Wendy, nine; Hugh, two years; Martin, one year; and April, three months old—and I agreed that none of them had ever been to school. I did not agree with school instruction, but I did approve of education.

Mr. Howard then asked me what I understood by the term 'education'—and my mind went completely blank. After what could only have been a few seconds, but seemed to me to be several hours, I found myself saying:

'Education is helping the mind to expand to its utmost and take in everything that it is capable of absorbing for the purpose of living a full and happy life.'

I went on: 'I believe that a child acquires knowledge when it needs to receive it and seeks it. I have made available to my children all the knowledge that they have sought as their minds have developed.

'A child is always learning. When my children meet with something that they do not understand, they ask for an explanation. The ages from five to fifteen are not the only ones for acquiring knowledge, and if the need for additional knowledge arises later, it can be supplied.'

Here the Chairman, Lord Evershed, intervened to say: 'If a child does not get a certain certificate, he or she may be at a disadvantage in later life. What do you say about that?'

I replied, 'I don't agree that it is necessary.'

Lord Evershed commented, 'Parliament provides that every child must have a full-time, efficient education.'

I returned, 'Parliament does not provide the children.'

Mr. Howard then continued my examination. Inevitably, this covered very much the same ground that I had already been over in the magistrates' court. I stated that the children learned to read and write. They learned geography and natural history; I did not agree with the early teaching of world history. They learned arithmetic by its practical application in their daily lives. They helped in the daily work and running of their home, and the girls learned housework and child care. They were taught to speak well and behave well.

Finally, Mr. Howard asked me, 'Have any of your children ever been in trouble with the police?'

'David was stopped by the local constable once when his light failed as he was coming home from Dereham with the week's shopping,' I said. 'There has been nothing apart from that.'

Mr. Howard sat down, and I was then cross-examined by Mr. Cassel. He began by pointing out that I had seven children, three under school age, who took up a great deal of my time. How could I give the older ones the 'full-time education' required by the Act?

'My household duties take up my hands a great deal,' I replied, 'but my mind is still available.'

Mr. Cassel doubted that this constituted a proper education.

'Education does not have to be restricted to set hours or set places,' I said. 'It starts when the child opens its eyes in the morning and only stops when it closes them at night.'

'But you only teach them by answering the questions that they ask you?'

'They ask questions constantly,' I said. 'Children want to know everything. It is only by trying to force knowledge on them when they are not ready or not interested that they stop wanting to know.'

'What happens if there is a day when a child does not ask questions?' asked Mr. Cassel.

There was laughter from the court when I replied, 'I have never known such a day or such a child.'

When, in answer to a further question, I said that the children were encouraged to read ordinary children's books, Lord Evershed intervened again to say, 'I may be old-fashioned, but what about the Bible?'

'The Bible is a beautiful book, but I do not think it is suitable reading for children under twenty-five,' I said. 'I don't believe in Christianity.'

'But you took the oath?' queried Lord Evershed. (Mr. Howard told me afterwards that he had a moment's panic at this point.)

'I believe in God,' I said, 'but not the Christian view of God.'

Replying again to Mr. Cassel, I said that the children were taught to know right and wrong.

'Do they play with other children?' Mr. Cassel asked.

'Sometimes,' I said. 'They don't like school-children very much because they so often behave in a stupid way—my children prefer more sensible company.'

At the conclusion of my evidence, Mr. Howard called David, and I asked permission to leave the court. This, which astonished everybody, had been agreed between David and myself previously; I knew he would feel less nervous if I was not present to hear his evidence. So I went back to the waiting room, where I found Felicity doing her utmost to console an outraged April, and I spent the time that David was in the witness-box soothing my baby to sleep in my arms.

I did, of course, learn later what took place. Replying to Mr. Howard, in what the newspapers described as a firm, clear voice, David said that the thing he liked doing best was farming—working with livestock. He was interested in Antarctica, which, he explained, consisted of snow and ice with, it was believed, land underneath. The Arctic was snow and ice with water underneath. He described Dr. Fuchs's crossing of the Antarctic; he explained the meaning of latitude and longitude, and he described the difference between oats and barley.

He told the court that he knew a little about history. He said that the Prime Minister ruled or helped Parliament to rule the country, and he knew that Mr. Butler was a former Chancellor of the Exchequer, but he could not remember the present Chancellor's name. He calculated that if he bought a dozen eggs at 3d. each, he would get 17s. change out of a £1 note. He was asked to read a passage from Volume 13 of Halsbury's *Laws of England*, which was handed to him by Lord Evershed; and he did so, having difficulty with only one word—'convened.'

Under cross-examination, he was asked by Mr. Cassel to write the phrase: 'The health of the people is the supreme law.' When he looked puzzled at that (which I found hardly surprising, as I was not quite clear what it meant myself), Lord Evershed remarked, 'If you don't like that, write 'What a silly question!' Take your pick.'

David, still more puzzled by this, wrote the original phrase, with two errors in spelling.

He did not know the date of King George III, which led Lord Evershed to quote a verse by which he could remember it in future—'George III said with a smile, 1760 yards make a mile.' In answer to further questions by Mr. Cassel, David said that he did all the handyman jobs about his home, and his sister Felicity spent most of her time helping in the house. He and his brothers and sisters did not get on with most of the other children in the locality, he said. They were happy living as they were—as a family.

I returned to the court after David had finished giving evidence.

'An extremely nice little boy, with very nice manners,' commented Lord Evershed. 'An intelligent, sincere, clean, and truthful boy. He does not get on with other children. His mother won't live forever. What is going to be the position when he is grown up?'

Lord Evershed turned to Mr. Howard and added, 'Mrs. Baker is a woman of very strong principles, but she has to consider whether she may not be sacrificing her children for her views. The children ought to be taught. We don't live on a desert island, and we have to be taught to live as Englishmen and Englishwomen. We are concerned with these seven children. Mrs. Baker can have what views she likes, but I don't want them to be put at a disadvantage.'

Mr. Howard agreed to put this point to me, and the court then adjourned for lunch. I returned to the children in the waiting room. David and Robin took the two girls out to a nearby coffee stall to get coffee and rolls, and I drank a glass of water and settled down to feed April, who was by now very cross and had no inhibitions about showing it. Her angry little mouth fastened on my breast, and peace at last descended over the Shirehall.

By the time April had finished and was comfortably sleeping, it was too late for me to get a meal, so I missed lunch. The other children came back, and Felicity took charge of April again. After a brief conversation with Mr. Howard in another empty conference room, I returned to my seat facing the window to hear Mr. Howard address the court.

It was apparent from the beginning that he had a lost cause; the Justices' decision had already been made, and all Mr. Howard's arguments had to be pushed up a very steep hill. He began by referring to the remarks made by Lord Evershed before the lunch adjournment. The views expressed by the Chairman had not fallen on deaf ears, he said, but Mrs. Baker did not concede that at the relevant date (July 1957), she was not educating the children as the law required.

Lord Evershed said that he and his fellow magistrates cared less about Mrs. Baker than about what was best for the children. 'If you want to be a John Hampden, it is all very well,' he said, 'but there are difficulties in the way.'

(I was restricted, unlike April, by not being allowed to speak at this stage of the proceedings; but it occurred to me that one of the main difficulties did appear to be the attitude of Lord Evershed and the magistrates.)

Valiantly, Mr. Howard pressed on. It was, he pleaded, a fundamental right of inhabitants of this country to bring up their children as they pleased.

'There is today more concern in this country about education than there has ever been—and there are also more appearances before juvenile courts. This seems to illustrate that education at school is only part of education. It is something to be said in Mrs. Baker's favor that none of her children has ever been in trouble with the police.

'It would be wrong to compare the education given by Mrs. Baker with that given in a state school. Many people think that the education given by state schools is inadequate. Hundreds of people impoverish themselves to send their children to public or private schools, for what the parents think is a more efficient education than that provided by the state schools. A person of sufficient means can have his child educated as he likes by employing a tutor.'

He agreed with Lord Evershed that these children would be at a disadvantage compared with others in some ways but maintained that it would be wrong to give it too much weight.

'The Baker children will also have some advantages. It would be a very brave man who would say that a child of David Baker's age from a secondary modern school would be as well educated as David, using the word in the broadest sense. The mere knowledge of facts is the least important aspect of education. Training of the mind is much more important.

'This is not a case of a parent with a bee in her bonnet, nor of a mother who has done nothing, however unorthodox her methods may have been. Had her financial circumstances been different, this case might never have arisen.

'In view of the manners and morals—the most important things in education—of David, of his obvious intelligence and ability to learn, I ask the Committee to say it is satisfied with the education given.'

This concluded my case, the Justices having decided that they did not require to see the other children; and Lord Evershed then gave judgment.

'Mrs. Baker sincerely holds the view that children are best brought up at home with their minds developing by natural processes,' he said. 'But it is her plain duty to consider her children. Unless the view of Mrs. Baker that education is little more than absorbing knowledge is accepted, they are not receiving full-time education.

'A parent with heterodox views should not sacrifice her children. These children, if this method of upbringing continues, will be unable to fit themselves in with the rest of the community as they grow up. It is impossible to say that they are being efficiently educated.

'I do not want to overstate the position, but I got the impression from seeing David, the eldest child, that he was getting little more than a conscientious parent would give a child in any case.

'The most impressive thing, I think, is that he seems to be growing up a creature apart from the rest of the people of England and Wales.'

Lord Evershed dismissed the appeal, adding that the local Education Authority in these matters always had an invidious task. 'It can never be very pleasant interfering in the home circle.' So far as he could judge, the Authority had dealt carefully and kindly with Mrs. Baker and would, no doubt, continue to do so in the interests of the children.

I sat and watched the grass and the cow parsley outside the

window, and the sheer idiocy of the whole proceedings struck me with renewed force. Here were my children, growing up peacefully in their own way, in a country that for centuries had sounded the cause of freedom throughout the world; and here we sat, in the courtroom beside the old castle, while learned judges and counsel strove to make these children conform to the rigid boundaries imposed by a newly introduced and as yet unproved Education Act.

It is an unfair aspect of English courts that you cannot reply to the judge, and it was the positive inanity of some of Lord Evershed's remarks that had impressed me most. Did he really suppose that because David was being brought up at home, he would be unable to manage without his mother when he grew up? Already, David was far more independent than most boys at school. Did Lord Evershed really mean that the purpose of school education was to teach children 'to live as Englishmen and Englishwomen'? His description of David as 'sincere, intelligent, clean, and truthful' seemed nothing for England to be ashamed of. Did he really believe that a child living at home becomes 'a creature apart' from the rest of the community? But I could not say any of this, so I watched the cow parsley and simmered inside.

As soon as it was over, I rejoined April, who was starting to protest again in her sleep, and the other children in the waiting room; and we all thankfully got into Mr. Bales's car and returned home.

Later that night, I was still telling reporters who called, 'I will never send my children to school.'

10

Warned by the Bench

After the first shock of losing the appeal—a shock only in the urgent anticipation of its possible consequences, since I had never really expected any other result—there came a period of suspense while we waited to see what the Education Authority would do next; a suspense growing rapidly into the realization that, although we knew that after further prosecution they could ask for a prison sentence on me or apply for an order to bring the children before a juvenile court, nothing was happening now because, at this stage, there was nothing drastic they *could* do.

There was now no question whatever of my giving in or seeking any compromise with the authorities. Not only was it obvious (a point which appeared to have been ignored by all concerned) that to send the children to school now, after all that had happened, would be from any standpoint the most arrant cruelty, but it was also now apparent to me that my system was, in fact, working out, and my theories were proving correct.

David could read, write, and do basic arithmetic without ever having had a formal lesson. He had a wide range of knowledge about subjects in which he was interested and practical ability in the work connected with his chosen career. He had the courage to stand up in court and answer with composure questions put by judge and counsel—questions on which his own future depended— which many adults would find a strain; and he had impressed the Chairman as being intelligent, sincere, clean, and truthful. Perhaps it was these qualities that would make it difficult for him to fit in with the rest of the community?

He did not know the date of George III—but then, nor did I. It was not a thing I had ever found any need for in the course of my life. When I was at school, we were once given sixty dates to learn for our weekend history homework. During the following week, we were asked forty of these, and I got twenty right. I don't even remember those now, and I have never needed to. But I do remember, while I was learning them, fixing one in my mind by looking intently at a lily and a delphinium growing in the garden as I learned it. I cannot remember now what the date was—but in my mind, I can still see the blue spire of the delphinium and the white purity of the lily against the summer evening sky. These are the lasting things. I had not taught David any dates in history, although he did, in fact, know some, like the date of the Great Plague and the Fire of London, because he had become interested in the sequence of these events. Knowledge is of no value unless it stimulates thought, and active, independent thought reaps knowledge.

All in all, David was, despite Lord Evershed's remarks, better equipped for his future than the average boy of his age at school. Out of a firmly held conviction, a growing theory, I began to see a practical pattern emerge, satisfying like that which I had reasoned it must be. My decision was made, my gauntlet flung. Now I must go on to the end.

The summer went by, and nothing at all happened until the middle of September, when I had a letter from the Chief Education Officer, Dr. Lincoln Ralphs, saying that he understood that I had still not complied with the requirements of the School Attendance Orders made in respect of my four older children, and asking me whether I proposed to comply with them or to make provision for the children's education 'in some other satisfactory manner.'

I replied, saying that I did not intend to comply with the Attendance Orders, I had not altered my views since the hearing of my appeal, and I was continuing to give the children a satisfactory education at home.

At the beginning of November, two notable events took place. David, who had entered a photograph of Felicity with two young racehorses for that year's photographic competition in Parents magazine, heard that he had won first prize—£30. And on the following day, four more summonses for 'failing to cause the children to receive efficient full-time education' were served on me by the local constable.

On November 28th, I made my third appearance in Dereham Magistrates' Court.

David went with me to give evidence, wearing the new tweed jacket, grey flannel trousers, and Burberry, which he had bought out of his £30 prize. We cycled to Dereham together against a strong wind, with squalls of rain beating into our faces, and arrived rather breathless and five minutes late.

By this time, the courtroom was almost as familiar to me as my own kitchen. I was again conducting my own defense, and as I walked in and sat down at the solicitors' table, I had the dream-like feeling that all this had happened before. There were, however, different magistrates this time, with an elderly man, Brigadier K. W. Hervey, in the chair.

The case for the prosecution was opened as usual by Mr. Brighton, who pointed out that the proceedings were brought under the 1944 Education Act and that children had to be taught at school unless it could be proved that they were receiving an efficient full-time education suitable to their age, ability, and aptitude otherwise than at school.

Mr. Earl then gave his usual evidence concerning the ages of the children and their failure to attend the schools named in the School Attendance Orders.

Cross-examining, I pointed out that it was now six months since I lost my appeal to Quarter Sessions, and in that time, I had received only one letter from the Education Authorities inquiring about my children's education. 'It does not therefore appear that they thought the matter very urgent?'

Mr. Earl replied: 'I don't know what they thought. I am the Welfare Officer—I cannot speak for the Authority.'

That concluded the evidence for the prosecution. I then went into the witness box, took the oath, and addressed the court:

'I think it is already clear that I am not trying to prove that I am teaching my children as they would be taught at school. I am educating my children at home because I do not believe in school education. The Education Act requires that children shall receive efficient full-time education, but in enforcing this regulation, the Education Authorities appear to assume that the only meaning of the term 'education' is that type of education provided in State schools. There are, of course, many types of education, and only by varying widely educational methods can any education be suitable to the child's ability and aptitude, as the Act also requires. It is, in fact, a contradiction in terms to require that education be suited to the child's ability and aptitude, and at the same time that it must follow only one rigid pattern as decreed by a Government department.

'If no one is ever to be allowed to carry out any different methods of education from that employed in schools, no progress in educational methods can be made.

'The law places on the parent the full legal responsibility for the children. It is surely, therefore, reasonable that the parent should have control over the influences that the children are subjected to and the matter introduced into their minds.

'We hear a great deal about the prevalence of juvenile delinquency, maladjusted children, the unhealthy addiction of teenagers to rock-and-roll, and the hero-worship of popular singers, and so on, but when someone makes a serious effort to undertake the education of their own family with a view to bringing about a more wholesome and natural approach to life, they are prosecuted in a criminal court.

'The ultimate test of all education is the value of the finished product—the young adult at the end of school life. The Education Committee is trying its hardest to prevent me from producing that ultimate evidence, but so far as I have progressed now, I have yet to be told where my methods have failed to produce an overall result that compares favorably with that turned out by any school.

'I maintain that many subjects taught in school are unnecessary, or unsuitable at that period in a child's life, or are taught at the wrong ages and presented in the wrong way, and many other things of value to the growing individual are not taught at all. My children's education has been based on the assumption that the ultimate purpose of education is to prepare the child for adult life. My children have been taught to speak well, to behave well, to develop a sense of responsibility, and to act sensibly on their own initiative—things not very noticeable in children at school.'

'My method of educating my children is to let them seek and acquire knowledge and abilities as they are ready for them, without giving set lessons. My contention is that no one can learn anything that is not already in them, and that all those abilities which are in any individual can be brought out by encouragement and help in the normal course of the child's development towards maturity; and that forced instruction on subjects which have no real meaning in connection with everyday life, and no real interest to the individual, only retard this natural development.

'Education is not the stuffing of minds with set facts on set subjects at set times. Education is the training of the mind along its natural course, the formation of character, the development of the individual. Instruction is only part of this, and formal instruction should only be given in those subjects in which the individual is interested and requires at the start of adult life in order to follow a career.

'Few of the subjects taught in school are of any practical value in adult life, and if the purpose of their teaching is to train the mind, it cannot matter on what subjects the mind is trained. What is called efficient education in school consists largely of the accumulating of a series of facts in which the child has little interest and less understanding, and the retaining of these facts until the taking of the appropriate examination, after which they are, in the great majority of people, mainly discarded.

'Children's minds become ready to absorb knowledge at different times and stages of development. No one would advise 'teaching' a baby to walk at a year, regardless of whether it was ready to do so or not. The school inspectors set an arbitrary standard of what children should do at a given age and appear to regard education as inefficient if it results in a child doing so at a later age than that. Yet children are only babies at a later stage of development. Facts taught before the mind is ready to take them in are only memorized, not understood, and do not benefit or educate the child.

'In educating my children, I have aimed at drawing out and

developing the natural abilities of the individual child and at the same time giving access to and encouraging interest in such subjects as geography, early world history, and natural history, without giving formal lessons in any of these. A child who has approached history or geography from personal interest will acquire as much knowledge of the subject as its mind can absorb at that stage and will at the same time be ready to undertake further voluntary study of these subjects at a later stage when the mind is better able to absorb them.

'None of my children has been taught to read. They have always been given access to suitable reading matter, and I have found that under these circumstances, they learn to read slowly but far more efficiently than a great many children formally taught at the expense of many wasted hours at a school desk. It appears obvious from this that the ability to read is latent in the human mind and will develop without teaching, and that by this method, a real understanding of words is reached at an earlier age than in children taught by conventional methods to start reading when very young.

'David and Robin have both learnt to read, without any teaching, over the last four years. Felicity, who had difficulty in starting to read, has now started recognizing and reading words which had previously remained meaningless to her. Wendy, who is young for her age compared with the other three, is now showing obvious signs of doing the same. It is apparent in the reading of a great many school children that they have been taught the words but not to read with understanding. Children who learn by themselves read with understanding from the start. I am told that my children are backward because they learned to read later than the accepted standard, but they have never so far suffered any disadvantage from this. Indeed, they have benefited from it, as they have not been able to contaminate their minds too young with unsuitable reading matter—and to a sensitive child, even children's stories can be unsuitable and have a distressing effect.

'Handwriting I have allowed to develop in the same way, with the result that although their writing is backward by accepted standards, by which they would now all be writing a uniform and characterless schoolboy or schoolgirl hand, they are developing, slowly, strongly individual handwritings. I believe that enforced immature writing is a great factor in the production of bad handwriting in adult life, and that to acquire a good hand, as little writing as possible should be undertaken until the necessary coordination of hand and eye is acquired, which does not often take place until after school leaving age; and should then, and not until then, be taught.

'Arithmetic they learn as it comes into their daily lives—which may start with adding up the number of kittens born to our cats and goes on to the handling of money in doing household shopping, weights and measures in farm work, cooking, and so on—until now, David and Robin are responsible for all our weekly shopping and can handle considerable amounts of money. They are encouraged to work out for themselves all the practical arithmetic that they encounter in daily life—which is, after all, where they will need it when they grow up, unless they want to take up anything which will require them to specialize in it later—and helped with all the information they need for this.

'History I do not believe should be taught to children at all. It is an adult subject, concerned with the actions of adults which no child can properly understand. Too early teaching of history results only in their having a disjointed and childish view which can never be reconciled to the facts. History should be read, in the right sequence, in full, at an age when it can be understood and seen in perspective—between the ages of fifteen and twenty years.

'Geography my children have learned through being encouraged to take an interest in places that come into the news, looking them up on the globe and in an atlas, and thereby regarding them from the start as real places with living people, not just as names and pages of facts to learn in a geography book. David has taken a great interest in the trans-Antarctic expedition, has collected all the newspaper cuttings about it from the start, and for months we had his *Daily Telegraph* map of the Antarctic hanging on the sitting-room wall. When one of the Sno-cats was in Norwich, he went to see it, and I took him to hear Sir Vivian Fuchs's lecture last July at King's Lynn.

'Languages I do not believe are necessary to the average child in the ordinary way. School-taught French is seldom any use as a spoken language; and if a child wants or needs to learn a language, it should be learnt preferably in the country concerned. If knowledge of any language becomes necessary for a child's chosen career, then is the time to learn it—including Latin, which if taught too young becomes too difficult too early, but at a later age can be appreciated and more readily understood.

'Natural history my children have learned by everyday observation, followed by questioning me, and looking up details in books. They all love animals; and fortunately, not going to school, have never been required to dissect them.

'They have read about, and listened to B.B.C. programmes on, the early history of the world; and David is interested in the stars and planets, and the weather—although not in spaceships and moon rockets.

'I do not believe in team games, cricket, football, hockey, and so on, and none of my children has ever felt any interest in them. They regard it as a stupid waste of time to chase a ball about over a field when they could be doing something interesting, and their physical energies are expended in more individual pursuits—riding, cycling, farm work, and climbing trees. As regards learning about 'fair play,' which I am told is the primary purpose of team games, they learn that as members of a family.

'Individually, these children are developing very different characters and abilities.

'Wendy, who is the most immature for her age of the four, has in the last few months taken a marked step forward towards maturity. She shows a good deal of practical and even mechanical ability; she delights in mending things and making things with her hands; she is also becoming efficient at all kinds of domestic work and is now developing an ability in handling the younger children, through which she is acquiring the sense of responsibility and coming maturity she had previously lacked. She is sensitive and imaginative; she loves poetry and music, she is fond of drawing and painting, and she shows signs of developing a more dominant personality than any other member of the family.

'Felicity, by contrast, is mature for her age. Her main interest is in babies and home-making, and she is learning in her own home the care and upbringing of children from birth. At the age of eleven, she can already take charge of her baby sister and brothers aged one, two, and three years, single-handed.

'She has also a great love for horses, and without ever having had a riding lesson has ridden cart-horses, riding ponies, and racehorses bareback. She has never been requested to write formal essays, but in the last few months, she has started writing stories showing marked originality of mind. In this, her lack of early reading has again been an advantage; her style is natural and entirely unaffected by anything she has read. It is too early to judge whether this may develop into a permanent talent, but reading her stories, I am reminded that Beatrix Potter never went to school.

'Felicity's ambition is to marry and have a family, and she is being educated with this in view. I am aware that this can be called Victorian, but in her case, I maintain that it is right. The avowed purpose of modern education is to produce scientists and technicians; I think it is of greater value to produce good mothers.

'Robin, at twelve, is a highly sensitive child and less mature in development than Felicity. He has been slow to decide what he wants to do, but his interests have been varied, including domestic subjects—cooking and knitting—as well as gardening and farm work. He has, in fact, become an efficient cook and has recently decided that he would like to be a baker—despite teasing on the lines that he is a master baker already. He has very considerable skill with his hands and is efficient in doing household repairs and any mechanical jobs. He loves music and animals and has great feeling for colour and beauty. He is a sociable child, more interested in people than things, but he does not have as strong a personality as David, and at school would probably have let his own interests and talents become submerged and tended to follow someone else.

'David, at thirteen, is now within eighteen months of school-leaving age. He is a child with a marked sense of responsibility, tenacity of purpose, and a serious approach to anything he undertakes. His ambition is to be a farmer, and he has been working regularly on a neighbouring farm—milking, tractor driving, ploughing, working on a combine—and learning all he can about practical farm work, as well as reading farming literature.

'Eighteen months ago, he took up photography when he received a camera for his twelfth birthday. Two months later, he won a prize in a photographic competition for adults in Parents magazine. He continued to study photography, and this year he entered again for the yearly competition in *Parents*. He won first prize—£30.'

Here I handed a copy of the magazine containing David's prize-winning photograph to the Bench.

'I have been told that I have no qualifications for the educating of my children. But I have the one qualification—and the only one—that fits or entitles anyone to undertake the education of a child—love for the children. That love is the first essential in the upbringing of any child and is now acknowledged by all authorities on child care. But the present Education Act now decrees that it is only necessary up to the age of five, when a child should be summarily removed from the love which has protected, encouraged, and educated it up to that age and set in a classroom to be made to receive the most lasting impressions of its life from complete strangers. Only through the understanding interest in the child that arises from love of the child can true education be given. Lord Evershed said in dismissing my last appeal that he 'had to consider' the children. I also have considered the children—not for an hour in a law court without seeing them, but unremittingly for thirteen years. I do not believe that Dr. Lincoln Ralphs ever lies awake at night considering whether the steps he is taking are in every way to the utmost benefit of the four individual children concerned; nor do I believe any schoolteacher would do so. Nothing that I have done for my children has been done without the utmost searching of my mind, the most vigilant watching of the results, that they should not be mishandled in any way. It is this that gives me the ability and the right to educate my children—that I care for them—that I am in a position to judge the results of what I am doing daily, hourly—that I have no hidebound red-tape system that takes no regard for the effect on the individual—that I can and do devote to their education and to their welfare all the hours of my life.

'I have been told that modern children need to be educated in a certain way, to a certain set standard of knowledge, to face up to modern life, and that if they are not, they will be at a disadvantage among their fellows. But it is still possible for individuals to develop in ways that are not covered by what we call modern life; even in this scientific age, it is still necessary and right for women to make homes and bring up children, and it is still necessary and good to harvest the fruits of the earth. Farmers and bakers, as well as mothers, are needed as much as mathematicians.

'The schools may try to impose modern education on all children, but this system overlooks one thing—children are an old-fashioned product to start with.

'God, not man, ordained the natural development of the young without the assistance of the present education authorities. God endowed women, in common with the females of all mammals, with the instincts which would enable them to bring up and train their young to a happy and secure maturity. Man alone thinks he can do better than God. I believe that God is the living power of life itself, and I do not think that Parliament is an adequate substitute. It cannot be beneficial for the growing child to be handed over to strangers who care nothing for and understand nothing of the child, for guidance during the formative years of its life. The young adult, at a later stage, can beneficially receive instruction in chosen subjects from those people who have specialized in those subjects, but the education of the child from five to fifteen should be carried out in its home.'

I laid down my papers and turned to face Mr. Brighton's cross-examination.

Mr. Brighton was brief. In an exasperated voice, he asked, 'Mrs. Baker, have you any intention of complying with these School Attendance Orders?'

'None whatsoever,' I said firmly.

Mr. Brighton sighed. 'Do you realize that there is a century of experience behind the Education Act?'

I replied, 'The fundamental right of a parent to educate her own children is even older.'

Mr. Brighton sat down abruptly, and I called David to give evidence.

David entered the witness box confidently, took the oath, and faced me cheerfully as I stood at the solicitor's table—it was the first time he had seen me pretending to be a barrister. In reply to my questions, he told the court that his chief hobby was photography, that he had just won first prize in a photographic competition, that he had bought the clothes he was wearing out of his £30 prize money, and that he wanted to be a farmer.

'I start work at half past seven in the mornings, helping on a neighbour's farm,' he said. 'I can milk on my own, by hand or machine, and I can drive a tractor, work a combine, plough, and drill corn.'

I then asked David to read to the court and suggested that the magistrates might like to choose something for him to read. The Clerk of the Court, Mr. Allwood, picked up the copy of *Parents* from the table and handed it to David, who read a passage from the editorial clearly and without hesitation.

Mr. Brighton declined to ask any questions, and David left the court. I turned to the magistrates again to give my final address.

'You have heard my evidence and that of my eldest son, and you are doubtless aware that if I lose this case, the Authority has the power to ask for the children to be brought before a juvenile court for the purpose of having them removed permanently into an institution.

'You are being asked to decide whether the education I am giving my children is efficient full-time education. So far as 'full-time' is concerned, I would point out that the education I am giving my children is full-time in the fullest sense of the word. Their learning extends over all their waking hours and is not limited to school hours or school terms. Further, the whole of my time is given to their educational needs, which compares rather favourably with the time that can be given by one teacher to the classes of thirty or more children often existing in schools.

'The question then remains, is their education efficient? You have here a boy of thirteen who has never been to school. He can read well and understand, or take steps to find out about, everything he reads. He has a background of general knowledge equal to many people's after they leave school. He has already developed two main interests which he wants to follow in adult life—farming and photography. He can already do most farm work efficiently and is a reliable and conscientious worker, taking an interest in every job he does. He has just won a £30 first prize in an adult photographic competition.

'Yet he is supposed to be at a disadvantage among his fellows because he will not have the General Certificate of Education in eighteen months' time. Is this really going to stand in his way? A farmer is not asked for his School Certificate before he is paid for the value of his work and produce. An editor does not ask for a School Certificate before accepting a photograph for publication. If he should have need for further studies in any particular direction, these can be undertaken when they are required.

'You have also to consider the younger children, each of whom is an individual with a sturdy approach to life. You have a boy of twelve developing on entirely different lines to his brother, despite their being brought up very closely together; a girl of eleven who is already showing promise of the woman she is going to become, and her younger sister, who at nine is also an individual with a mind of her own.

'Can you say that these children are not making progress in their own method of education? When the children were examined by the schools' inspector three years ago, he reported that Felicity 'could not write words'—she is now writing stories; he said that David was 'eighteen months behind in reading'—but you have heard David read today, and six months ago he read in court from the Laws of England to Lord Evershed.

'You may say that these children have not had a conventional education or that you do not personally agree with or approve of their education. But that is a matter of opinion, not of law. You may say that they are not being educated in accordance with school methods; but can you say that this education has not been efficient or is not producing a favourable result?

'Because these children's absorption of knowledge follows a different pattern from school methods of teaching, and many school subjects are being held back, spread over a different period of time, or approached in a different way for a considered purpose, does this make their education inefficient? If my methods produce—as it is apparent to all who know the children that they are producing—intelligent, healthy, well-balanced children with active minds, continually acquiring knowledge; potential sound men and women, good husbands and fathers, wives and mothers, is it reasonable to say that their method of education must be altered to produce a different result?'

'It is the contention of the Education Committee that, despite the length of time for which these children have been educated by my methods, they should now be precipitated into school life, to adapt themselves as best they can to an entirely different method of education. It must be obvious to anyone that such a change could not produce efficient education and could only be harmful to the children concerned.

'I have not been trying to prove that these children are receiving the same kind of education as they would receive in school. The Education Act does not make any mention of that. I have been trying to prove that these children are receiving a better educa-tion—with regard to their ages, abilities, and aptitudes—than they could at school; that it is producing better results, in their individual cases, than education at school would.

'You are not being asked to decide whether you think these children ought to be at school or should receive any other method of education. You are being asked to decide whether they are receiv-ing an efficient full-time education within the meaning of the Act.

'I am asking you to say that these children are being properly educated within the meaning of the Act; to dismiss these summonses which threaten the children's future and leave me to educate my children in peace.'

I sat down, and Police Inspector Goldthorpe got up and gave details of my previous convictions under the Education Act in November 1957 and June 1953. Then I stood up as the magistrates left the court and sat down again to wait.

Time went by, and I began to be apprehensive and tried not to be hopeful. What were they preparing for me in their little back room? The clock on the courtroom wall moved on and on. Finally, when my nerves were being strained to breaking point, the door opened. Again, we all got to our feet, and the magistrates filed in.

The Chairman, Brigadier Hervey, eyed me with a stony stare as he announced their decision:

'We have taken a considerable time not in deciding whether you are guilty, but with the very serious consideration as to whether at this stage we require the attendance of your children before a juvenile court. The court warns you most severely that if you persist in your present attitude, the time will assuredly come when steps may be taken in a juvenile court to remove your children from you.'

In sudden anger, I interrupted to say, 'I shall not abandon my duty because of threats.'

There was a few seconds' dead silence, and Brigadier Hervey then went on to announce that I would be fined £1 on each summons. I immediately gave notice that I would appeal.

I found David in the little ante-room outside the court and told him that our court proceedings were now beginning to resemble those involving Toad of Toad Hall, who was sentenced to seventeen years' imprisonment for cheeking the police, 'without, of course, giving him the benefit of the doubt, because there isn't any.'

We were joined by a group of reporters, inevitably wanting to know, 'What would I do now?' 'I shall not give in,' I told them. 'And my children will never come before a juvenile court.'

It was now past lunchtime, and the reporter from the *Daily Mirror* offered to drive us home. This meant leaving our bicycles in Dereham to collect later, but it was still raining and blowing hard, and I felt I had battled with the elements enough for one day. Several other press cars accompanied us, and when we got into the house, our sitting room was illuminated by the intermittent glare of successive flashbulbs as we posed for photographs—much to the babies' astonishment. In the intervals of this, and talking to the reporters, we tried to feed the babies and get ourselves something to eat, but with only limited success. Altogether, we were rather relieved when the last car disappeared down the field, and we were able to pick up the used flashbulbs, put the babies to bed, and get ourselves a substantial high tea in peace.

The next day, the headlines announced: 'No Surrender, Says Mother,' and 'I Won't Let Children Go to School—or Court'—and following this, I received the usual batch of letters, almost always from sympathizers, and including one postcard beginning: 'Brave and wonderful woman!' Meanwhile, I prepared Notices of Appeal and sent them to the Education Authority and the Clerk of the Court. What one paper now described as my 'long, lone, legal battle' went on.

II

Danger—Children Not at School

THERE was not a great deal of time between the case in the magistrates' court and the hearing of my appeal, which came before the Quarter Sessions Appeals Committee on February 10th, 1959. I intended to conduct this appeal myself, and as so far none of the Justices concerned had ever been sufficiently interested to ask to see the children when they were brought to the court for that purpose, I proposed to call all four children to give evidence in court. We were all, therefore, in a state of considerable excitement and apprehension by the beginning of the New Year.

There were two matters arising out of the hearing in the magistrates' court on which I believed I might have a specific case for appeal on points of law. One was that the record of my previous convictions had been read to the magistrates before their decision had been given; this should not have been done until after I was found guilty, before the sentence was imposed. The second only occurred to me when I was drawing up the Notices of Appeal, which I copied from those Mr. Hipwell had prepared for me the previous year; and that was that, in each case, the date given for the committing of the offence—the date of the School Attendance Orders, July 19th, 1957—was the same. So it appeared that I must have been convicted and sentenced twice for the same offence.

I raised both these points with Mr. Hipwell, and while he agreed that it was entirely wrong for the previous convictions to be announced before the magistrates' decision, he doubted whether this was a point which could be helpfully raised at the appeal, which would be a rehearing of the whole case. Regarding my sec-

144

ond point, he was puzzled by this, as he found on looking up the papers that no date for the actual committing of the offence was given, as is usual, on the summonses; they merely charged me with having failed to comply with School Attendance Orders made on July 19th, 1957, and he did not know why the Notices of Appeal had been worded as they were. But he promised to give it further consideration and let me know.

The appeal was heard in the Crown Court at the Shirehall in Norwich, before Judge Carey Evans, sitting as Chairman of the Quarter Sessions Appeals Committee. I arrived at the Shirehall, which by now was also becoming very familiar, with Robin, Felicity, and Wendy. David had stayed at home with the three younger ones to look after them until Felicity and Wendy came back. I left the three of them in the waiting room and went into the court.

The proceedings were opened by Mr. Michael Havers, representing the Norfolk County Education Department. Mr. Havers said that as a consequence of my actions my children were now in peril of being brought before a juvenile court. Dire penalties could follow there, and it might be better if that were fully realized by everybody.

'The time has come to be perfectly frank,' he said. 'The selfish obstinacy of Mrs. Baker—maybe she thinks she is striking a blow for freedom—is in fact really depriving her children of the chance of getting that education which is available and which the State provides, and which the State says should be provided unless she can provide as good an education at home.'

Here Judge Carey Evans intervened to say that to use the words 'as good' was 'putting a slight gloss on the statute.'

Mr. Havers agreed. 'Mrs. Baker,' he continued, 'has three other children in addition to those concerned in this case—one of them a baby. She is not qualified in any way to teach.'

As usual, the only witness called for the prosecution was Mr. Earl, who caused a slight diversion when asked to state his employment by starting to say, 'Administrative...' stumbling over the word, and being helped by Mr. Havers to finish—'Administrative assistant.'

'Promotion, I take it,' said Mr. Havers; and Mr. Earl, still looking rather flustered, agreed that this was so. I wondered whether he had been promoted on account of the progress he had already made in getting my children to school—or perhaps in order that he might devote more of his time to trying to do so?

After this opening, he gave the same evidence as he had in the magistrates' court and sat down.

At this point, a written message was handed to me from Mr. Hipwell, who had not been able to get to the court. It stated simply: 'Press for *autrefois convict*.' This threw me into a state of some confusion, as my school education had not taught me this phrase; and although I assumed, correctly as it turned out, that it referred to my contention that I had been convicted twice for the same offence, I didn't know whether I should use these words, and, if I did, I didn't know how to pronounce them. However, I decided that the judge would doubtless understand even if I did not; and the basic meaning of the message was clear. So I left the solicitors' table and entered the witness box to present my case.

'Before giving evidence regarding the education of my children, I would like to draw the attention of the court to the fact that it appears that I have been convicted, and sentenced, twice for the same offence—according to my solicitor, *autrefois convict*. On November 15th, 1957, and November 28th, 1958, I was convicted and fined for having unlawfully failed to comply with four School Attendance Orders dated July 19th, 1957. No date on which the offence was alleged to have been committed was given in any of the summonses served on me, but in each case, the summonses gave the date for the School Attendance Orders, July 19th, 1957. My solicitors, in preparing the Notices of Appeal, worded these: 'I appeal against a certain conviction of me for having on the 19th day of July 1957 unlawfully failed to comply with the requirements of a School Attendance Order made on the 19th July 1957.' This same date was repeated, as it had to be, in my Notices of Appeal against my second conviction. Since these Notices were accepted and were both held to be valid by the court, it would appear that I was in fact convicted and fined on each occasion for the same offence.'

Judge Carey Evans disagreed with this, and I went on to describe my children's education. As this appeal was in fact a complete fresh hearing of the same case that had been put before the Dereham magistrates, the greater part of my evidence now consisted of the same statement of facts which I had made in the lower court.

As I started to describe the children's individual interests and achievements, I asked if I might put an album of David's photographs, including his prize-winning entries, before the Appeals Committee. Judge Carey Evans rather grudgingly agreed, saying, 'But they are really quite irrelevant.' I handed up the album, which was passed perfunctorily around the magistrates.

A little later, I mentioned Felicity's stories and suggested that I should put these before the court. The Chairman stopped me. 'They are quite irrelevant,' he said again. 'It does not prove whether or not she is having efficient full-time education.'

'If she becomes a second Beatrix Potter, it may be relevant,' I returned in some anger. 'She did not go to school either.'

I continued my evidence and finally concluded:

'You cannot develop an individual if he or she is one of a class of twenty or thirty children, all being told the same thing at the same time. No system of mass education can be suitable to each child's ability and aptitude. I am bringing up my children to be well-balanced, well-informed individuals, mentally, physically, and spiritually equipped to lead a full adult life.'

Cross-examining, Mr. Havers asked me, 'Do you ever intend to comply with these School Attendance Orders?'

I replied: 'No. I do not believe it would be right; and I don't think it can be right to do what I believe to be wrong.'

I then returned to the solicitors' table and addressed the court:

'I now propose to call my four children as witnesses. I would like to make it clear that it is not my intention to put them through the ordeal of giving evidence in a formal sense, nor to give them a test of knowledge in the unnatural surroundings of a law court, but to let you see and hear the children themselves.'

I then called Wendy to give evidence. She seemed very small looking over the edge of the witness box, with her short, curly red hair and wide green eyes. She was too frightened to take the oath, but in reply to my questions, she answered readily, in her surprisingly deep voice, that she was ten years old; she liked making things, looking after the babies, drawing, and climbing trees; and her last birthday presents were a dolls' house, a carpentry set, and a propelling pencil. She smiled tremulously at the Justices as she left the court, and Felicity, composed and self-possessed, took her place.

Felicity startled everyone at the outset by taking the oath in a clear, precise voice—'I swear by Almighty God that the evidence I shall give to the court shall be the truth, the whole truth, and nothing but the truth'—which, as the Clerk pointed out, was the oath as given before the magistrates; at Quarter Sessions, the words 'to the court' are omitted.

Gravely, looking very Victorian with her sea-blue eyes and long copper hair, she told the court that she was eleven. Her little brothers and sister were three, two, and one year old. She could look after all of them by herself. She liked writing fairy stories and riding horses; for her last birthday, she had a camera, and she had started taking photographs.

When I asked her if she liked the local schoolchildren, she replied, 'No.' Indignantly, she added, 'When we were out with Hugh in his pram, some of them followed us, and one of them pulled Hugh's hair and made him cry.'

In reply to Mr. Havers, she said that she helped with the work of the house and had some free time to herself each day. Asked how much time that was, she replied primly, 'It depends how quickly the work is done.'

At the conclusion of her evidence, the court adjourned for lunch. Immediately after the adjournment, I sent Wendy and Felicity home so that David could come to the court. Robin and I went to a nearby restaurant, and I was glad to see that he ate with an unimpaired appetite.

At two o'clock, we were back in our places, and I called Robin to give evidence. At the same time, a note was handed to me saying that David had arrived at the court.

Robin, looking rather nervous, entered the witness box. He took the oath without hesitation and told the court he was twelve, and he liked gardening and cooking. He could cook roast beef and Yorkshire pudding, roast lamb with onion sauce, and roast chicken with bread sauce and stuffing. He could make pastry and cakes, and he wanted to be a baker. He liked going down to the village bakery and watching the bread being made, and they let him help. He liked classical music, painting, and cycling.

When Robin had left the court, looking very relieved, David came in. He entered the box and took the oath with the assurance of a veteran and gave virtually the same evidence as he had in the magistrates' court.

It occurred to me that there was one aspect of my children's education which had not been mentioned in my evidence, although it must be becoming increasingly apparent: a knowledge of court procedure and elementary law.

When David left the court, I stood up to give my final address, in which again I covered the same points as I had before the magistrates. I went on:

'I have been fighting for the right to educate my children now for nearly four years, and I have appeared in court on five previous occasions—three times before the Dereham magistrates and twice before the Appeals Committee. I have been interested to note that the reasons given for the magistrates' decisions have been varied on each occasion.

'When I appeared before the magistrates in May 1955, the Chairman stated simply that they did not think the children were receiving 'enough education' at home. 'When I appealed against this decision and won my appeal on a point of law, the Chairman said that they 'would not express an opinion' of the education my children were receiving. 'When I appeared before Dereham magistrates again in November 1957, the Chairman gave no decision after hearing my evidence on the children's education but required the older children to attend the court for a private examination by the magistrates and the Justices' Clerk. This examination was one of the most terrifying ordeals that could well be imposed on a child—they were conducted through the court to the magistrates by uniformed police. Felicity, who was then only nine, was at first too frightened to speak and was then asked only two questions, both of which she answered correctly. David, who was then twelve, chose to go alone before the magistrates. He was not told what questions he had failed in, but from the account he gave afterwards, it was obvious that he had answered a great many correctly—as well as correcting the magistrates on the contents of the camel's hump.

'When Lord Evershed dismissed my appeal against this conviction, he suggested that my children were being brought up 'to live on a desert island.' I think anyone who knows these children would realize that this is absurd. For although I would like to think that my children would have the energy and resource to tackle life on a desert island if they had to, they are in fact being brought up to deal with life as it is—as they will have to live it when they reach adult status—which they certainly would not be in the artificial surroundings of school.'

'School is indeed the only place where we are forced to live in a totally unrealistic and artificial atmosphere, which bears no relation to future adult life whatsoever. The first thing—and it is very often a hard thing—that a child has to learn on leaving school is to discard the outlook, ideas, and behaviour practised in school and to face life as an individual. The effect of school is to crush individuality on all sides; if the teacher doesn't, the other children certainly will; and this does put the school-child at a disadvantage from the time he leaves school. Whereas my children are now recognizably embryo adults, slowly progressing towards maturity, the effect of school is to keep the child away from contact with normal adult life until he or she leaves school and is pushed suddenly into an adult world for which the school-child has no preparation whatever. It is not a coincidence that the rise in juvenile delinquency has followed the introduction of the present Education Act.

'Far from being cut off from their fellows as Lord Evershed suggested, my children are growing up as part of a community in a very real sense; first, in the close community of the family—and no child can grow up in isolation in a family of seven—and then in the larger community of people in which the family takes its place. It is children at school who are brought up isolated from the normal daily lives of the adult people they will soon become.

'Lord Evershed said that my children would be 'at a disadvantage' through not having gained the General Certificate of Education. I was told exactly the same thing when, knowing that I was years ahead of my class in English and years behind in mathematics, I elected not to take the School Certificate. My headmistress lectured me about this for the best part of an hour and reduced me to tears, but I didn't take the School Certificate, and I have never experienced any disadvantage as a result. But I have often been at a disadvantage through the soul-destroying years I spent at school, which produced in me a total effect of abnormal nervousness, self-consciousness, and lack of self-confidence, which took me years of personal effort to overcome after I left school. If any of my children wish in the years to come to take up any profession for which the General Certificate of Education is necessary, they can study for it then, with the added incentive of wanting it for a specific purpose and knowing what they are studying for.

'What disadvantage will it be to a boy growing into manhood if he is able to deal with all kinds of situations and people with assurance, and tackle any job with determination and common sense; if he has a strong sense of responsibility and is already deeply interested and experienced in the work he has chosen to do in adult life?

'What disadvantage will it be to a girl growing into womanhood if she is fully capable of running a home and looking after half a dozen children, if she is able to groom and dress herself with pride and good taste, and has at the same time an original and imaginative mind?

'I only wish my education had included these advantages.

'When I appeared again before the Dereham magistrates in November 1958, the Chairman announced, after retiring for some time, that they had taken considerable time 'not in deciding whether I was guilty' but in very serious consideration of what penalty to impose, and added that the time 'would assuredly come' when steps would be taken to remove my children from me. If these steps are to be taken without first considering whether or not I am guilty, the proceedings will resemble the trial of Toad of Toad Hall rather than those of a serious court.

'Mr. Havers now suggests that I think I am 'striking a blow for freedom' in refusing to send my children to school. I would ask you to bear in mind that all I am really doing is claiming the right to bring up my own children myself, in their own home, as I believe is right. After all, I had the children in the first place.

'Mr. Havers now states openly that the children are in peril of being brought before a juvenile court, and 'dire penalties' can follow. I would point out that these penalties can only be inflicted deliberately by justices such as yourselves, and the only peril in which my children now stand arises from the actions of the members of this Appeals Committee, the Education Committee, and Mr. Havers himself.

'Many people would believe it impossible in this country that my children could be brought before a juvenile court and taken away from me on the sole grounds that I do not send them to school. They cannot be said to be in need of care on this or any other grounds; they are not neglected, ill-treated, or damaged in any way.

'Throughout all these proceedings and in face of these threats, I still stand steadfast in my beliefs. I ask you to say that the education these children are receiving does in fact constitute efficient full-time education within the meaning of the Act, and let me continue their education in their own home.'

I sat down and waited, without hope, for Judge Carey Evans to announce the decision of the Committee.

'We have listened, with such patience as we could muster, to Mrs. Baker's very bitter attack upon schools, school-teachers, school-children, and school authorities, but we disagree with a very great deal of it,' he said. 'It has been largely irrelevant, however, to the question of whether her children are receiving an efficient, full-time education, suitable to their ages, abilities, and aptitudes, otherwise than at school.

'They have no lessons, no teacher, and, to use her own words, they are left to develop on their own. The unanimous view of the magistrates is that they are not receiving efficient full-time education within the meaning of the Education Act.'

Referring to the question of whether an order should be made to bring the children before a juvenile court, the Chairman said they thought it best to leave it to the County Council to decide what steps to take.

The appeal was dismissed, and I was ordered to pay an additional ten guineas costs. We went home to consider the next move.

There did not seem to be any point now in waiting to see what the Education Committee would do next. They had already made it only too clear: four happy, well-brought-up children would be taken away from a united home and put into the misery of an institution—because the method of their education did not conform to that approved of by the State. But there seemed to be no way in which I could attack this peril at its source, particularly being still hampered by the belief that such an attitude, let alone action, was impossible in a country priding itself on freedom of thought, speech, and human rights.

It appeared that my only hope was to fight a delaying action, in which I would be helped by the fact that the children were steadily growing towards safety with every passing year. I went to Mr. Hipwell and asked his advice about the procedure for appeal, and he advised me to apply to the Justices for a case to be stated, on which I would appeal to the Queen's Bench Division of the High Court.

I immediately started to set the preliminary stages in motion, copying out the NOTICE OF APPLICATION FOR A CASE TO BE STATED there and then in Mr. Hipwell's office, on the back of my Quarter Sessions notes.

'To His Honour Judge Carey Evans,

Mrs. M. C. Sargent,

Mrs. M. E. Aspin,

Mr. G. E. Denney,

Brigadier T. B. Trappes-Lomax, of Her Majesty's Justices of the Peace for the County of Norfolk, and to the Clerk of the Magistrates' Court sitting at the Shirehouse, Norwich.

'Whereas informations wherein Frederick Joseph Earl was informant and I, the undersigned Joy Elsbeth Baker, was defendant were heard before and determined by the Magistrates' Court sitting at the Shirehouse, Norwich, on the 10th day of February 1959. Now I, the undersigned, being dissatisfied and aggrieved with your determination upon the hearing of the said informations as being wrong in law, hereby, pursuant to the provisions of the Magistrates'

Courts Act, 1952, S. 87, apply to you to state and sign a case setting forth the facts and grounds of such your determination for the opinion thereon of the Queen's Bench Division of the High Court of Justice.'

This I duly signed and sent to the Clerk of the Peace, with a covering letter, on February 14th:

'Appeals to Quarter Sessions
Joy Elsbeth Baker v. Frederick Joseph Earl

'With regard to the above hearing, I wish to apply for a case to be stated, on the grounds that the Justices were wrong in law in stating that I had not been convicted twice for the same offence, and that they misdirected themselves as to the meaning of the term 'education' in the light of the evidence adduced.

'I am not represented and have little knowledge of the legal procedure, but the proper procedure appears to be to make application to you, under Section 20, Sub-section 1 of the Criminal Justice Act of 1925, Stones Justices Manual 1958, Volume 1, page 101, note 5.

'I therefore enclose herewith formal notice of application to state a case.'

At the same time, I applied for legal aid to conduct the appeal, but this was refused on the grounds that I 'had not shown that I had reasonable grounds for taking proceedings.'

I therefore prepared to 'resume my role as a modern Portia,' as the local paper had put it, in the Divisional Court.

12

See How They Grow

ALTHOUGH I did not know it at the time, it soon appeared that I could not have chosen a more effective course for the purpose of delaying matters than my Divisional Court appeal. It was, in fact, a year before this appeal was heard; a year during which, although there were still the storm clouds hanging over our heads, the long knife of the Education Committee was at least temporarily rendered harmless.

At the beginning of March, I received a letter from Mr. Peter Hutchinson, Acting Deputy Clerk of the Peace for Norfolk, asking me to prepare a draft case or a statement for submission to the Justices. On Mr. Hipwell's advice, I replied to this on March 24th:

'With reference to your letter of March 10th, in which you ask me to submit a draft case or statement, as I am not represented and in view of my lack of knowledge of the formal procedure of drafting a case, it would appear that the proper course would be for you to ask the prosecution to draft the case and submit it to me for approval, comment, or amendment. I enclose herewith my statement enlarging on the two points in question.'

With this letter, I sent a statement covering the main points of my arguments in court.

A month later, I received from Mr. Hutchinson a copy of the draft case which, he said, had been 'prepared by the Norfolk County Council and settled by Counsel.'

He added: 'I think you will find that it deals adequately with the points made in the statement which you sent me, and I should be glad if you would kindly return it to me approved, or with any amendments you would like to make, as soon as possible in order that I may submit it to the Appeal Committee for signature on 30th April.'

It was an imposing document, headed:

IN THE HIGH COURT OF JUSTICE

QUEEN'S BENCH DIVISION

BETWEEN: JOY ELSBETH BAKER, Appellant

and

FREDERICK JOSEPH EARL, Respondent

'CASE STATED by Justices for the County of Norfolk acting in respect of their adjudication as the appeal committee of the general quarter sessions of the peace holden at The Shirehouse, Norwich, in and for the said County.

'1. On the 4th day of November, 1958, an information was preferred by the Respondent as a duly authorized officer for and on behalf of the Local Education Authority for the County of Norfolk against the Appellant that on the 19th day of July, 1957, the Local Education Authority made a School Attendance Order in accordance with Section (2) of the Education Act, 1944, in respect of David Baker, a child of compulsory school age as defined by Section 114 of the said Act, requiring such child to become a registered pupil at the school named in the Order, to wit, East Dereham Secondary Modern School, and that such School Attendance Order was still in force and had been served upon the Appellant, the parent of the said child, and that the Appellant had unlawfully failed to comply with the requirement of the said School Attendance Order and had failed to cause the child to receive efficient full-time education suitable to his age, ability, and aptitude, otherwise than at school, contrary to Sections 37(5) and 40 of the Education Act, 1944.'

'2. On the same day, three further informations were preferred by the Respondent against the Appellant, similarly alleging unlawful failure to comply with the requirements of three further School Attendance Orders made by the said Local Education Authority in respect of three other children of the Appellant, namely, Robin Baker, Felicity Baker, and Wendy Baker.

'3. The said informations were heard by the Magistrates' Court sitting at East Dereham in the said County on the 28th day of

November, 1958. The Appellant pleaded not guilty to each of the said informations and was convicted and fined £1 upon each charge.

'4. On the 10th day of December, 1958, the Appellant gave Notices of Appeal against the said convictions.

'In the said Notices of Appeal, the Appellant erroneously stated the date of the alleged offences to have been 19th July, 1957.

'5. By the consent of the parties, we heard the appeals against the four convictions together on the 10th day of February, 1959.

'6. The following facts were proved before us:

'(a) The Respondent was duly authorized to institute proceedings for and on behalf of the Local Education Authority for the County of Norfolk.

'(b) The children named in the said informations were of compulsory school age.

'(c) The Appellant was the parent of the said children.

'(d) The said School Attendance Orders had been duly made and had been duly served upon the Appellant and were still in force.

'(e) The Appellant had failed, up to and including the date of the hearing of the said appeal, at any time to cause any of the children to become registered pupils at the school named in the said School Attendance Orders.

'(f) None of the said children had any lessons, lesson periods, prescribed courses of study, or hours of study. None of them received instruction in any subject, but the Appellant (who is without any educational qualifications) encouraged them to follow up any subject in which they were interested. The eldest boy spent most of his time working for a neighboring farmer; the younger boy in cooking and housework; the two girls in looking after the younger children and in other domestic tasks. All four children were called before us as witnesses, and we observed them.

'(g) The Appellant had been convicted on the 8th of November, 1957, of breaches of the same four School Attendance Orders, contrary to Sections 37(5) and 40 of the Education Act, 1944, and her appeals to the magistrates sitting in an

Appeal Committee on the 10th day of January, 1958, had been dismissed.

'7. It was contended by the Appellant:

'(1) That she had already been convicted of the same offences on informations laid on the 12th day of October, 1957, and was autrefois convict.

'(2) That in encouraging the said children to develop 'naturally' and to gain experience through farm work, domestic work, and in the home generally, she was causing the said children to receive efficient full-time education suitable to their ages, abilities, and aptitudes, otherwise than at school.

'8. It was contended on behalf of the Respondent that the children were not receiving efficient full-time education suitable to their ages, abilities, and aptitudes. Counsel for the Respondent was not called upon to make any submission upon the plea of autrefois convict.

'9. (a) We were of the opinion that the contention of autrefois convict should not be upheld for the following reasons:

'(i) Such plea must be raised before pleading to the charge, but the Appellant pleaded 'Not Guilty' before the magistrates at East Dereham.

'(ii) No such contention was raised in the 'grounds of appeal' in the Appellant's Notice of Appeal.

'(iii) The Appellant, after the dismissal of her appeal as aforesaid on the 10th day of January, 1958, had subsequently failed to comply with the said School Attendance Orders, which continued in full force and effect; and the informations preferred against the Appellant on the 4th day of November, 1958, could only have referred to offences subsequent to the dismissal of her said appeal.

'(b) Having considered the evidence, observed the children, and heard the Appellant's argument, we found as a fact that the Appellant had failed at all material times to cause any of the said children to receive efficient full-time education suitable to their ages, abilities, and aptitudes, otherwise than at school. We did not hold that any particular form or pattern of efficient full-time education, otherwise than at school, was required as a matter of law.

'(c) The Appellant, having failed to comply with the said School Attendance Orders and having failed to cause any of the said children to receive efficient full-time education suitable to their ages, abilities, and aptitudes, otherwise than at school, we upheld the convictions in the Magistrates' Court and dismissed the appeal.

'QUESTION

'10. The question for the opinion of the High Court is:

'(1) Whether we came to a correct decision in point of law, and if not, what should be done in the premises.

When I had read this, it appeared to me that it was singularly devoid of any mention of the points I had made and did not, indeed, cover adequately any part of my evidence. I therefore wrote to Mr. Hutchinson, saying that I did not approve the case as stated and asking if I might have time to consult a solicitor regarding what amendments I should make before returning it.

I was now in fact in some difficulty over this, as I was getting well out of my depth in these unknown legal waters, and Mr. Hipwell was unable to help me further as I could not ask him to instruct his London agents without having legal aid; and being a Divisional Court case, it needed the advice of a London solicitor.

In an attempt to clarify the position, I also telephoned Mr. Hutchinson; but I met with a surprisingly unhelpful reception. Mr. Hutchinson at first informed me that I could not make any amendments to the draft case; and when I drew his attention to the contents of his own letter of April 24th, he made no direct response to this but said that it would not matter if the draft was not returned by the 30th of April, despite the request in his letter. I could get no further with him than this, and I rang off, feeling that the position was distinctly unsatisfactory.

I had still been unable to obtain legal advice when, on the 6th of May, I received a further letter from Mr. Hutchinson, informing me that the case stated by the Appeal Committee was now signed and ready to be delivered to me, and should be lodged without delay at the Crown Office and Associates Department, Royal Courts of Justice, London. Before this could be done, however, I had to pay to the Clerk of the Peace 'his fees as provided for in the Criminal Justice Act, 1925', which amounted to £1 18s. 4*d*., made up as follows:

'To drawing case (14 folios at 1s.).. ..	14	0
'For copy thereof (14 folios at 4d.) ..	4	8
'For attending Chairman settling case ..	10	0
'For engrossing case as settled	4	8
'For attending Chairman for signature ..	5	0

'The following documents', the letter continued, 'must accompany the case:

'(a) Three copies of the case.

'(b) The Memoranda of the decisions of Quarter Sessions sent to you on 13th February, 1959.

'(c) Three copies of the judgements appealed from.

'(d) Three copies of the Notices of Appeal.

'(e) Your recognizance to prosecute the appeal (which is in my possession).

This last item I had signed earlier at the Justices' Clerk's office in Dereham.

'So far as copy documents are concerned,' Mr. Hutchinson added, 'if it would assist you, I would be prepared to supply these at the cost shown below:

'12 copies of decision of Quarter Sessions ..	15	0
'12 copies of Notices of Appeal	12	0
'12 copies of convictions	9	0.'

The number of copy documents required apparently grew like a snowball with each paragraph; three, I assumed, were for the three judges who would hear the appeal, but would I, I wondered, really need the other nine, or was it simply that they could not be supplied in less than dozens? The more I read Mr. Hutchinson's letter, the more unlikely it seemed that I would ever get my appeal into court.

By now, I felt that I was altogether up to my neck and floundering in all these complications of legal procedure; and it was at this point that I was given an introduction to a London solicitor,

Mr. Edward Iwi, who agreed to take the position in hand for me, obtain the necessary documents, and handle the matter up to the actual hearing, when I would conduct my own case in court.

I went to see Mr. Iwi in June and thankfully handed over to him my correspondence with the Acting Deputy Clerk of the Peace; and at the end of July, the case was officially lodged at the Crown Office of the Law Courts.

Meanwhile, the pattern of our lives continued to weave its course throughout the passing year.

In April, David started working regularly, six mornings a week, on the 400-acre farm of one of our neighbors, with the purpose of gaining a full twelve months' experience there before his fifteenth birthday. This, however, was stopped in July by the Education Authorities. I received a letter from Dr. Lincoln Ralphs stating that, although David was not being paid and was in fact receiving instruction, his 'employment' under the age of fifteen constituted an offense under the Norfolk County Council's by-laws; and an official from the Council called on the farmer for whom David was working and warned him that if he continued to have David on the farm, he would be liable to heavy penalties. David was then fourteen, and we had begun counting off the months to the next June, when he would be free.

The previous December, David had given Felicity his first camera as a birthday present; I had given him a more advanced model for his birthday that year. Felicity's approach to photography was quite different from David's; with no knowledge of, or interest in, the technical side, she aimed her camera at whatever caught her eye and broke all the rules with careless abandon; but she produced thereby some quite startling results, showing both originality and a flair for artistic lighting and composition.

In August, David won another prize for a photograph of Felicity with one of the racehorses in *Pet Life* magazine. The prize was a camera similar to the one he had given to Felicity, but a newer model; so he gave this to her also, and she gave hers to Wendy.

As she became increasingly interested in photography, Felicity gradually gave up writing fairy tales and put aside the stories that Judge Carey Evans would not read; her Little Stories of Dido (pronounced Dee-doo)—the imaginary place where, all through her childhood, for as long as she could remember, she had played. Perhaps they would not have impressed the judge, but they gave a clear insight into the mind of the ten-year-old child.

'One day I went for a walk and I found a little place and I called it Dido. Dido was shaded by trees, especially so no one could see in, and it had a little running stream beside the house. A quiet little place this, with a lot of wild animals, rabbits, birds, and other kinds of animals, and when no one is looking, a cherub babe may run past.

'Tiptoe is a little horse, and sometimes she will give the cherub babes rides. Tiptoe is white with a long mane and tail. She is a sweet little horse, and her companion is named Snowball.

'One night in Dido, when the fairies were going home, a white horse with a baby fairy on its back dropped down into Dido. The fairy climbed off and looked round and she said suddenly, 'I am Prill! Anybody about?'

'Just at that moment, Dido's owl flew over and saw her, and fluttered down beside her, and called all the other animals and birds and cherub babes of Dido, and she looked very startled because she didn't expect there would be so many animals and birds and cherubs.

'The cherubs told Prilly how sweet she was, but she was very shy. Snowball offered to give her a ride. Tiptoe offered too, so by now, Dido was getting quite noisy with the cherubs and Prilly riding up and down.

'One morning, when Dido was very quiet, everybody noticed that Snowball was missing. It was several days and nights before he came back. Then he told his story to everybody.

'He said, "A man caught me and put a saddle on me, and put a pair of reins on me, and then climbed on me, but I reared up and threw him off. Then I got my reins and saddle off and I galloped back to Dido."...

'There is a lot of Dido and of animals in it, and small babes called cherubs. There is a mother fox with four cubs, and here is the story about them. The mother fox hadn't been seen since last night. 'I wonder where she is?' said all the animals.

'Days went past, but there was no sign of her. All the animals thought she must have been killed, but one break of dawn, they heard a lot of little feet and noises. They all looked out and saw her with four little cubs. They were so pleased they had a lovely party, and they were very happy.

'Once upon a time, there lived two cherubs, Small Cherub and Little Cherub. One day they were playing in the woods when a man rode up on a big black horse, picked Little Cherub up, and rode away again. Little Cherub sobbed. The man took Little Cherub to a big house, locked him up in the attic, and put bars across the window.

'Small Cherub ran in and told the fairies. Little Cherub had sobbed so much the fairies could follow his tear marks. They got to the house, flew up to the window, and touched the window with their wands. The bars vanished, and Little Cherub flew out, and they all flew home.

'The man was very cross indeed, and he never came near Dido again, and the fairies and the cherubs were happy ever after.

And then there were the poems:

> Before I was born, I was at Dido,
> Before I was born, I was very new,
> My hands and legs were crumply things,
> I had two little smoothed-out wings,
> And now I remember a long time ago,
> Around me little flowers did grow...'

The court should perhaps have been interested in her growing ability to handle words expressively and in her early appreciation of the idea of reincarnation, even if they had not liked the clarity with which she brought out, in allegory, her attitude toward the Education Authority.

Perhaps it was natural that, following her fairy tales and her photography, Felicity should now start to take an interest in ballet. I had taken her in the spring to see *Coppélia* at the theatre and later in the year to see the film of the Bolshoi Ballet, with Galina Ulanova dancing in *Giselle*; in July, I took her to the Bolshoi Ballet's film of *Swan Lake*. She was entranced, but it was not enough for her to watch. She began to want to be a ballet dancer.

At the same time, David started taking an interest in music. He was first attracted by the music lessons in the *Children's Encyclopedia*; and, having absorbed all these, he bought himself a handbook, which he studied with increasing interest, and after a time, he started writing music himself. He also bought himself a mouth organ and learned to play tunes by ear; and in the summer evenings, he used to provide the accompaniment, as well as operating an ingenious 'curtain' on the linen line, while Felicity and Wendy danced ballets of their own invention on the lawn. On these occasions, Robin helped with the 'curtain,' worked a 'spotlight' with a torch from the landing window, and announced the programme. The backcloth was a bed of roses and sweet peas, and I was the audience, seated under an apple tree in one of the sitting-room armchairs.

It had been, on the whole, a happy year, with the immediate danger of the Education Authorities held at bay, and the children continuing to grow steadily in the general direction I wanted them to go; although we had all received a shock when, in April, our landlord gave us formal notice to quit, saying that he objected to press reporters, photographers, and television vans coming up the field to the house. (Earlier in the year, we had recorded a ten-minute interview for the B.B.C. television programme Tonight.)

In May, I saw a house advertised to let in the next village; but when, after going to see it, I offered for the tenancy, I was refused because, the owner said, he could not have as tenant 'a woman who was constantly appearing in the local magistrates' court.' He was Sir Bartle Edwards—Chairman of the Dereham Bench.

Eventually, however, this threat to our security also died down. Our landlord retired, although grumbling, without pursuing the matter further, and our tenancy continued without interruption.

And then, in August, there came to me the one irreparable tragedy of my life. On August 7th, my fourth baby girl, two months premature, was stillborn in the Norfolk and Norwich Hospital. A black curtain descended over my heart, and for many months, I did not think I would ever be able to face life again.

For the children also, this was a time of sadness and pain. It had happened with a suddenness that inflicted a severe shock on us all. I had gone to have lunch with my mother at her home in Norwich, but by the time I arrived, I was in labour, and within an hour, I was on my way to the hospital in an ambulance. The children were left without warning to deal with a world turned suddenly upside-down. I was in hospital for five days, during which time eleven-year-old Felicity looked after the household and three babies, and all four older children combined to keep the home together until I was well again. While I was in hospital, Felicity sent me a photograph of April, then eighteen months old—'with love from all the babies'—and wrote: The babies are all right. The airing is in order; so is the running of the house. When the ambulance brought me home, I found them all shaken and sad, but they were all there to welcome me home, and 'the running of the house' was still in order.

It was suggested at the time that I might have lost my baby due to the worry caused by the Education Authorities. But I do not think this could be said to be so; the cause of the stillbirth was toxaemia, and although the strain of continual court proceedings had certainly aged me and might not have improved my condition, this could not have been caused by worry alone. The approach of my Divisional Court appeal did indeed have the effect of forcing me to take an interest in life again, sooner perhaps than I would otherwise have had any incentive to do.

In October, I had to go to London again to see Mr. Iwi; the case might now be heard at any time, and I had to be prepared to go into court. To help me with this, Mr. Iwi arranged for me to come up to London for a third time and spend the morning in the Lord Chief Justice's court while a case was being heard, so that I might have some idea of procedure when I came to conduct my own case. I sat at the back of the court and was deeply impressed by the clarity of mind and fairness with which Lord Parker handled his judgments. I was also rather overcome by the realization that soon I would have to stand up in front of that court and address the judge myself. Particularly terrifying was the thought of calling the judge 'My Lord.' I practised this at home on the children and the cats, but doing it to a real, live judge, robed in crimson and

black, was quite a different matter. I also made several alterations
to my previously prepared brief when I got home from the court;
consisting for the most part of deleting the words 'I maintain' and
substituting 'In my submission, my Lord' instead.

At the end of October, Mr. Iwi let me know that my case was
not likely to be heard before January, so I had a few more months'
respite. It was, in fact, not until the 5th of February 1960 that I
appeared before the Lord Chief Justice in the Divisional Court.

Despite my earlier introductory visit, I was literally scared stiff
when I entered the court. Hardly conscious of my surroundings
or the people on all sides of me, I walked to my place immediately
below the three judges, got out my papers, and tried to relax as I
listened to the conclusion of the preceding case, which concerned,
so far as I could make out, an appeal over the sale on a Sunday of
a pound of sugar.

When it was finished and my name was called, I stood up, very
frightened, to open my case.

I had to start by reading the case stated, copies of which had
already been put before the judges, and I then went on:

'Before continuing my case, I would like to make a submission
regarding the preparation of the case stated.' I then gave details
of the events following my application for a case to be stated, my
correspondence with the Acting Deputy Clerk of the Peace, and my
telephone conversation with him, concluding, 'I wish, therefore,
to make it clear that the case stated has not been approved by me,
and I would like, if I may, to place before the court the statement
which I originally submitted to the Acting Deputy Clerk of the
Peace.' I had copies of this statement prepared, and these were
handed up to the judges. 'It appears to me that the case has not
been properly stated, and I submit that under Section 7 of the S.J.
Act of 1857, it should be sent back for amendment.'

The judges, however, did not uphold this, and I could not
debate it as I had only the bare reference and was not sure what I
was talking about; so I therefore continued:

'As set out in my statement, which you have before you, I claim
that I have been convicted twice for the same offence. In the case
stated, it is stated that in my Notices of Appeal against my convic-

tions of the 15th November 1957 and the 28th November 1958, I erroneously stated the date of the alleged offences to have been the 19th July 1957, which is the date of the School Attendance Orders. This wording was set down for me by the solicitors who assisted me in preparing the Notices of Appeal. If this were not the date on which the offences were said to have been committed, it appears that no date on which I was alleged to have committed the offences referred to in the summonses has ever been given.

'My Lord, in my submission, I cannot be summoned for an offence if the date of the offence cannot be given.

'The Justices state that this contention should not be upheld because (1) such plea must be raised before pleading to the charge, and (2) no such contention was raised in the grounds of appeal in my Notice of Appeal. On these points, I can only say that I was not represented and was not aware of these technical points of procedure, which do not affect the correctness or otherwise of my contention in law.

'The Justices further state (3) that after the dismissal of my appeal on the 10th January 1958, I subsequently failed to comply with the School Attendance Orders, and the informations preferred against me on November 4th, 1958, could only have referred to offences subsequent to the dismissal of my appeal. My Lord, I submit that this wording is too vague to have meaning in law, and if the informations referred to specific offences, this should have been made clear; failing which, the only date given in the proceedings against me is the same as in the preceding proceedings, namely, July 19th, 1957.

'I would draw your attention to the wording of the School Attendance Orders, which is, 'Now, therefore, you are hereby required to cause the child *forthwith* to become a pupil at the following school.' The dictionary definition of 'forthwith' is 'immediately, without delay,' and this presumably refers to the date on the School Attendance Orders, July 19th, 1957; and it is this injunction that I have been summoned for failing to comply with. In each case, therefore, I have been summoned for failing to send my children to school 'immediately' on July 19th, 1957. In my submission, my Lord, it cannot be said that this could refer to a date during the following year.'

I paused, consciously wondering how long it would be before I had finished and could sit down. Then I started on the main part of my argument.

'The second point of my appeal is on the meaning of the term 'education,' as laid down in the Act.

'The Education Act requires that children shall receive efficient, full-time education suitable to their age, ability, and aptitude, but does not state what type of education this must be or that it must bear any relation to that given in the State schools. There are a great many types of education, and only by varying widely the educational methods employed can these be made suitable to each child's individual ability and aptitude.

'Education is defined in *Webster's Dictionary* as the 'process or manner of training youth,' and by Spencer as 'preparation for complete living.' The term 'education' does not mean mass instruction—nor wholly instruction of any kind—it means the bringing up of a child to a well-balanced, well-informed young adult, mentally, physically, and spiritually equipped to live a full adult life. It is education to teach and encourage a child to seek and acquire knowledge voluntarily, to develop his individual ability, to gain a sense of responsibility, to conduct himself properly on all occasions; and this is what I am doing in the education of my children.

'The Justices state that none of my children had any lessons, or lesson periods, or prescribed courses of study or hours of study, and that I had no educational qualifications. My Lord, I would draw your attention to the fact that there are still schools, approved by the Minister of Education, run and taught by teachers with no more qualifications than I possess. There are also schools approved by the Minister of Education, employing a method of 'free' education, at which no set times or courses of study are laid down. In the State schools, the emphasis is laid on the teaching, and it appears to be on this point that the Justices regarded my children as not receiving efficient education. My Lord, in my submission, education is not what children are taught or the qualifications of their teachers, but what they learn.

'The Justices stated that my children had no teacher, received no instruction in any subject, and were left to develop on their own. My Lord, this is not supported by the evidence. Because I have not taught my children according to school methods does not alter the fact that I have been their teacher from birth; because they do not sit at desks to have lessons in the sense used in a school does not mean that they do not receive instruction and learn; the fact that they are being trained in such a way that they will each develop their own individuality is not 'being allowed to develop on their own'; their whole education is being carried out under my close guidance and supervision.

'It is surely not the method of teaching, nor the teacher's qualifications, that constitute education, but the effect of these on the child. The parent who has lived with and studied the child from birth onwards is a far better judge of its present and potential ability and aptitude than any schoolteacher can be whose knowledge of the child is limited to a few hours daily as one of a large class.'

'Children can leave school unable to read or write, but having attended school for the prescribed period, they are regarded as having received efficient education under the Act. It cannot be said that all children leaving school today are what was understood, in my childhood at any rate, to be well-educated persons.

'By an educated person, I understand a well-behaved, well-spoken individual with a wide and varied knowledge of many subjects and a serious interest in those most suited to his or her own ability and aptitude; able to talk intelligently, behave intelligently, and act in an adult way. I do not think anyone really regards the absorption of the standard subjects taught in the secondary modern schools as resulting in an educated person. Formal tuition in subjects for which the individual has ability and aptitude can and should be given when the mind is ready for them; but I regard the value of instruction during the years between five and fifteen as less important than the development of individual characters. Study can be undertaken at any age, but character is formed and developed during the years when school education requires children to receive continuous teaching in one subject after another, in many cases when they are not ready to take advantage of it. Many children lose interest in subjects which, at a later age, they would find interesting through being taught them when they were not ready to learn.

'The primary purpose of education I take to be the preparation of the child for adult life, but mass instruction in set subjects does not achieve this, and no one faces adult life properly equipped through having received it. Adult life requires people to act as individuals, and education is that method of upbringing which makes an individual, not that which tends to standardize the mass. Ideally, education should give the opportunity to each child to find its own course and set its own pace, should provide help and encouragement along that course, and fulfill the educational need of each stage of development at whatever ages these occur.

'The value of competition in school education is often stressed, but I doubt its value. Competition more often than not gives the forward child a chance to look down on the backward child and causes the backward child to lose heart. No two children develop at the same rate, and the backward child of one year may be the forward child of the next—provided no importance is placed on his relative position at the start and he is not discouraged by the false values induced by the spirit of competition.

'Importance is also placed on the value of mixing with other children. But forced mixing with others is not education, and being forced to mix does not make the shy child less shy; it makes the child either withdraw into himself or, going to the other extreme, become artificially over-aggressive. A child only develops normally when given the opportunity to choose for himself company or solitude. The natural community of a large family is of real value to a child, not the indiscriminate mixing of children in school.

'No training is of any value to a developing child that does not leave room for the encouragement of the child's expanding independence and the use of his own initiative. But by its very nature, school training cannot do this. The majority of children leave school without any preparation for a more independent life.

'In planning my children's education, I have had to bear in mind that, in my own education as a child, I attended school for eight years; during which time, although I tried hard to learn, I did in fact learn nothing that has ever been of any use to me—whereas those things which I have needed in adult life, and in which I have ability, I learned myself, and in spite of, not because of, the education I received at school.

'The Justices have stated in regard to my children's education: 'The eldest boy spent most of his time with a neighbouring farmer; the younger boy in cooking and housework; the two girls in looking after the children and in other domestic tasks.'

'My Lord, this is not an accurate record of the facts which were brought out before the court. My eldest son, David, who is now fourteen and a half, wants to be a farmer and has worked on several different types of farm in our area during the past two years, gaining practical experience of farm work during the time that, if he had been at school, he would have been playing games. Last year, he started spending the mornings, six days a week, on the 400-acre farm of one of our neighbours, learning the full routine of the work in which he wishes to make his career. But I then received a letter from the local Education Authority informing me that this constituted an offence under the bye-laws, and the farmer was warned that if he continued to have David on the farm, he would be liable to heavy penalties. I find it difficult to understand how team games can be regarded as education when studying for a future career is treated as a breach of the law.

' David has also studied photography and has already achieved considerable success in this. He has won, first a £1 prize, and then the following year the £30 first prize in Parents magazine photographic competition—a competition intended for adult photographers—and he has had a number of other photographs published in national magazines.

'He has recently taken an interest in music; and starting by reading the music lessons in the *Children's Encyclopedia* and then other books on the subject, he now knows a great deal more about it than I did after years of music lessons at school. He can play tunes by ear, whereas my teacher never taught me to play anything, and he has started to write music himself.

'Robin, who at thirteen is a less mature child than David, is developing more slowly. He is interested in farming but is more interested in gardening, for which he shows considerable aptitude. But his main interest up to the present is in cooking, and he wants to make it his career. He is, in fact, by now a skilled cook, and it appears to me that this knowledge will be of considerably more use to him than the enforced study of some more academic subjects which he has not at present the ability to acquire.

'My eldest daughter, Felicity, now twelve, is a born housewife and mother. She has learned to care for babies from a few weeks old to three years and is capable of taking complete charge of her three younger brothers and sister, aged three, two, and eighteen months—a task which is regarded as formidable by a fully trained children's nurse. She can run a full household, cook, sew, and iron as well as most women.

'She can also do anything with horses, although she has never had riding lessons, and she can and does ride almost any horse bareback. She has never been set formal essays, but she writes fairy stories by way of recreation. And a year ago, she took up photography and has shown in her photographic work considerable artistic ability and skill.

'Wendy, who is nearly eleven, is entirely undomesticated in her interests, although she also has learned to care for the younger children and do practical housework, because I regard this as an essential part of education for any woman. But her main interests are outdoor ones, and she is waiting impatiently for the time when she will be allowed to drive a tractor. Like Felicity, she writes her own stories instead of school essays; although she is the most immature of the four, she is also in many ways the most dominant personality and shows an incredible amount of efficiency and organizing ability in any practical work she undertakes, which she would certainly not have a chance to develop in school.

'At the hearing of my appeal to Quarter Sessions, my eldest son's prize-winning photographs were placed before the Justices, but the Chairman stated that this was irrelevant. As my son has studied photography in place of other school subjects, his achievements in this field are, in my submission, very relevant to the efficiency of his education.

'I also proposed to put some of Felicity's stories before the Justices as part of my evidence, but the Chairman refused to permit this, saying that it was irrelevant and would not prove whether or not she was receiving efficient full-time education. In my submission, work produced by my children in the course of their education was essential proof of my case.

'It does not appear to me reasonable to say that if a child learns without being formally taught, he is not therefore receiving education. None of my children has ever had a set reading lesson, but they have learned to read. They have had access to reading matter in which each would be interested and help with words whenever they needed and asked for help; and the ultimate result has been more efficient than the methods practiced in school.

'My children have learned arithmetic by its daily use instead of by set lessons; they have learned history and geography by reading and discussing them; they have learned many subjects not taught in schools at all, which are likely to be of far more use to them than orthodox subjects would ever be. It is my submission, my Lord, that what they have learned by my system of education constitutes a more efficient full-time education, more closely suited to their abilities and aptitudes, than they could have received in school.

'Education includes the training of the mind, but the Act does not specify on what subjects the mind shall be trained. For this purpose, the choice of subject is immaterial; provided the mind is trained to think, farming, photography, child care, or music are as beneficial as Latin or geometry.

'The Justices state: 'All four children were called before us, and we observed them.' They do not, however, give any indication of what actual conclusions they drew from their observation of the children, and they do not state in what way they found them uneducated.

'The evidence of my children in court did establish that they spoke well, were well-mannered, and had the general appearance of children receiving a good private education. The Justices do appear to have based their conclusions on the fact that I could give them no timetable of lessons or hour-by-hour curriculum. In my submission, the Act does not require this. No one who knows my children has any doubt about the ability of their minds. I don't want to stand out as a crank, but I do believe that I am doing what is best for my children. After all, I have the living evidence before me every day.

'My children have learned some subjects later than they would have been expected to in school—but it does not follow that they *would* have learned them earlier if they had been at school. The Act does not lay down at what age a child should reach any set standard—it is only assumed that they should be at the standard accepted by the school authorities, but the Act does not require this—it only requires them to receive *efficient education*. In my submission, it is immaterial at what age a child learns any given subject, provided that at the end of his school life he is properly educated within the meaning of the Act. 'Since my children's education has produced, in the case of my eldest son, who is now within six months of school-leaving age, results that compare favorably with the average child on leaving school, it is, in my submission, my Lord, demonstrably efficient education.

'And I do not think that anyone could reasonably suggest, my Lord, that David could receive any benefit from attending school now for the period of less than six months during which he will remain within the limits of compulsory school age as defined by the Act.

'The Act requires the child to receive 'full-time education,' but it does not define the number of hours meant by 'full-time.' It is apparently merely assumed, and not laid down by law, that this means the hours kept in most schools. The education I am giving my children is full-time in the widest sense of the word, since it goes on all the time as an integral part of their upbringing throughout all the waking hours of their lives.

'The Chairman of the Justices stated that my views on education were 'largely irrelevant.' But the law places upon the parent the responsibility for causing the child to receive efficient education suitable to his age, ability, and aptitude, and it must therefore follow that the parent should be permitted to decide what type of education should be given; and, in my submission, my Lord, it cannot be properly said that the views of the parent are irrelevant in the matter of the child's education.

(*a*) Hugh (4) and Martin (3) in 1960
– photograph by Felicity (12)

(*b*) Martin (5) in 1962 – photography
by Wendy (13). In the background
in Heath Farm House

(*c*) April (3) in 1961 – photgraph by
Felicity (13)

The author outside the Shirehall, Norwich, after her successful
appeal to Quarter Sessions in November 1961

'My Lord, it is not my wish to defy the law—I am asking only that the law be reasonably and considerately interpreted.

'It does not appear to me that the schools can ever provide, in the mass teaching of classes, education suitable to any child's individual ability and aptitude; and it is therefore only by educating my children according to my own views that I can comply with the requirements of the Education Act.'

I sat down, still trembling, after talking for three-quarters of an hour; and I did not take in one word of Mr. Paul Wrightson's reply for the Education Committee. I sat in a state of acute tension, waiting for the Lord Chief Justice to speak.

I was fascinated by the way the judges got up one at a time and stood conferring over each other's shoulders; and then at last, they all seated themselves in their places, and Lord Parker gave his judgment.

He began by giving details of the original charges against me, my conviction by Dereham magistrates, and my Quarter Sessions appeal.

'This lady—and one cannot help feeling a certain amount of sympathy with her—does not believe in the school curriculum; she thinks that a lot of subjects which are learned at school up to the age of fifteen do not serve any useful purpose in after-life and that the children can be better trained for their future at home. She, in fact, prides herself on the fact that she has brought up these children extremely well, that they are just as capable, or better capable, of being good citizens and making their way in life than if they had been to an ordinary school.'

He went on to quote the relevant sections of the Education Act and continued: 'Accordingly, before anybody can be found guilty of an offense, it follows that they have an opportunity of satisfying the local Education Authority before a School Attendance Order is made, and if the parent fails to do that, the parent has a further opportunity of so satisfying the Justices.'

'The whole trouble in the present case is that Mrs. Baker failed to satisfy the local Education Authority in the first instance, and then both before the Justices at East Dereham and before the Appeal Committee failed to satisfy them that the children were receiving efficient full-time education. That is primarily a question of fact, and the Appeal Committee found as a fact that the Appellant had failed to cause the children to receive efficient full-time education otherwise than at school.

'That is a finding of fact which cannot be challenged in this court, unless it is said that the Justices have in some way gone wrong in law or misdirected themselves in arriving at that finding. Indeed, that is what the Appellant suggests. The Appellant suggests that the Justices had in mind that efficient full-time education necessitated fixed lessons at fixed hours, prescribed courses of study, and matters of that sort. The truth of the matter is that the Justices thought no such thing, because they said, 'We did not hold that any particular form or pattern of efficient full-time education was required as a matter of law'; so the Appellant failed to prove before them that the children were receiving efficient full-time education.'

I was puzzled by this since the Justices' 'finding of fact' that my children had 'no lessons, lesson periods, or prescribed courses of study' *had* been one of their main grounds for dismissing my appeal.

Lord Parker continued: 'Apart from that, the Appellant takes the point that she has already been convicted of this offence. It is quite true that in neither of the informations were any dates stated as to when the breaches of the School Attendance Orders occurred. A breach could not occur until, firstly, the School Attendance Order had been made, and secondly, until it had been served; but, in my judgment, there was no necessity to do more than to recite the date of the order and its service, and every date after that up to the date of the information would be days when breaches of the order occurred. Accordingly, in my judgment, the Appeal Committee came to a perfectly correct decision, and this appeal should be dismissed.

'I would only add this, a matter which really does not concern this court directly, but it appears that the eldest boy, David, is now fourteen and a half years of age; and it would seem wrong that he now, at fourteen and a half, should be required to go to school.'

Mr. Justice Davies and Mr. Justice Ashworth agreed.

I stood up again and asked, 'My Lord, is there any further right of appeal?'

Lord Parker replied, 'No—this is the final court.'

In view of my experiences over the last five years, it did seem very unlikely. And I was tired of this assumption of absolute supremacy over other people's lives by officials who were only human beings themselves, after all.

So I smiled and replied, 'Not quite.'

As it turned out, I was absolutely correct.

To the reporters who questioned me as I left the court, I said: 'I still won't send them to school. There is no question of my giving in. I believe that what I am doing is right.'

I returned home, arriving late in the evening, and was greeted by Robin with a bouquet of daffodils. I felt that I didn't really deserve them—I had not brought victory. But at least I had chipped one little corner off the strength of the opposition. The Lord Chief Justice had said that David should not go to school.

13

Not Quite, My Lord

On the day following my appeal to the Divisional Court, we got all the newspapers as usual and found the position summed up by the *Daily Sketch* in very black headlines: 'Home-school Mother says again—I'll defy the law.'

This was all very well, but I had to deal with the practical aspect of the matter. The children were now again exposed to an attack by the Education Authority, and it seemed to me that it would be a good idea if I made a move first. I therefore wrote that same day to the Minister of Education:

'I wish to draw your attention to the position that has arisen as a result of the dismissal of my appeal against my conviction for failing to comply with School Attendance Orders in respect of my four older children, heard in the Divisional Court yesterday.

'For the past ten years, I have carried out the education of my children at home, and these children, the eldest of whom is now aged fourteen years and eight months, have never received any other form of education.

'As a result of this, I have been repeatedly prosecuted by the Norfolk Education Committee, and they have stated that it is their intention to apply for an order to bring these children before a juvenile court, with a view to their being taken into the care of the local authority.

'It is reasonable to suppose that this provision of the Act was intended to apply in the case of children whose education had been willfully ignored or neglected; whereas in this case, it appears that it is to be used as a weapon to force a parent, whose views on education differ from those of the majority, to subject the children concerned to a form of education regarded by the parent as inefficient and unsuited to the children's ability and aptitude, contrary to Section 36 of the Education Act.

'You, as Minister, are responsible to Parliament for the administration of the Education Act, and if these children should be removed from their home on these grounds, the matter will become a national scandal. I request an interview with you to clarify the intentions behind the provisions of the Act.'

To this, I received a reply from the Ministry, dated February 18th, stating that the Minister could not intervene in a matter which had been decided by the court. I wrote again on March 5th:

'Thank you for your letter of February 18th, but I would point out that it was not suggested in my letter that the Minister should intervene in the decision of the court.

'I would, however, again draw the Minister's attention to the position that has arisen as a result of that decision.

'While my appeal was dismissed, the Lord Chief Justice stated that in the opinion of the court, it would be wrong if my eldest son—who is still 'a child of compulsory school age'—was now required to go to school.

'But the dismissal of my appeal leaves it open to the local authorities to take proceedings in the juvenile court for the removal of all four of these children from my care. And it has been stated on a number of occasions in open court by the solicitor for the Education Committee that it is the intention of the Committee, acting on behalf of the Ministry, to take such proceedings against me.

'It is not in the matter of the decision of the court, but in this matter of the declared policy of your Ministry, that I seek an interview with the Minister; and I shall be glad, therefore, to know if the Minister will make an early appointment to see me as I have requested?'

The reply from the Ministry, dated March 18th, stated:

'I have been asked by the Minister to reply to your further letter of the 5th March about your children's education. Having considered the contents of that letter, I am to repeat the view expressed in our previous letter that the Minister does not consider an interview would serve any useful purpose.'

I replied on April 25th:

'With reference to your letter of March 18th, I note that the Minister does not consider that an interview would serve any useful purpose, but I cannot agree with this view, and I would suggest that the Minister would be better able to assess the purpose served by an interview if he would agree to its taking place.'

To this, I received a reply from the Ministry, dated May 6th, stating:

'With reference to your letter of 25th April, I have been asked by the Minister of Education to say that there is nothing he can usefully add to previous correspondence, in which he has already indicated his inability to agree to an interview.'

Whether or not this correspondence had any bearing on the local Education Committee's change of ground for their next attack, I shall never know. But on Thursday, May 12th, Mr. Earl and Mr. Brighton called at our house and served on me a writ applying to have Robin, Felicity, and Wendy made wards of the Chancery Court.

The writ asked specifically:

'1. That the three children should be made wards of court. 2. That direction should be given about their education. 3. That such other orders may be made as the welfare of the children requires.'

Mr. Earl and Mr. Brighton served the writ without comment and left. Two unmentioned facts stood out: the Council, for whatever reason, was reluctant to carry out their threat to bring the children before a juvenile court; and they had accepted the Lord Chief Justice's remarks about David and were letting him go free.

It remained to be seen just how long the Chancery proceedings could be made to assist in continuing our delaying action and, of course, what would be the ultimate result. I was quite well aware that if the children were made wards of court and I then refused to send them to school, I could be sent to prison for an indefinite period for contempt of court. My release could then only be sought if I agreed to send them to school, which meant that I would face the prospect of remaining in gaol until April reached school-leaving age—which would mean for the next thirteen years.

When I let myself think about it, the future was terrifying. But I did not give it much thought at that time, being a believer in dealing with things when they happened. All that had actually happened then was the service of the writ, and that had to be dealt with immediately.

On Sunday night, a reporter from the *Daily Mail* called and asked to see the writ to verify its terms for his report. We had always been on good terms with the Press, and I asked him in and showed him the document. Previously, we had received very fair treatment from the newspapers, and I was totally unprepared for the extraordinary description of our home that appeared in the next morning's *Daily Mail*—May 16th, 1960.

The report stated: 'The paint was peeling. Behind Mrs. Baker, a blanket served as a door. Several of the windows had been replaced by wire netting.'

I was shocked and angry. There was no paint peeling in the house, although the younger children had chipped the paintwork in places. Behind me, as I spoke to the reporter, was a green velvet curtain hung between two communicating rooms, our sitting room and the babies' playroom. We had repaired some broken window panes temporarily with Windowlite until we could get them glazed again. The degree of poverty and neglect indicated in the report could hardly have existed in a household fit for children to live in, and this was the start of a battle to keep my children in their own home!

The ensuing acrimonious correspondence with the *Daily Mail* produced no helpful result, and no acceptable correction was ever agreed to. It was a long while afterward that I realized I had in my possession a photograph taken by the *Daily Mail* the previous year, showing the children grouped in front of the same velvet curtain that the *Daily Mail* now described as 'a blanket serving as a door.'

On the day that the *Daily Mail* report appeared, another 'television van' came up the field, and I was interviewed with the children outside my back door by Anglia ITV. The interview subsequently appeared on the news that night—'But do you feel you have any special qualifications that fit you to educate your children, Mrs.

Baker?'—'That comes in the same category as whether I am fit to bring them up; they are my children.'

The next day, I took the writ to Mr. Hipwell and left it in his hands. Within twenty-four hours, I had entered an appearance to the writ and made an application for legal aid. It was not long before I heard that this had been granted, and Mr. Hipwell went into action. The matter was passed up to the firm's London agents, Messrs. Piesse and Sons, who attended the hearing of the Originating Summons before the Master in Chambers and did their utmost to oppose the determination of the Council's solicitors that the case should be heard before the end of the current Law Term—'in order,' the Council's solicitors explained, 'that the children could commence their attendance at the designated schools on the 6th of September next.' The Master was sympathetic to the Council, and, as my solicitors put it, 'considerable argument ensued,' resulting in the case being provisionally set down for hearing on the 25th of July.

Meanwhile, the children, the source of all this legal controversy, continued to develop naturally and satisfactorily through the passing year.

David continued with his photography, taking the final illustrations for my book *The House on the Hill*, which was accepted by Phoenix House in April. He also continued, without further comment from the Council, to work part-time on the farm, waiting until, at fifteen, he would be able to take his first real job. And while he was waiting, he also dug up and re-laid our main drain, which had been continually getting blocked up, very efficiently; this apparently being one of the many useful things he had found out how to do which he would not have learned in school.

Wendy, having now a camera of her own, also started taking photographs but with an approach entirely different from David's or Felicity's. She took close-ups of the younger children, Hugh, Martin, and April, with a total disregard of the limits of her camera's focus but often with very striking results. She dressed them up and got them to play make-believe games for planned pictures, in which the realism and unselfconsciousness of her 'models' revealed both her organizing ability and her creative imagination.

Robin continued to make our garden grow and supplied us

with lettuces all through the summer, as well as producing a magnificent row of sweet peas flowering several weeks before anyone else's in the locality.

In June, David reached his fifteenth birthday—in our family, a very real coming-of-age. Now he could look back on all the law courts, the magistrates and judges, the cross-examinations, the worry and strain and fear; he would never have to face them again. He was free. Free to learn what he wanted to, when he wanted to, without battling with the law; free to take a job and do the work he cared for most.

During the past year, he had taken a good deal of interest in veterinary work, having frequently helped the local veterinary surgeons on the farms, and for a time he considered whether he would like to become a vet. He had patience, an observant mind, and skill in handling animals; but he had also a sensitive heart, and in the end, he decided that he would rather work to keep healthy animals fit than be continually dealing with the pain, sickness, and tragedies of farm life.

He was offered several jobs as soon as he was fifteen. Two farmers from villages some miles away called at our house to ask him if he would come to them when he wanted work. But none of these was what he really wanted, so he decided to wait and make inquiries farther afield, and meanwhile, he continued to help the neighboring farmers with harvest and sugar beet.

In the middle of June, I took a job—under my pen name because I didn't think any sane employer would take on a woman with seven children—at a television advertising agency, Willsmore and Tibbenham, in Norwich. I answered their advertisement in the first place out of sheer curiosity, to see if, without any scholastic qualifications or any actual experience of the work involved, I could obtain an executive position.

I went twice to be interviewed by the directors, but I was thoroughly taken aback when I heard that I had been successful. I had then to consider the question of whether I could be absent from home all day for five days a week, but the children were confident that they could manage, and we all felt that I ought to take the opportunity of trying to improve our financial position. After considerable discussion, I took the job for an initial period of three months at a salary of £450 a year. I proposed to continue after that time only if I could then obtain an increased salary which would enable me to employ domestic help in the home; and it was agreed that if at any time the children found the responsibility too much for them, I would give up the job immediately. The only drawback proved to be that, with fares, lunches, and a certain necessary outlay on clothes suitable for working in, we were for the first two months no better off than we had been previously. In the end, my employment was terminated by my employers after they found out who I was; but for two and a half months, Felicity ran the household as she had done while I was in hospital. She and Wendy shared the housework, Robin did the shopping and cooking, and David dealt with the other errands and the heavy household jobs.

Every morning before I left the house at seven-thirty to catch my train to Norwich, I wrote out the day's menus, details of the work involved in their preparation if needed, and the day's shopping lists, with any other necessary instructions for the day; and these lists were pasted onto the sitting-room door, where they could be referred to by any member of the family. Every evening when I reached home again at six-thirty, I found a meal waiting for me, the babies bathed and ready for bed, and the house clean and tidy.

Throughout this time, Robin not only cooked and served three meals a day for everybody and carried out each day's written orders efficiently; he also added to these of his own accord and, whenever it was possible, made cakes for tea. Wendy showed herself capable now of taking charge of the household single-handed and took over this responsibility gallantly when Felicity was in bed for two days with a cold, coping with the additional handicap of being without her sister's help and having to look after an invalid. And it was a further triumph for Felicity, who might be said to have graduated during this time in the art of being a housewife and mother.

All through the past year, Felicity had maintained her interest in ballet, and by now it had developed into a passionate desire to be a ballet dancer. She listened to radio programmes about ballet, collected pictures of ballerinas, studied books on ballet, and tried to copy all the steps and positions in the pictures herself. I made enquiries about dancing lessons, and in August I arranged for her to start attending the Anglia Academy of Dancing in Norwich for two ballet classes every Saturday afternoon and a private lesson every Wednesday. It soon became obvious that her longing to dance was not just a wish or a dream but a practical ambition. She progressed rapidly and showed a natural talent for dancing combined with the almost equally necessary requirements of a capacity for hard work and an indefatigable determination. From now on, ballet was her main interest in life, superseding everything else. Into it, she poured all her feelings, all her energies, and all her artistic and creative ability; and she wanted to train for a career on the stage. This was not what I would have chosen for her, but I believed in my daughter, and I supported her choice.

Meanwhile, in London, the Chancery proceedings continued on their complicated course, and at the beginning of July, I went to London for a conference with my counsel, Mr. W. A. Bagnall, Q.C. The County Council was doing all they could to expedite matters, but Mr. Bagnall was not to be hurried. Before they could be taken any further, he threw the Council into some confusion by suggesting that the whole proceedings were *ultra vires* by virtue of the fact that the Council was a corporate body created by statute and therefore had no power to sue.

The County Council then made an application to join Mr. Earl as co-applicant in the proceedings in case this submission was accepted. Mr. Bagnall promptly objected to this, as Mr. Earl derived his interest in the proceedings only as an agent for the Council. Master Dinwiddy, before whom the application was first heard, took the view that if the Council were able to sue, there was no need for the addition of Mr. Earl to the proceedings; and if they were not able to sue, then Mr. Earl had no power to take proceedings.

The Council's application was then heard before Mr. Justice Pennycuick on July 19th. During the hearing, the Lord Chief Justice's judgment in the Divisional Court was referred to, including the final exchange between Lord Parker and myself when I asked if there were any right of appeal:

'No—this is the final court.'

'Not quite.'

Mr. Justice Pennycuick commented drily, 'Mrs. Baker must have had pre-knowledge of these proceedings.'

The hearing lasted some two hours, with Mr. Sparrow, counsel for the County Council, trying to say that Mr. Earl was intended to be joined in his individual capacity and not as an agent of the Council. This was again opposed by Mr. Bagnall, who commented that while he was sure Mr. Earl was a very worthy citizen, he doubted whether he spent his Sunday afternoons, when he was off duty, worrying about the Baker children. He also pointed out that if Mr. Earl were joined as an individual, he and not the Council would be liable for the costs if he lost the case. (I should imagine that this latter point probably caused some considerable panic to Mr. Earl.)

Eventually, the application was dismissed, and the Council continued their efforts to have the case heard before the end of the term. But in this, they were unsuccessful, Mr. Bagnall being, as the London solicitors put it, 'a very wily counsel'; and it was nearly a year after the writ was served on me before this 'unique and complex piece of litigation' came before the Chancery judge. So, for the rest of the year, the lives of the 'Baker Infants' continued undisturbed, although technically, from the making of the application to the hearing of the case, Robin, Felicity, and Wendy were, in fact, wards of court.

In October, David started work on a farm in the next village, about two miles away. He had enquired at the local Youth Employment Office about getting a job on a dairy farm, but they could offer little help. All they could do was give him the address of the one farm vacancy for a boy that they had on their books, but this turned out to be a farm with a small herd of pedigree Jersey cows, which was what David wanted. We had heard a good deal about the services of the Youth Employment Officer, but it did appear that his chief function was helping children at school decide what they wanted to do when they left, and he was nonplussed by a boy who had already chosen his career and required only advice as to the best way to start.

David already knew a good deal about cows and dairy farming, and his ability, coupled with his desire to learn more, impressed his employer. After he had been working on the farm for only a few months, his employer went away for a week's holiday and left David in charge of the cows. This meant his tackling single-handed the twice-daily milking; the feeding, each cow having its own balanced rations; and the cleaning out. He also had to bring in and tend two calves that were born in the field during the time his employer was away. His successful handling of that week's work was a worthwhile testimonial in itself.

In January 1961, we had a number of repairs done to our house: windows mended, walls plastered, floors re-laid. The builders were working in the house nearly every day for five or six weeks, and Robin was fascinated by the work in progress. He helped to mix and carry cement and plaster, watched the men at work, and wanted to learn how it was done. When we had our old kitchen range taken out and the rough brickwork of the resulting recess needed covering, he borrowed a trowel from one of the men, made himself a 'hawk,' and cemented over the bricks himself.

As the workmen finished, we got paint and distemper, and Robin started work redecorating each room—walls, ceilings, and woodwork—and when he had finished inside the house, he started painting the outside doors and windows as well. By the end of February, he had redecorated the entire house single-handed, inside and out, and he had made up his mind that he wanted to enter the building trade.

At the beginning of February, Felicity took her first ballet exam and passed, 'Highly Commended.' This was certainly a contrast to her last 'exam' at the magistrates' court. As I watched her go confidently through the door in her white tunic to curtsey to the examiner, I thought how much she had grown up in the years between—to say nothing of there being, this time, no police.

On February 19th, Hugh entered the arena that David had just left: he reached his fifth birthday. Like David, Hugh had a vivid and essentially practical imagination. When he played pretend games, he liked to rig something up that really did some part, at least, of what he was pretending it would do. He had already decided that he wanted to be a farmer, and tractors, ploughs, and combines featured largely in his play. He had started taking an interest in letters and numbers and was learning to copy the alphabet and write his own name. He could count up to ten, and he liked me to read to him. After I had finished, he would take the book and spell out words letter by letter, asking me what they meant.

At the end of February, I heard from Mr. Hipwell that the Council's application would be heard in the Chancery Court on March 9th, and I went to London again for a final conference with Mr. Bagnall. On my return, late in the evening, I found April and Martin in bed, and Hugh in his pajamas on Felicity's lap, waiting for me to read to him before he went to sleep.

'We went for a walk around the fields this afternoon, and he's been telling me who all the pigs and cows and horses belong to,' Felicity explained.

'And who do you belong to?' I asked him as I carried him up the stairs.

He put his small arms around my neck. 'To *you*,' he said.

And that, my Lord, I thought, as I tucked him into bed, is the case for the defense.

The next day, our case opened in the Chancery Court.

14

Three Little Wards of Court

On the morning of March 9th, 1961, I set off again to London, accompanied by my 'three little wards of court.' David had asked for a day off work so that he could stay at home and look after the babies.

Robin, Felicity, Wendy, and I left home in the gray darkness of the early morning to catch the first train to Liverpool Street. There, we were met by a clerk from the London solicitors, who took the children to wait in their offices. It was not known whether the judge would want to see the three 'infants' or not, but they had to be available in case they were needed, so I left them in the solicitors' hands and went on to the Law Courts.

The case was being heard in *camera*, and as I took my seat at the back of the court, I was approached by an official who asked in a hushed voice, 'Are you connected with the case?' I replied, 'I am the defendant, the children's mother,' and he smiled and withdrew.

Then the judge, Mr. Justice Pennycuick, entered the court, and Mr. Sparrow, Q.C., for the County Council, stood up to open the attack.

He began by outlining the facts of the case, as given in the affidavit sworn to, and now produced in court by, Mr. Earl.

Headed: 'IN THE MATTER OF ROBIN BAKER, an Infant,

FELICITY BAKER (Spinster), an Infant,

and WENDY BAKER (Spinster), an Infant,'

this imposing document contained copies of all the Notices, School Attendance Orders, and relevant letters served on me by the Norfolk

Education Committee and included a full transcript of the judgment of the Lord Chief Justice in the Divisional Court.

'The object of these proceedings,' said Mr. Sparrow, 'is to ensure that the said infants shall receive efficient full-time education as provided for by statute. The said infants were born as follows: Robin, 14th August, 1946; Felicity, 16th December, 1947; Wendy, 19th March, 1949. Thus, each of the said infants has reached compulsory school age. The respondent also has a child, David, who was born on the 9th of June, 1945, and has therefore already reached school-leaving age.

'David,' Mr. Sparrow explained to the judge, 'is the one that got away.'

'There are also three other children,' Mr. Sparrow continued, 'who are not yet of compulsory school age, Hugh, Martin, and April. None of the said infants has ever attended school. The respondent is under a duty imposed by Section 36 of the Education Act 1944 to provide her children with efficient full-time education. She has contended, and still contends, that she is satisfying this duty by herself looking after the education of the said infants at home. As hereinafter appears, this contention has been held by the courts to be unsound.'

Mr. Sparrow then gave details of all the legal actions in which I had been involved. 'Notwithstanding these prosecutions,' he went on, 'the respondent refuses to comply with the said orders. The Norfolk County Council can see no likelihood of a satisfactory result from further prosecutions, and the previous hearings have attracted to the said infants undesirable public notice. In these circumstances, this honourable court is respectfully asked to grant the relief sought.

'Apart from matters of education,' Mr. Sparrow added, 'the Norfolk County Council believes that the respondent is providing the said infants with a good home and general upbringing.'

Mr. Earl then went into the witness box to be cross-examined by Mr. Bagnall.

Mr. Earl stated that he thought all children should go to school. He did not think there were any exceptions. He did not think it would be unwise for children aged fourteen, thirteen, and twelve

Felicity dancing in a cabaret given
in 1961 by students of the Anglia
Academy of Dancing at Norwich

With her is Janet Bygrave

The author with April (4) and Wendy (13), Felicity (14), Martin (5), and Hugh (6), after her victory in the Divisional Court in July 1962.

years to go to school now for the first time in their lives. Special arrangements would be made for them and had indeed already been discussed with the head teachers of the Dereham secondary modern schools.

Asked if this would mean that they might, if it were difficult to fit them in with other classes, be placed with children who were mentally defective, he agreed that this might be so. In reply to the question, did he not agree with the Lord Chief Justice that it would be wrong for a boy to go to school for the first time at the age of fourteen and a half, Mr. Earl said, 'No.' As wards of court, he said, the children could be kept at the designated schools after the age of fifteen for as long as the court thought necessary.

Following Mr. Earl, I went into the witness box to face cross-examination by Mr. Sparrow. Mr. Bagnall had explained to me that the question of whether the children were receiving a proper education or not did not really concern this court, as we were contesting the application only on grounds of law, so he was making no submissions on that point. However, it appeared that Mr. Sparrow either did not appreciate this or intended to take the fullest possible advantage of it.

'Mrs. Baker,' he began, 'would you agree that you have a very strong personality? Your mind has been the greatest influence in your children's lives?'

'I don't think so, necessarily,' I said. 'My mind is only one of many factors which influence my children's lives.'

Mr. Sparrow referred to a thick pile of newspaper cuttings in front of him; he appeared to be conducting his cross-examination almost entirely from press reports.

'You have described your methods of educating your children as 'giving them the light and warmth of natural education at home'?' he asked.

'I used that description of my children's education during the hearing of my successful appeal to Quarter Sessions in 1955,' I said, 'when the children were six, seven, eight, and nine years old.'

'But in fact,' Mr. Sparrow went on, 'your methods involved the children doing a great deal of domestic work, helping in the house and looking after the babies?'

'When I used that description of my children's education,' I said, 'the children were all under ten years old. At that time, none of them had done any serious domestic work, and the babies had not been born.'

'But you did apply that description to your method of educating your children?' Mr. Sparrow persisted.

'I applied it to the education of children under ten,' I said again. 'And I would apply it as a basis to the education of my older children. As children grow older, they obviously need to learn how to work.'

'Domestic work?'

'Not necessarily,' I said. 'My eldest son is totally undomesticated and has never had to do any domestic work other than household repairs. He has always wanted to be a farmer and is now working in his first job on a dairy farm where he has taken sole charge of a herd of ten pedigree Jersey cows. Robin is a more domesticated boy and is a keen gardener and a very good cook. The two girls have both learned housework and baby care as part of their education, but they have many other occupations—riding horses, nature study, photography—and my eldest daughter, Felicity, wants to be a ballet dancer and has just passed her first ballet examination 'Highly Commended' after only six months at a Norwich ballet school.'

Mr. Sparrow referred again to his newspaper reports.

'At one time in the magistrates' court, you said that David had the mind of a barrister. Has he ever wanted to study law?'

'He was interested in the law when he was younger, largely as a result of being involved in these continual education cases,' I said. 'I think he might have made a very good barrister, but after seeing so much of the law in action, he decided in favor of working with cows—and I think probably he was right.'

'He was not prevented from going further with this by lack of educational qualifications?'

'No. If he had wanted to take it further, he would have been given expert tuition in the subjects required to take the necessary exams—as Felicity has in ballet, which I am obviously not qualified to teach her myself.'

Mr. Sparrow again referred to his press cuttings.

'At the hearing of one of your appeals to Quarter Sessions,

Felicity said in evidence that she had some free time each day. In answer to a question, how much free time did she have, did she reply, 'It depends how quick the work is done'?'

This was a stenographer's error, which had irritated me for years.

'No,' I said. 'What she actually replied was, 'It depends how quickly the work is done."

Mr. Sparrow appeared to be suppressing his feelings with difficulty.

'Then,' he asked very slowly and deliberately, 'she did say, 'It depends how quickly the work is done'?'

'That statement was included in her evidence,' I said.

'And is it true that during last year you took a job which involved leaving this little girl of twelve in charge of the home and six other children?'

'It is true that Felicity took charge of the home while I was away five days a week,' I replied. 'It was a valuable part of her education. It is not true that she had to look after six other children—David was out at work, and Robin and Wendy are not babies and did not have to be looked after. They helped her to run the house—Robin cooked the meals, and Wendy helped with the housework and looking after the three babies. Felicity is fully capable of taking my place in the home. It is one of the first things she will have to know when she marries.'

Mr. Sparrow looked pained. 'And what are these three children doing now?'

I stared at him, incredulous.

'Sitting in my solicitors' office here in London, waiting to know whether you will succeed in breaking up their lives!' I burst out.

Mr. Bagnall intervened to explain that the children had been brought up to London so that they would be available if they were needed in court.

Mr. Sparrow murmured apologies and looked through his press cuttings again.

'Early last year, there was a report in a newspaper stating that in your home the paint was peeling, a blanket was serving as a door, and some of your windows had been replaced with wire-netting. Is this the case?'

Angrily, I replied, 'It is *not*. None of that was true, and but for my financial circumstances, I should have taken legal action against the *Daily Mail* for libel.'

Mr. Sparrow picked up another press cutting.

'During the hearing of one of your appeals to Quarter Sessions,' he said, 'did the Chairman, Lord Evershed, remark that your children were growing up as creatures apart from the rest of the community?'

'He did, and it is absolute nonsense,' I replied.

'Lord Evershed was talking nonsense?' Mr. Sparrow turned a shocked face towards the judges.

'Definitely, yes,' I said.

'Mrs. Baker.' Mr. Sparrow appeared to be trying, not very successfully, to look benign. 'Do you appreciate that the Education Authority has been doing all that it can for your children's welfare?'

'I don't,' I said. 'I regard the Education Authority as a tigress would regard a hunter who was seeking to catch her cubs and put them in a zoo.'

'You are very bitter about schools, Mrs. Baker?'

'I was continually unhappy for eight years during my own school days. It was an embittering experience.'

'But why should you have been so unhappy?'

'I was laughed at the whole time because I was considered different from everyone else. To be different means to be scorned and humiliated in a school.'

'In what way were you different?'

'Largely because I was unable to share the other girls' adoration of film stars and dance-band leaders and could not join in their conversations, which were almost entirely about this kind of thing. I was never able to become part of a crowd.'

'But don't you think that it is valuable to a child to learn about the team spirit?'

'I loathe the 'team spirit.' It is only another term for the herd instinct. Children should be brought up to be individuals. Felicity's dancing teacher remarked to me, 'Schoolchildren don't realize that the important thing is to be different.' At school, you are supposed to do everything because everyone else does, which is the worst possible reason for doing anything—and it can be a very dangerous one if a child gets into bad company. But at school, if you are not like everyone else, you are laughed at and made an outcast. I was even laughed at because I had fair hair.'

'You were so unhappy because a few children laughed at you?'

'Two hundred children was quite enough.'

'And they all laughed at you?'

'For eight years,' I said. 'No educational qualifications could offset the damage done by that, and, in any case, I never learned anything of any value whatever while I was at school.'

'But it doesn't follow that your own children would have this unhappy experience?' Mr. Sparrow suggested.

'I would not take the risk,' I said. 'In my experience, the effect of school is always detrimental, either for or to the child. An intelligent and sensitive child either turns into a bully or becomes unhappy and cowed. I think the State schools as they are now should be abolished.'

'Mrs. Baker,' said Mr. Sparrow, 'would you say that the people in this court were intelligent?'

I looked around the courtroom, at the judge, the lawyers, the opposing counsel, and I thought of my three children, waiting in the solicitors' office to know whether they were going to be taken away from their mother and their home.

'I would say most of them were intelligent,' I replied, 'but they have obviously lost their sensitivity, or I would not be standing here now.'

Mr. Sparrow appeared to have come to the end of his news-paper reports.

'Mrs. Baker,' he said, 'you are a very plausible woman?'

'I object to the word 'plausible,'' I said.

'Very well, then,' said Mr. Sparrow. 'You are a very eloquent woman.'

I considered this for a moment. Then I asked, 'Is that a question?'

In the court below me, I heard Mr. Bagnall chuckle and mur-mur, 'Fair enough!'

'In any case,' I said, as Mr. Sparrow showed signs of exploding, 'I don't think that I am the right person to ask.'

This cross-examination went on for over an hour. Mr. Sparrow ranged some distance from the subject of the children's education, his questions including details of my married life and all the events which had taken place during the last ten years. It was one of the most unpleasant attacks I had ever faced in any court, and my only consolation was the knowledge that if Mr. Sparrow had been on stronger ground with his legal points, he would not have resorted to trying to make bricks out of this very doubtful straw. At last, it was over, and I returned to my seat at the back of the court, while Mr. Sparrow stood up again to make his submissions to the judge.

The County Council, Mr. Sparrow maintained, was in order in bringing these proceedings and was doing so in the best interests of the children concerned. The Council had done everything they could to get these children to school and had taken all the steps authorized by the Education Act. But it appeared that although the Act had been planned to cover every possible situation, it had in fact no adequate provision for anyone simply steadfastly refusing to comply with it.

'Parliament,' explained Mr. Sparrow in some exasperation, 'never visualized a Mrs. Baker. There has never been another Mrs. Baker.'

In order to get these children to school, he continued, something more was required than the steps laid down in the Act. School Attendance Orders had been made and fines imposed, but the children still did not go to school. Someone, Mr. Sparrow pointed out, had to actually put the children on the bus or train to school, and this the County Council had no power to do.

The only other step that the Council could take was to ask for the children to be brought before a juvenile court, where they could be taken into the Council's care; but this could not be said to be in the best interests of the children. As wards of court, the wardship judge could make whatever directions he thought right in order to get the children to school.

Here Mr. Justice Pennycuick intervened to say, 'You are in fact asking me to act as an enforcement officer for the Education Authority?'

Mr. Sparrow said this was not really the case.

'But surely,' objected the judge, 'the whole point of the Council's application is to ensure that the School Attendance Orders made in respect of these three infants are obeyed?'

Mr. Sparrow said yes, that was so.

'And as wardship judge,' continued Mr. Justice Pennycuick, 'I would have no authority to decide whether or not compliance with these orders would be in the children's best interests?'

Mr. Sparrow assented. But no one, he maintained, would doubt that it was in the best interests of these children, or indeed of any children, to go to school. And even if this were a matter on which the judge would wish to exercise his own discretion, there were still some parental rights remaining to him under the Act.

Mr. Sparrow then proceeded to detail an incredibly long list of powers, extending in all directions, now vested in the County Council, which left the impression that very little indeed of any-one's life was beyond interference by the local authorities; and he ended by explaining again that the few remaining shreds of parental rights left to the parents of a child would, in the event of the child becoming a ward of court, be available also to the wardship judge, to exercise his discretion as he thought fit.

The more Mr. Sparrow talked, the more hopeless the position seemed; not that his arguments appeared even to me to hold a great deal of legal force, but as he went on talking, the extent of the powers against us seemed overwhelming, and I felt the inescapable cords of State control and its bland inhumanity winding tighter and tighter around my children, like a ball of string around the hub of a wheel.

I was appalled by the obvious impossibility of putting the human facts before the judge, of making him understand the real position regarding the children, their feelings, and their needs, which certainly bore no relation to the ones which Mr. Sparrow was now describing to the court.

These children, Mr. Sparrow maintained, were in dire need of help. The court, he urged, should not be guided only by the 'dry bones of the law'; they had to consider the children. He drew a horrifying picture of these 'poor little children,' who, he said, were being 'used as servants,' learning nothing, receiving no preparation for their future life. These 'unfortunate infants' were in jeopardy, and even if the procedure were not strictly in accordance with the law, he asked the Chancery Court to come to their rescue.

My mind went back again to the three children, waiting apprehensively in the solicitors' office. Robin, who was planning to take a job with a local builder when he was fifteen in five months' time, where he could train as a plasterer; Felicity, whose career as a ballet dancer would be wrecked if her training were now summarily interfered with; Wendy, whose deep-rooted shyness was slowly giving place to self-assurance, and who would be annihilated by this proposed legal upheaval of her life. And I wondered just what my self-possessed, efficient, thirteen-year-old eldest daughter would say to being described as a 'poor little child.'

I began to wish that we could return to the purely primitive—blanket, say, over the head of Mr. Sparrow, and a half-brick shattering the complacency of Mr. Earl. It seemed improbable that anyone in the court had any comprehension of the children as personalities. But I did rather like the look of Mr. Justice Pennycuick; his clear blue eyes conveyed some measure of reassurance, and here at least, I felt, was someone who would be singularly fair and guided by nothing but his own conscience and its meticulous interpretation of the law.

Mr. Sparrow was still speaking when the court rose at four o'clock, and the hearing was adjourned until the following day. I collected my three 'infants' from the solicitors' office, and we went back to Liverpool Street station, where Felicity, unused to being shut in all day, did jetés and arabesques on the platform, much to the surprise of the other people catching the train. At least I would not have to bring the three children to London again; the judge had said that he did not want them to be brought into court.

We arrived home to find the household at first sight chaotic, but the babies had been fed, looked after, and kept clean, safe, and happy; David, although not domesticated, could do practically anything in an emergency. And it took Felicity only a few minutes of tidying and cleaning up to restore order also to the outward appearance of the household, she and Wendy putting into it all their suppressed energies; which was just as well because by then

I was nearly exhausted, and I still had to prepare for going up to London again the next day.

On that Friday morning, I again caught the first train to London, but when I arrived at the Law Courts, there was some doubt whether the case would be continued that day, and after waiting until two o'clock, I was told that it had been adjourned until the following Monday.

On the Monday morning, I returned to my seat at the back of the Chancery Court, and Mr. Sparrow went on talking. He talked throughout the whole day until my mind became numbed, and, being very tired anyway, I kept dropping off to sleep and waking up with a jerk to hear him saying very much the same things as he had been saying an hour or two hours before. At least Mr. Sparrow was thorough; although by the end of the day, I was left more impressed by his sheer ability to keep going than by the wisdom or otherwise of his utterance. He still showed no signs of finishing when the court adjourned at four o'clock, and I went home until the next day.

On the Tuesday, I took my seat hopefully, feeling that Mr. Sparrow must run down sometime; and he had indicated at the close of the previous day's hearing that he had not a great deal more to say. In fact, he went on saying it until lunchtime, after which, at last, Mr. Bagnall rose to put his arguments before the court.

In contrast to Mr. Sparrow, Mr. Bagnall was refreshingly brief. The Chancery Court, he maintained, had no jurisdiction in a matter already fully provided for by statute under the Education Act. He elaborated this theme, which was obviously well received by the judge, who showed immediate appreciation of Mr. Bagnall's points of law. On the question of whether or not the children were being properly educated, Mr. Bagnall made no submissions at all; a course which I accepted with regret, as it allowed Mr. Sparrow's very damaging accusations to go unchallenged. But the important thing at the moment was to defeat the Council's application to have the children made wards of court, and by now it appeared fairly clear that this was what Mr. Bagnall was going to do.

At three-thirty, Mr. Bagnall concluded his submissions, and Mr. Justice Pennycuick informed us that he would adjourn his judgment until the following day. I went home to the children feeling quite confident about the result.

On Wednesday, March 15th, I was in my seat in court at ten-thirty, and Mr. Justice Pennycuick delivered his judgment.

'This is a summons taken out by the Norfolk County Council,' he began, 'in the matter of three infants, Robin Baker, Felicity Baker, and Wendy Baker.' He went on to give details of the Council's application, the ages of the children, and the other children of the family.

'The mother has a rooted objection of principle to sending her children to school,' he continued, 'and has waged a prolonged defensive battle on this issue against the local Education Authority.' He gave details of the previous cases in which I had been involved and added:

'The Council now seeks to enforce school attendance by means of these proceedings.

'I have come without hesitation to the conclusion, so far as I am concerned to do so, that the mother is not causing the children to receive efficient full-time education as required by the Education Act.' Here, he read out the relevant sections of the Act in full and continued:

'The effect of the provisions which I have just read is that the parent is bound to cause the child to receive efficient full-time education, either by regular attendance at school or otherwise. If the local authority is not satisfied that the parent is performing this duty, the local authority must serve on the parent a School Attendance Order requiring the parent to cause the child to become a registered pupil at the school named in the order, as to which the parent has a limited power of selection. If the parent fails to comply with the requirements of the order and is unable to prove that he is causing the child to receive efficient full-time education otherwise than at school, he is guilty of an offence, and on summary conviction for this offence, he is liable to fines of a specified progressive amount, and, on the third offence, to imprisonment also.

'It is clear to me that the Education Act 1944 has, by necessary implication, restricted the inherent jurisdiction of the Sovereign as exercised by this court, to the extent that the court cannot give any direction at variance with the provisions of the Act. In particular, the court cannot prevent the making of a School Attendance Order; nor, so long as a School Attendance Order is in force, can the court direct that the child shall receive education otherwise than in accordance with the order; that is to say, by becoming a registered pupil and attending regularly at the school named in the order.

'Counsel who appears for the Council accepts and, indeed, asserts this proposition, but he contends that, subject only to the limitations imposed by the Act, the inherent jurisdiction of this court remains unimpaired, and that, in exercise of this jurisdiction, the court can give a direction, the effect of which will be to enforce the School Attendance Orders made by the Council. That is, indeed, the whole purpose of the present application.

'In my judgment, the Act, by placing outside the jurisdiction of the court the decision whether or not a child should receive education in accordance with a School Attendance Order, has equally put it outside the proper jurisdiction of this court to enforce such an order. The court, in the exercise of its inherent jurisdiction, can only properly give a direction after it has decided that the act directed to be done is for the benefit of the infant concerned. It seems to me necessarily to follow that the court cannot properly give a direction where the decision whether the act is to be done rests with some other authority, so that the court is not itself able to decide whether or not the act is for the benefit of the infant.

'Counsel appearing for the Council sought to meet this difficulty in a number of ways. First, he contended that this court, although precluded by the Education Act 1944 from making a decision whether the children should receive education in accordance with the School Attendance Orders made under the Act, may yet consider whether such compliance would be for the benefit of the children, and, if satisfied that it is for the benefit of the children, enforce the School Attendance Orders. I find the greatest difficulty in the conception that this court can or should conduct an independent inquiry of this kind into a matter on which the decision has been entrusted to the local authority.

'Secondly, he contended that this court is bound to assume that compliance with the School Attendance Orders was for the benefit of the children concerned. No doubt the Education Act 1944 was passed in what Parliament conceived to be the interests of children generally, but Parliament legislates for the community as a whole, and I do not think there is anything in the Act or in general law which entitles the court to assume that its provisions are necessarily for the benefit of every particular child between the ages of five and fifteen.

'Thirdly, he contended, with truth, that the Act has by no means wholly excluded the parent from control of his children's education; and he referred to the general provision in Section 76, and, more particularly, to the limited powers conferred in Section 37. Therefore, he says, the jurisdiction of this court stands unimpaired to a corresponding extent. But this does not meet the present point: namely, that the court is being asked to enforce the School Attendance Orders, in the operation of which the court has no discretion.

'It may be that these specific contentions do not do justice to the forceful arguments of counsel on behalf of the Council. In broad terms, he urges that these children are in jeopardy and that the court ought to come to their rescue. I feel much sympathy with this plea, but the court can only act within its proper jurisdiction, and it seems to me that I am not entitled to stretch that jurisdiction in order to meet the unusual circumstances of the present case. I have come to the conclusion that enforcement of these School Attendance Orders lies outside the proper function of this court, and that the Council must rely on the sanctions contained in the Act itself.

'I should like to make it clear that I do not intend to express the slightest agreement with the mother's views on the education of children in general, or of her own children in particular. Equally, I do not intend to express the slightest disagreement with the views expressed by the Norfolk Justices or the Queen's Bench Divisional Court.

'I propose, therefore, not to make any direction as to the education of the infants. I direct that these children cease to be wards of court.'

So it was over. At least it was over for a time, but Mr. Sparrow immediately asked for, and was granted, leave to appeal.

I arrived back in Norwich in the middle of the afternoon, and at the station met Felicity, to her great surprise, as she returned home from her dancing lesson. By then, the evening paper was on sale, and on the front page, we saw the headline: 'MRS. BAKER WINS IN HIGH COURT.' I knew that this was neither a personal victory nor a permanent one, but it was a comforting thing to have. I felt too worn out with the strain of the last five days to look any further ahead just then. I sat and looked at that headline all the way home.

15

Tigress at Bay

WHEN I considered the Chancery case in retrospect, one point became very clearly apparent. The Chancery judge had refused to make the children wards of court because the parental rights taken over by the Council in respect of the education of the children left him no power to exercise his own discretion. But those remaining rights, which he regarded as insufficient for the proper consideration of the children's welfare as wards, are the only rights now remaining to all parents of all children in this country. And if those rights are insufficient for the care of children as wards, then it must follow that they are also insufficient for the care of children by their own parents. This is illustrated by one particularly objectionable aspect of the Education Act: a parent has no right, on the grounds that attendance at school is causing suffering to the child, to keep that child away from school. As Mr. Justice Pennycuick said, it does not follow that attendance at school is in the best interests of *every* particular child. But what, under the present Education Act, is to happen to the 'unfortunate infants' for whom it is not?

My victory in the Chancery Court, although it revealed with a new clarity this aspect of the matter, did nothing to offer a solution. And it was not long before I heard from Mr. Hipwell that the Council was appealing against the judge's decision.

The County Council's appeal opened on Tuesday, May 30th, 1961, in the London Court of Appeal before Lord Justices Ormerod, Upjohn, and Pearson. Again, I traveled on the early train to London and sat this time in the well of the court, watching the faces of the three judges who were to decide this stage of the battle for my children's freedom. I took an immediate liking to Lord Justice Ormerod, who reminded me of my father and seemed to be regarding me throughout the proceedings with very much the same expression of kindly disapproval; but Lord Justice Upjohn exactly resembled an aunt of mine who had refused to speak to me for years and, oddly enough, couched his remarks about me in very similar terms.

Being an appeal against a previous decision, there were no witnesses called and no evidence given; it was a battle between the two counsel, Mr. Bagnall and Mr. Sparrow. Mr. Sparrow again opened the attack for the County Council. As before, he appeared to be conducting his case very largely from press reports; and although he had previously expressed horror at the 'undesirable publicity' the children had received as a result of the earlier court proceedings—he had in fact stated that this was one of the reasons for the Council's deciding to make the Chancery application—he now proceeded to read out in open court parts of the evidence given in camera at the previous hearing, which added very considerably to the publicity he had previously complained of.

He began, as before, by outlining the facts of the case. The only issue before the court, he said, was that of jurisdiction. He went on to give details of the previous court hearings, the School Attendance Orders, the fines imposed, and the appeals.

'Not one of these children,' he said, 'has spent a single day at school.'

Mrs. Baker, he said, claimed to be able to educate her children, although she herself had left school at the age of fifteen. She said she wanted her children to acquire knowledge by wanting to know, asking questions, and being told. There were no formal lessons or hours of lessons, and they learned mainly from experience. She thought children reached out physically and mentally for what they were capable of learning, and that was when they should be taught.

She said, continued Mr. Sparrow, that she thought school was definitely harmful to an imaginative child, and many sensitive children suffered and were unhappy at school. She regarded schools as a form of imprisonment and had referred to children being sent to school as tiger cubs being put in a zoo.

At this point, Lord Justice Ormerod intervened to say: 'This lady takes the view that the education provided by the Minister of Education is unsatisfactory. She is entitled to that view whether it is misguided or not.'

Mr. Sparrow said, 'Yes, my Lord.' Mrs. Baker, he went on, had described her teaching methods as giving her children 'the light and warmth of natural education,' but in fact, this involved their doing a great deal of domestic work. The elder girl, Felicity, was said to have exceptional domestic ability and was capable of running the entire household, including cooking and looking after the babies. Wendy was following in her sister's footsteps. Even the boy, Robin, said Mr. Sparrow, was said to be 'domesticated' and cooked meals for the family.

Here, Lord Justice Ormerod commented, 'Perhaps it is as well for a boy to learn something about housework in these days when most men have to help in the home.'

'Yes, my Lord,' said Mr. Sparrow. But apart from domestic work, he maintained, the three children were learning little or nothing. They could read and write and do simple arithmetic, but if they went to school, they would be quite unable to cope with the standards of the other children.

'These children,' Mr. Sparrow declared, 'are being denied something which is the right of every child—a respectable and decent education. They are being used as unpaid domestic servants.'

This, he went on, was the 'most disquieting feature' of their education. Mr. Justice Pennycuick had held that although the children were not being efficiently educated, the Education Act fettered the court's jurisdiction. But the Council's application was brought under the Wardship Act, not the Education Act.

'This case,' he maintained, 'concerns not the remedies of the local Education Authorities, but the rights of these children to a respectable education.'

There was no doubt, Mr. Sparrow went on, that Mrs. Baker was devoted to her children; but their home conditions were not satisfactory. The children were in grave need of help—they were in grave moral danger, even physical danger, being left all alone in the house.

Here Lord Justice Upjohn commented: 'Your argument would have greater force if you could suggest an alternative method of upbringing. All you are suggesting is that they should be educated at the local school. You cannot control them outside school hours.'

'My Lord,' Mr. Sparrow replied, 'these children are in grave need of the assistance of the court in one way or another. They are growing up isolated from the rest of the community.'

It was infuriating to be unable to point out that properly brought-up children of twelve, thirteen, and fourteen should not be in moral or physical danger even if they were alone in the house—they were probably safer in any case than they would have been traveling home from school—and that normally they were only left alone in the house for any length of time when I had to defend the continual legal proceedings brought by the Education Authorities.

Throughout the previous court cases, Mr. Sparrow was saying, these children had been the subject of a great deal of unfortunate publicity; their pictures had been published in the newspapers, they had been continually interviewed by the press, and they had appeared on television. (This must surely, I thought crossly, interfere with their 'isolation'?) It was most undesirable, Mr. Sparrow declared, that they should be held before the public gaze in this way. Then, to my intense irritation, he added, 'Mrs. Baker has even written a book about the case.' This statement was nearly two years premature, and it made it obvious that he had not read my book, *The House on the Hill.*

Mr. Sparrow was still arguing on very much the same grounds when the court rose at four o'clock, and the hearing was adjourned until the following day.

The next morning, on the train to London, I saw the newspapers—with the headlines: CHILDREN USED AS SERVANTS—'COUNSEL: THAT'S WHAT LIGHT AND WARMTH OF MOTHER'S NATURAL EDUCATION MEANS.'

When I reached the court, I showed this to Mr. Bagnall and asked him if he could counter these accusations when he came to present our case. But Mr. Bagnall insisted that he must confine himself strictly to points of law. Mr. Sparrow was out of order, he said, in not doing this, and it would not be in order for him to reply. It would not, he assured me, influence in any way the decision of the court. But it had certainly influenced the press; it was, in fact, the first wholly 'undesirable publicity' we had received. To me, the 'most disquieting feature' of this case was having to be shot at when I could not fire back.

While we waited in court for the judges to enter, Mr. Bagnall showed a copy of one of the newspapers with its banner headline to Mr. Sparrow, saying, 'I thought you objected to undesirable publicity?'

Mr. Sparrow merely shrugged his shoulders and said, 'Not my fault.' He then continued his attack, on very much the same lines as during the previous day.

Mrs. Baker's refusal to send her children to school, Mr. Sparrow submitted, was 'quite shocking.'

Lord Justice Ormerod commented: 'We may or may not agree with you about that, but need we go into it? There has been a finding by the trial judge that these children are not getting an efficient full-time education, which is not challenged.'

Mr. Sparrow replied that he thought the court could not be absolved from inquiring into 'the state of these children.' Not only had they not been taught 'where Australia is, and that sort of thing,' but, he declared, they had been brought up 'as little hermits.'

Here Mr. Bagnall did rise to object. There was, he said, no evidence of that.

I also, although silently, objected. Not only were they by no stretch of the imagination 'hermits,' but even five-year-old Hugh knew 'where Australia is.'

Mr. Sparrow suggested that the children had no more tuition at home than the conscientious parent gave in addition to schooling.

Lord Justice Pearson intervened to say that he did not think it would be right for the court to interfere in school attendance matters, which were expressly conferred by statute to the local education authority, with provision for penalties.

Lord Justice Upjohn said the maximum penalty for failing to send a child to school was a month's jail, but even if Mrs. Baker were sent to prison, there was no officer of the court, so far as he knew, with power physically to take the children to school.

Mr. Sparrow said that if the matter were to be dragged through the magistrates' court again, with full publicity, how could that be said to be for the benefit of the children?

Lord Justice Ormerod said there would be publicity if Mrs. Baker were committed to prison in the present proceedings.

'All you are asking us to do,' he pointed out, 'is to substitute a possible penalty of imprisonment for an indefinite period for disobeying the order of the Chancery Court, for one of up to one month's imprisonment which might be imposed by the local magistrates. Mrs. Baker,' he added, 'has not yet had a prison sentence imposed on her by the magistrates. It has yet to be seen how she would react if threatened with imprisonment.'

Here he looked at me sternly, and I met his eyes, hoping that mine conveyed exactly what I *would* do if faced with the threats he described.

These children, Mr. Sparrow argued, were not being given a fair chance in life. Mrs. Baker had said that at one time David had been interested in the law and had also considered becoming a vet. But he could not have trained for either of these professions without a knowledge of Latin, and he had not been taught Latin.

Here Lord Justice Ormerod intervened again to say: 'I understand that the School Attendance Orders made in respect of these children required the boys to attend Dereham Secondary Modern Boys' School. I don't think Latin is taught at the secondary modern schools, Mr. Sparrow.'

'Er—no,' admitted Mr. Sparrow. 'No, it isn't, my Lord.'

There was an audible chuckle from Mr. Bagnall.

Mr. Sparrow continued to press for the assistance of the Chancery Court. The Education Act, he maintained, had failed to provide for the circumstances of this case. He began to deal with the technicalities of the law, returning frequently, with numerous interventions by the judges, to the most operative question: how, whatever direction might be given by the court, were the children to be actually taken to school?

As he had at the previous hearing, Mr. Sparrow spoke at great length. When Lord Justice Ormerod said, 'I think, Mr. Sparrow, you have already covered that point quite adequately,' Mr. Sparrow replied, 'I would just like to put it this way, my Lord'—and did, although to me it sounded exactly the same as it had when he said it before.

I sat, increasingly uncomfortably, on the very hard seat and felt already defeated by the futility of it all; the whole legal façade with its dignity and its tradition and its undoubted capacity for justice, yet turned into something of a mockery when it was all directed to interference with the lives of three young people who neither wanted nor needed the help of this, or any, court; particularly when this help could only be construed, when they got down to it, as a choice between their mother serving a sentence of a month's imprisonment or imprisonment for an indefinite period.

My mind began rejecting the interminable legal flow of words, which after a time became very largely meaningless. These are living children, I thought wearily, not cold items in a book of law. I found myself imagining Felicity in her white ballet dress, poised in perfect arabesque on the bench in front of the judges, her hair gleaming gold in the harsh lights of the court—perhaps this would bring home to them what they were really dealing with; and Wendy, vivid and mercurial, turning an aerial somersault over the judges' heads, her copper hair flying; or sitting, pensive and dreaming, at the judges' feet, looking into their faces with her green eyes filled with tears. These, my Lords, are the realities; what you are saying and doing is no more real than the wigs you wear—they are symbols, and no more—symbols of an authority which should be used to right wrongs, not to hurt children and wreck homes. It was maddening—although, I am sure my counsel would have said, just as well—that I couldn't speak.

As only lawyers could take part in the appeal, I was not permitted to say anything in court at all; strictly speaking, I don't think I was supposed to be there. It was difficult to keep quiet when there was so much I wanted to say. At one point, I nearly caused an uproar by merely trying to be helpful. The question was raised by Mr. Sparrow as to how long I was working with Willsmore and Tibbenham. No one apparently had any record of this. Mr.

Bagnall, questioned by the judges, didn't know either. The entire court was debating the issue—and there I sat, silent, until I could bear it no longer. I lifted my head and said clearly, 'I was there for two and a half months.'

Immediately, everyone in the court looked at me in horror, and Mr. Bagnall said, 'Shshhh!' There was a long silence. Then Mr. Bagnall cleared his throat and said, 'I am instructed that the time was two and a half months, my Lord.'

At last, towards the end of the day, Mr. Sparrow concluded his submissions and sat down, while Mr. Bagnall rose for the defense and returned at once to his points of law.

'When a decision of the magistrates is prescribed by statute,' he argued, 'one cannot substitute a decision or the discretion of someone else.'

Mr. Bagnall was still speaking when the court adjourned at four o'clock; and he continued when the case was resumed at the beginning of the following day.

It would be wrong, he said, to make a girl start school life at the age of thirteen, projecting her into a way of life she had never known. It would cause emotional and other upsets. Clearly, no order should be made in respect of Robin, who would be fifteen in August. No order, he submitted, should be made in respect of any of the children. Mr. Justice Pennycuick was right in holding that the Education Act had fettered the jurisdiction of the Chancery Court.

Mr. Sparrow, in his final address, replied that the Council was seeking a remedy additional to the remedies provided for by the Education Act.

'These children, who have never spent a single day at school, have slipped through the scheme of the Act,' he said. 'They have slipped through the net.'

He finally concluded his submissions shortly before the court was due to adjourn for lunch, and then Lord Justice Ormerod announced that they would take time to consider their judgment. The court rose, and I returned home. I was told that they might give their decision within a few weeks, but in fact, they took nearly two months. It was not until July 15th that I returned to my seat in court to await the outcome of 'judgment day.'

Lord Justice Ormerod first pronounced judgment. After giving the relevant facts in the case, he went on: 'In this appeal, we are concerned with three children, and they are Robin, Felicity, and Wendy, who are aged fourteen, thirteen, and twelve respectively. There appears to be no doubt that Mrs. Baker has persistently refused to allow any of her children to attend school. She has contended that by her own methods she is educating her children, and they are receiving at home an efficient education. She has referred in her evidence in one or other of the numerous cases which have been before the courts to the fact that she was giving the children the light and warmth of natural education, and she spoke of schools sometimes as a form of imprisonment and sometimes as a zoo. Be that as it may, the local Authority, as was their right and, indeed, as was their duty, came to the conclusion, after investigating the matter, that Mrs. Baker was not affording to the three children concerned an efficient education as required by the Education Act, 1944, and in these circumstances conceived it their duty to take such steps as they could to ensure that the children received the prescribed education. It is no part of the duty of this court to comment on the behavior of Mrs. Baker or to remark on the correctness or otherwise of the decision taken by the local Authority, but it should be noted that the judicial bodies concerned with the attendance orders, that is to say, the magistrates and, in due course, Quarter Sessions, have each in their turn confirmed the view of the local Education Authority that these children were not receiving a proper, or indeed any, education; and although Mrs. Baker has insisted that she is bringing the children up in such a way that they will get the benefit of a natural education, the fact remains that they are learning very little as education is understood at the present time, and they are associating little, if at all, with other children of their own age, and indeed that they are doing a great deal of the housework and work about the farm and land where they live.'

Here he quoted details of the previous court cases, concluding with the judgment of Mr. Justice Pennycuick.

'In the result,' he continued, 'the position would appear to be that the Education Act, 1944, provides for the education of children of compulsory school age, and it is enacted that it is the duty of the local Education Authority to satisfy themselves that such children are being properly educated, and if in the view of the Authority they are not being so educated, it is the duty of the Authority to see that they are and to take such steps as are prescribed by the Act of Parliament to attain that end. The position is therefore that the jurisdiction of the Crown in relation to the matters vested in the local Education Authority should not be exercised in these circumstances. The judge recognized that this was the position, and consequently refused to continue the order of wardship. Although I have every sympathy with the local Education Authority in the difficulty in which they have been placed, it does not appear as a matter of law that the proceedings which they have started in the Chancery Court are likely to be of assistance to them.'

'There is one matter to which I think I should draw attention. Section 40(1) of the Act of 1944, as I have already pointed out, provides for certain punishments to be administered by the magistrates in the event of a breach of an order made by the Education Authority. In this case, the parent has been summoned before the magistrates twice, and in each case, penalties little more than nominal have been inflicted, which may, of course, have been perfectly proper in the circumstances. The Act does provide, however, that on a third summons for neglect to obey an order, the magistrates may inflict a penalty of a maximum fine of £10 or imprisonment for not more than one month or both, according to the circumstances of the case. No third summons has been issued in this case in a magistrates' court. It is impossible, therefore, to say how the mother would behave if she were threatened with a sentence of imprisonment. That may not be a matter of any great importance, but it is some indication of the way in which the court should exercise its discretion in deciding whether a wardship order should be continued. If there is another remedy available with a sanction which would appear on the face of it to be similar to the sanction within the power of the Court of Chancery, it is difficult to see why the discretion of the court should be exercised in any other way than by putting an end to the wardship. In these circumstances, I would dismiss the appeal.'

Lord Justice Upjohn then delivered his judgment. 'I agree that the appeal fails,' he said. 'I do so with the greatest regret, because it is clear, on the evidence adduced before the learned judge, which has been read to us, that these unfortunate infants, the subjects of this appeal, are not receiving any education in a true sense of the word to enable them to take their proper place in the community when they are older. Though the appeal fails, I have no criticism to make of the local Authority for endeavouring to invoke, for the first time so far as I know, wardship proceedings to assist them in their statutory duties as Education Authority. It is obvious that the mother is not only in complete breach of her duties under Section 36 of the Education Act 1944, but that she is also in utter disregard of her natural moral duties as the mother of these children.

'Counsel on behalf of the local Education Authority has argued this case with great persuasiveness.' ('Plausibility,' I murmured under my breath, and hoped Mr. Sparrow heard.) 'In the first place, he argues on a broad basis that we ought to approach the case apart altogether from the powers and duties conferred and imposed on the Authority by the Act, and give directions as to the future education of the children because the mother is in serious breach of her duties and it is in the paramount interest of the children that direction should be given by the court exercising powers and duties in relation to wardship proceedings. He invites us to do this on the application of the local Authority. At first sight, that is an attractive argument, but on the whole, I am unable to accede to it, for it involves the proposition that the Authority are entitled to seek the direction of the court rather than discharge their duties under the Act. This the local Education Authority plainly cannot do, for, where it appears to the Authority that a parent is not giving a child efficient full-time education, they are under a duty to serve a notice under Section 37(1) on the parent to satisfy the Authority that the child is receiving efficient full-time education. If the parent fails to satisfy the Authority, they are under a positive duty to serve on the parent a School Attendance Order. If the parent fails to comply with the order and does not show that the child is receiving efficient full-time education, he commits an offense, and under certain circumstances, the Authority are under a duty to prosecute. These specific and positive duties cast on the local Education Authority cannot be delegated, and the court has no power to interfere in relation thereto. It seems to me that the Authority cannot approach the court on this wide basis but are bound to carry out their duties under the Act.

'The second submission which counsel for the local Education Authority makes goes to the real kernel of the point. He invites the aid of the court to assist the Authority to enforce the statutory duties which are cast upon them by the Act. I find this a more attractive argument. The real question may, I think, be posed in two ways—first, whether the Education Act 1944, in imposing duties on the local Education Authority only, intended those powers and duties to be compendious and exclusive, to form in effect a complete and exhaustive statutory code, so that they have no right to invoke the assistance of the court in carrying out these duties; secondly, whether, if the Act does not go so far as that, it would be right to lend the assistance of this court having regard to the conflicting jurisdiction thereby created. During argument, the point was made that, if the local Education Authority have some power to resort to the court for the purpose of assisting them to carry out their statutory powers and duties, yet in this case, the point has not been reached when it would be proper to invoke these powers, for, it is argued, the Authority have not yet fully pursued their powers under Section 40 of the Act by prosecuting the mother. Although the Authority have twice prosecuted the mother for her failure to carry out School Attendance Orders, the point has not yet been reached when it is open to the local magistrates to impose on the mother the punishment of imprisonment.

'Speaking for myself, I do not agree with this point. The mother has shown herself in persistent and flagrant disregard of the orders made on her; she has made no effort whatsoever to remedy her course of conduct or to comply in any way with the duties cast on her by the Act and orders made thereunder. She is plainly contumacious, and I see no reason why the Authority, in the particular circumstances of this case, should not invoke the powers of the court, if they are entitled to do so, until there have been three or more prosecutions under the Act. In the circumstances of this case, the sooner the court makes an order in aid of the powers and duties of the Authority, so much the better. The Authority take the view, in which I concur, that if the infants are made wards of court, the court, exercising those powers, is in a position to exercise a more effective control over the mother than is available to the Education Authority in continued prosecutions under Section 40 of the Act. Therefore, it seems to me that the sole question is that which I have already posed: Is it proper for the court to make an order to assist the local Education Authority in the discharge of their duties under the Act?

'I have reached the same conclusion as the learned judge, though I prefer to put it in my own language. I think the Education Act 1944 has imposed on local Education Authorities a complete code which they are bound to carry out, and it would not be proper for the court to lend its assistance to them in carrying out these powers and duties—and therefore that the appeal must be dismissed.'

Finally, Lord Justice Pearson gave his judgement. 'I agree,' he said. 'Mrs. Baker has persistently omitted and refused to send any of these children to school, and they are not receiving efficient full-time education otherwise; indeed, they are hardly receiving any education at all. Norfolk County Council, as the local Education Authority, have endeavoured persistently and, so far, unsuccessfully, to persuade or compel Mrs. Baker to send her children to school.' He gave details of the steps already taken by the Council and continued: 'If the Chancery Court were to give a direction duplicating the obligation already imposed by the School Attendance Orders, for the parent to send the child to school, subsequent questions would arise as to amendment, revocation, or enforcement of the obligation. Then who would decide? Would the local Education Authority surrender their discretion to the Chancery Court, or would the Chancery Court surrender its discretion to the local Education Authority, or would they each exercise their own discretion so that a conflict could arise? It is clear that, at any rate in the absence of some very peculiar situation calling for and justifying intervention by the Chancery Court in the sphere of activity of the local Education Authority, there should be no such intervention.

'In the present case, the remedy under the Act is specifically provided and has not been fully tried out. In my opinion, although the local Education Authority have all the merits in this case and it must be regretted that no help can be given to them, the learned judge was right in declining to give the directions desired by the local Education Authority, and consequently terminating this wardship. I agree the appeal should be dismissed.'

Mr. Sparrow then got up and asked for leave to appeal to the House of Lords. This was a case of considerable importance and might, he said, have a wide application. 'There are many of these cases where parents have refused to send their children to school.' But Lord Justice Ormerod announced that the court would not grant leave to appeal. The Chancery battle was over.

But although this battle was over, it was obvious from the terms in which judgment had been given that victory here was only the prelude to the next stage of the conflict. It was interesting to see how the appeal judges, while agreeing with and arriving at the same conclusion as the Chancery judge, had yet formed a different view of the legal aspect of this decision. In their opinion, the Education Authority could not receive assistance from the Chancery Court because the steps they were empowered to take were already provided for under the Act, and they had not yet fully made use of these powers in dealing with my case. And the Education Authority had now received from the court the strongest possible adjuration to take fresh proceedings in the magistrates' court and to ask for a sentence of imprisonment. I had therefore won the Chancery case only to find myself again facing prison.

However, this might, by virtue of the slow-moving machinery of the County Council and the law, be a little way off yet; and it seemed probable that nothing more would happen until the start of the schools' autumn term. I went back to my children to give them news of our latest victory, and we settled down to enjoy a few months, anyway, of peace.

16

'...to prison for two months...'

THE YEAR 1961 was undeniably our peak legal year; I fought four law cases during the twelve months, attended five separate hearings, traveled to London in connection with the cases ten times, and spent a total of eleven days in court. And altogether, twelve different judges and justices were concerned in adjudicating in the actions heard in that year alone.

But at the same time, the children who were the subject of this flurry of litigation went on steadily growing up, reaching and passing milestones in their lives and careers; and remained, for the most part, sublimely indifferent to the portentous certainty expressed by some of the best legal minds in the country, that the things they were, in fact, now doing were those which they would never be able to do.

In May, David came home from work one evening broken-hearted; his employer was getting rid of the cows and, it later turned out, giving up the farm. Anyone who has worked with Jerseys will understand something of what David felt; to him, it was like a personal loss. The farm and stock were finally sold in June, and David was looking for a job again; but farms with Jersey herds were few and far between.

At the end of June, we went to the Royal Norfolk Show, and there we saw the prize-winning Jersey cattle of the year. Suddenly, it occurred to me: here were the people who had Jersey herds, and we had their names and addresses in the show catalogue. David picked out the one he liked best, in Cambridgeshire, and wrote asking if they wanted a boy. Soon, he received a reply: they did and wanted him to go for an interview.

He set off early in the morning and returned proudly that evening; he had got the job, on a farm of 3,000 acres, with a herd of seventy pedigree Jersey cows.

At the end of July, two weeks after judgment was given in the Chancery appeal, he left to start a new life in his new job in Cambridgeshire. Nothing had been said about his education; he liked his employers, and they liked him, and it was not until the news of our next law case appeared in the papers that they learned who he was. By then, they had already formed their judgment; they told me, 'He's a wonderful boy.'

Felicity's days continued to be seriously and purposefully tied up with pink satin ribbons; she had started on the 'long road from barre to ballerina,' and she asked nothing more of life than that. Two days before the Chancery appeal judgment, she took part in the Anglia Academy's Summer Show at the Theatre Royal in Norwich. She was practically the only girl out of the Academy's two hundred pupils who was not nervous about appearing on the stage; happy and excited, she danced in three numbers with complete poise and assurance, looking very lovely and attracting admiration and praise from everyone.

In August, Robin reached his fifteenth birthday; and a few weeks later, he started work, learning plastering with a local builder. Like David, he had been offered a number of different jobs as soon as he was fifteen, but he kept to his decision to go into the building trade. Far from my children experiencing any difficulty in obtaining employment as they grew up, it did appear that, in fact, the demand for 'Baker infants' would exceed the supply.

And in September, after only one year's training, Felicity took her next two ballet exams, Grades II and III, both on the same day, and passed both with Honours. Her teacher described this as 'a record,' saying she had done three years' work in her first year. On several occasions during that autumn, she danced in cabaret shows given by the Anglia Academy in Norwich; and I watched her with an ache in my heart as, in her gleaming white ballet dress, brilliantly illuminated by the spotlights, she danced alone on the floor.

But with the coming of September, with the yellowing leaves and the damp, misty evenings, danger again lay ahead. The school term had started, and the Education Committee again moved in to the attack. There was no doubt at all now about what lay ahead of us; this was to be the last, bloody, hand-to-hand battle with nothing barred, which would decide my fate and my children's future once and forever.

By way of a flank attack, the Education Committee had already served on me a: 'NOTICE TO PARENT OF FAILURE OF DUTY REGARDING EDUCATION OF CHILD' in respect of Hugh, offering, as usual, the services of their inspectors to assist in satisfying them that he was receiving efficient full-time education. I received this within two weeks of the dismissal of the Chancery appeal and replied to it on the 5th of August, saying that I would be willing to agree to the Committee's Inspectors visiting Hugh, provided that they would agree to my conducting an inspection of a school child of similar age and assumed educational standard; that is, a child who had been attending for six months at the local primary school.

The Education Committee retired for some time to consider this, and it was not until September 25th that Dr. Lincoln Ralphs replied, saying that the Committee had 'decided not to accept' the arrangement which I proposed as a condition of accepting the offer of the services of the Committee's Inspectors; and they had therefore authorized the issue of a second Statutory Notice in accordance with Section 37(2)(a) of the Education Act 1944, in respect of my son Hugh, which was enclosed herewith.

To this, I replied on October 7th that although I was interested to note that the Education Committee was unwilling to agree to my 'examining' a child of Hugh's age attending the local school, it did not therefore follow that I was unwilling to agree to the Committee's Inspectors visiting my son Hugh; and perhaps they would suggest a suitable date for this?

But by then their main attack had already opened fire; at the end of September, two summonses had been served on me in respect of Felicity and Wendy, and I heard nothing more about the proposed inspection of Hugh until after these had been heard by the magistrates. I took the summonses to Mr. Hipwell and asked him to get an adjournment of the hearing if he could, so that I might have as much time as possible to prepare for the presumably inevitable consequences. I applied for, and was granted, legal aid, and the date of the hearing was finally fixed for Friday, October 13th.

There was not really any question about what the outcome would be if I lost. Although nearly everyone I spoke to said incredulously, 'They'll never do that!' it did seem obvious that, in view of the appeal judges' remarks, the magistrates would have no option but to send me to prison. The only question that remained was, how long for?

I said I thought that they would be reluctant to hit me too hard and risk appearing vindictive; that they would consider a short prison sentence sufficient to meet the judges' requirements and bring home to me what I would be in for if it happened again. I predicted a sentence of seven days on each summons, to run concurrently, making only seven days in all.

Mr. Hipwell disagreed. He said that now they had the opportunity and the approval of the appeal court, they would give me the heaviest sentence possible. But he agreed that they would want to make it look as lenient as possible too. He predicted that I would get two weeks on each summons, to run consecutively, making a month in all—which would amount to my serving exactly the same term as the more usual one month on each, concurrent, but would sound less.

It made a most interesting discussion, but personally, I was beginning to feel rather queer inside. We were all in a state of extreme apprehension when Friday the 13th came, and, accompanied by Felicity and Wendy, I met Mr. Hipwell at Dereham Magistrates' Court.

Once again, back in these familiar surroundings, I heard Mr. Brighton open the case for the Education Authority. He described, at some length, the previous legal history of the case.

'In bringing these proceedings today,' he continued, 'I am asking you, if you find Mrs. Baker guilty, to impose a sentence of imprisonment. And I am asking you also to make an order committing these children to come before the Dereham Juvenile Court.

'It is not sufficient,' he told the magistrates, 'for Mrs. Baker to say that she is against all types of formal education and is in favor of what she terms 'natural development.' She has to prove that her children are being adequately educated at home.'

What Mrs. Baker held as her own method of educating her children, he claimed, was nothing more than the normal out-of-school assistance that any ordinary parents gave to their children.

'We hold,' he said, 'that the kind of education that these children have been receiving is not adequate within the requirements of the Education Act.'

Mr. Earl then got up and stated that he was an Administrative Assistant employed by the Norfolk Local Education Committee. He produced copies of the School Attendance Orders served on me in respect of Felicity and Wendy, and the amendments to these, with Post Office forms relating to their dispatch and receipt. He also produced a certificate from the head teacher of Dereham Secondary Modern Girls' School relating to their non-attendance at that school.

He was then cross-examined by Mr. Hipwell. In reply to questions, he said that he last visited Mrs. Baker's home in May 1960. Before that, his last visit was in 1957. He saw some of the children, he said. He had no reason to suppose that they were other than carefree, healthy, and happy.

'I am not suggesting,' he added kindly, 'that, apart from the education aspect, Mrs. Baker is not doing what she can.'

The Education Authorities, he said, were at present proceeding with the preliminary notices in respect of Hugh. He agreed that there were schools, accepted by the Authorities, which did not have qualified teachers.

That concluded the evidence for the Education Committee. I then went into the witness box to give evidence.

In reply to Mr. Hipwell, I told the court that I lived at Heath Farm House, Thuxton, and I had three younger children: Hugh, aged five; Martin, aged four; and April, aged three. David was away at a job in Cambridgeshire, and Robin was working with a local builder.

'I contend that I am providing Wendy and Felicity with efficient education suitable to their age, ability, and aptitude. I think that all that is necessary can be provided in the course of a normal home life.

'As far as Felicity is concerned, her whole life interest is in ballet.' Here, Mr. Hipwell produced a testimonial from the principal of the

Anglia Academy of Dancing, stating what Felicity had achieved in her first year's training, and adding that she stood a good chance of eventually getting into a ballet company. But if that ambition was not fulfilled, she was assured of a worthwhile career as a dancing teacher. Mr. Hipwell also produced the certificates showing Felicity's success in her examinations. In reply to a further question, I said that Felicity had been going to the Anglia Academy for several months before anyone knew that she did not go to school. Her teacher had never come up against any difficulties in teaching her as a result of her education at home—quite the reverse. Felicity was more supple physically and better able to concentrate than the girls who went to school.

Felicity, I agreed, was thirteen; she would be fourteen in December. She could read and write; she read mostly books on ballet; she had written fairy stories. She had never been taught arithmetic in the formal sense, but she could do the calculations necessary for efficient housekeeping, 'which,' I said, 'is all I have ever been able to do.' She was well spoken, happy, and cheerful. And she was here at the court if the Justices wished to see her. (They didn't, of course.) In reply to a question from the Bench, 'Did she have any exercise?' I pointed out that, apart from her normal recreation of riding horses bareback, ballet training was a very strenuous form of exercise itself.

'What do you think would be the effect on her,' Mr. Hipwell asked, 'if she was now projected into a State school?'

'I think she would be very unhappy and would probably become anti-social in her outlook,' I said. 'She would develop into a very difficult character. At present, she gets on well with the other children at the ballet school. She accepts the fact that she does not go to school while other children do, in just the same way as she accepts the fact that she has red hair while other children have not. If she had to go to school, this would be about the worst time in her life to force her to go. She could not be expected to take any interest in school lessons.'

Asked about Wendy, I replied that she was twelve and would be thirteen in March. 'She is not interested in ballet like Felicity—she is an entirely different personality.' I agreed that she was a happy, healthy, cheerful child.

'If she was now sent to school,' Mr. Hipwell asked, 'what do you think would be the effect on her?'

'I think she might be completely annihilated,' I said. 'She is a courageous, even fierce, but very sensitive child; she would either break down or become fiercely anti-social. She would be much better left to grow up as she is.'

The children did, I pointed out, get the companionship of other children. Felicity did so at the ballet school; she had danced with two hundred others at the Theatre Royal. Both children helped in the house.

'Would you be prepared to send the children to the school named in the orders?' Mr. Hipwell asked.

'No,' I said. 'I should not consider doing so. I would not allow my daughters to attend a school where the manners and morals of the other children, at least outside their homes, are such that I would not wish any of my children to be contaminated by them.'

'Would you consider sending your children to any school if you had the choice?'

'I am opposed in general to formal education, to mass education, and to compulsory education,' I replied. 'I am prepared to accept that there might be a school somewhere to which I would send my children. If I knew of such a school, I would consider it, but I have not been offered the choice of any other schools. If I had the means, I should probably employ a private tutor.'

The children had been with me all their lives, I continued. Robin and David, who were now aged fifteen and sixteen, had been educated at home by my methods. Both had obtained jobs in the work they had chosen and were doing well. I had shown that I could prepare my children at home for the careers for which, by temperament and talent, they were best suited. 'A child will follow that career which expresses itself in its own personality.'

I remembered Mr. Earl's visit in May 1960, I said. That was when he called with Mr. Brighton to serve the Chancery writ. Apart from that, he had not been to the house since 1957.

'When I had to be away in London for four or five days during the hearing of the Chancery case, I left David in charge. Everything was in order when I returned,' I said.

'So far as my experience goes,' I concluded, 'I do not think state schools are suitable places for the education of the young.'

I was then cross-examined by Mr. Brighton.

'Do Felicity and Wendy do a good deal of housework?' he asked.

'They both help in the house,' I said.

'Do you have any timetable of schoolwork?'

'No,' I said. 'I think the important thing is what a child learns, not the time of day at which he learns it.'

'Have you any teaching qualifications?'

'Yes, sixteen years' experience,' I replied.

'You had no objection to sending your child to a school of dancing?'

'No,' I said. 'It is part of my method of education that the children should receive instruction from a qualified teacher in specialized subjects when they need it. Felicity went to the dancing school at her own request.'

I agreed that there were ballet schools that also provided a general education.

Mr. Brighton asked, 'Would you object to sending your daughter to such a school?'

'I could not know unless I had seen it,' I said. 'I should make a personal and individual judgment.'

'But you said you would be prepared to send your children to a suitable school?'

'I said I would be prepared to consider a school and refuse if I did not think it suitable. I do not know of any school that would meet my requirements, but I do not reject the possibility that there might be one.'

'You do not agree with school education?'

'I do not like state education.'

'Do your children know that mathematics exists?' asked Mr. Brighton.

'Yes,' I said.

'Do they know what it means?'

'Yes, I think so,' I said.

'Don't you think they should learn mathematics?'

'When they have a reason for doing so, or show an interest in it,' I said. 'That is the right time to learn.'

'Mrs. Baker,' said Mr. Brighton, 'do you realize that this case involves the possibility of your children being taken away from you and that the County Council will send them to school?'

'I realize that,' I said. 'But does the County Council realize that it will have to catch them first?'

'Have you no intention at all of sending these children to school?' Mr. Brighton asked.

'In view of the suffering that would be inflicted on them if they were compelled to go to school, I have no option but to refuse,' I said. 'It would be grossly unfair if I sent them to school now when I am threatened with imprisonment.'

Mr. Brighton sat down, and I went back to my seat at the front of the court. Mr. Hipwell stood up to make his final address to the magistrates.

Mrs. Baker, he said, had been fighting for a long time for the right to educate her children at home. She had appeared in every court in the country except, so far, the House of Lords. Last year, the County Council had attempted to have the Baker children made wards of court. Their application was refused, and this decision was upheld on appeal. Now the County Council appeared to have taken the advice given by the Court of Appeal and sought fresh redress before the magistrates in the cases of Felicity and Wendy.

'But,' said Mr. Hipwell, 'it is a bit late in the day. Both David, sixteen, and Robin, fifteen, who were included in earlier proceedings, have never attended school. Yet both of them have managed to get and hold responsible jobs. Felicity, who is now thirteen, is making excellent progress in her training at a ballet school. At this late stage, more harm than good would be done by sending these two girls to school.'

It would be wrong to break up the family by the action which the Council proposed, he said. 'No one contends that Mrs. Baker is not a fine mother. All her children are happy, healthy, well spoken, intelligent, and have loving care at home.'

Mr. Hipwell concluded his submissions, and the magistrates filed out. After a short absence, they returned and announced that they found me guilty on both charges. They then retired again to consider the sentence.

We seemed to be waiting for a very long time. I looked out of the courtroom window, and everything seemed rather unreal. Then, at last, the magistrates came back, and the Chairman announced without preamble:

'You will go to prison for two months—one month on each count, to run consecutively. And we make an order for the two children to be brought before the juvenile court.'

Mr. Hipwell immediately rose and gave notice of appeal. He had brought the forms of appeal with him, already prepared, needing only my signature. As I leaned over the table to sign them, I murmured: 'You were right. But they needn't have used a steamroller!'

I was granted bail until the hearing of the appeal. As I left the court with the two girls, a policeman stopped us in the hall and produced summonses for Felicity and Wendy to appear before the juvenile court. This was more than I could bear—that they should have summonses served on them as if they were delinquents. Furious, I snatched the documents from him as he handed them to my daughters and tore them in half. The torn halves I presented to Mr. Hipwell as he descended the stairs into the hall, so he left the court cheerfully grasping a handful of severed summonses.

At least these could not be proceeded with until after the appeal. And while there was an appeal to come, there was hope. We returned home singing my new version of the song from *Oklahoma*:

> 'Oh, what a horrible morning,
> Oh, what a horrible day—
> I've got a horrible feeling,
> Everything's coming my way—
> The policemen are standing like statues,
> The policemen are standing like statues,
> There's a look grim and sly,
> In the magistrates' eye—
> And it looks like they're giving me two months inside…'

'Whatever happened, the girls would have to be kept out of the juvenile court. But it never occurred to me to give in.

17

The Final Court

THERE was only a month between the magistrates' court and the hearing of my appeal to Quarter Sessions. I spent these few weeks trying to make arrangements for a two-month absence from my family. As time went on, people started remarking that I wasn't looking very fit. To be honest, I wasn't feeling very fit either. By the time that the day of the appeal drew near, the prospect of prison was looming over me like a nightmare.

During that time, I received a letter from Dr. Lincoln Ralphs, dated November 1st, in which he suggested that, 'without prejudice to the validity of the second Statutory Notice' concerning Hugh, it would be possible for the Committee's Inspectors to see Hugh on either the 7th or the 9th of November. To this, I replied that in view of the forthcoming appeal, the meaning and implications of which my son Hugh was fully aware, I felt that to have him subjected to a visit from the Committee's Inspectors at this time would be wholly unreasonable. I suggested that the inspection should be postponed until after the hearing of the appeal, when, I said, I would communicate with the Education Committee again. Dr. Ralphs replied on November 8th, agreeing to this.

On the day before the hearing of the appeal, I received a letter from Mr. Hipwell, asking me to telephone him as soon as possible. When I did so, he was out, but I spoke to his secretary, who said he had left a message for me, saying that we must appeal against sentence only, not conviction. Horrified, I said, 'No, no, NO!'—and she agreed to tell Mr. Hipwell this.

The appeal was heard, as before, at the Shirehall in Norwich, on

November 15th, 1961. When I arrived at the Shirehall, I met my counsel, Mr. Geoffrey Leach, who explained that he must advise me to appeal against the sentence only, as, in view of the long series of court cases in which the Justices had rejected my views, he felt he should warn me that if I appealed again against conviction, I would almost certainly go to prison.

There were only a few minutes before we had to go into court, and I was faced with a difficult and frightening decision. I had no wish to inflict more suffering on the children by quixotically courting a prison sentence for the sake of my views. If it came to that, I was terrified myself at the prospect of going to prison.

But nothing could alter the fact that I believed in my own views, and I felt that I could not possibly do other than stand by my plea of not guilty to the charge of failing to provide my children with a proper education. I told Mr. Leach that while I appreciated his point, I could not agree; and so my appeal against conviction and sentence began.

Up to now, the proceedings at the Quarter Sessions and the surroundings of the Shirehall had been familiar to me; but this time, there was one big difference. When Mr. Leach left me, I was put in the custody of a woman prison officer from Holloway Gaol. She led me into the dock through a door on which was painted the notice: I pointed to it and asked my escort, 'Who painted that?' She grinned and replied, 'Someone who had been to school!'

As we entered the dock, she took my handbag away—from now on, I was a prisoner. She sat beside me and shut the door. The Justices entered—Mr. Roger North, the Chairman, and one man and one woman magistrate. Counsel for the Education Committee—Mr. Ives, an old opponent of mine—rose to open their case.

It was the duty of an Education Authority, said Mr. Ives, to see that every child in its area received an efficient, full-time education suitable to its age, ability, and aptitude. It was also the duty of the Authority to take proceedings against parents who failed to conform to this statute.

What Mrs. Baker had to do, he said, was to satisfy the court that her children were receiving efficient, full-time education within the meaning of the 1944 Act. In the opinion of the Education Committee, the education these children were receiving was not adequate.

Mr. Earl then went into the witness box and repeated the evidence he had given in the magistrates' court. He had visited Mrs. Baker in May 1960, he said, and before that during 1957. Asked by Mr. Leach whether he saw either Felicity or Wendy in May 1960, Mr. Earl said he did not think so.

'There is no suggestion that Mrs. Baker is not doing her best for these children?' Mr. Leach asked him.

Mr. Earl looked down his nose and replied, 'She provides food, clothing, and shelter.'

'She is a good mother?' pressed Mr. Leach.

'I prefer not to comment,' replied Mr. Earl.

At the conclusion of Mr. Earl's evidence, I went into the witness box.

None of my children, I said in reply to Mr. Leach, had ever been to school. They had all learned reading, writing, and basic arithmetic. They had learned history and geography from the school programmes on the radio and from books. In their everyday life, they had learned natural history, riding, cookery, and photography, and the girls had learned household management and childcare. They had all been taught to speak well and behave well.

'Education is a training for life,' I said. 'It is too wide a subject to be confined within the four walls of a classroom. My children do not sit at desks to study set lessons at set times. They are taught a subject when they show interest in it. When they are interested, they ask questions and are told what they want to know.'

Everyone who had met the children, I said, agreed that they appeared well educated, that they were well spoken, well mannered, and well behaved.

'Felicity,' I went on, 'is already an accomplished young lady. By my standards, she is better educated than she would have been at school. She shows considerable talent for ballet and attends a ballet school in Norwich, where she has now passed three examinations in one year. She is also a skilled photographer and a very good housewife, and her favourite recreation is riding horses bareback. At the ballet school, she has a distinct advantage over the other girls, who are often tired by the long hours of school and homework, while Felicity is fresh in body and mind.

'Wendy is a far more immature child than Felicity and the most sensitive of all my children. I think she would be very greatly harmed by going to school.'

In reply to another question from Mr. Leach, I said that the children had not learned languages. 'I think the only way to learn a foreign language is to go to the country where it is spoken and learn it there. But Felicity has had to learn the very comprehensive French terms relating to ballet, and she has done so better than many of the girls who learn French at school.'

At this point, the Chairman, Mr. Roger North, turned to me and said, 'Can we get this down in order? What subjects do you say these girls are learning? Give me a list.'

'Reading and writing,' I said, 'and basic arithmetic; geography and history; natural history; photography and riding; cooking, household management, and child care. They are taught correct speech and good behaviour. And, in the case of Felicity, ballet and French where it relates to ballet.' I paused. 'May I include the art of living?'

'Well—I don't know about that,' said Mr. North, writing it all down. 'No science?'

'No,' I said. 'I want to produce children who are going to do something creative, not destructive. I do not want to encourage anything which might destroy the world.'

'You have two older children, Mrs. Baker,' resumed Mr. Leach, 'who have been educated in the same way?'

'Yes,' I said. 'My two eldest sons are both out at work now— David, who is sixteen, on a dairy farm, and Robin, who is fifteen, with a local builder.'

'It appeared from certain newspaper reports,' said Mr. Leach, 'that David had sole charge of a herd of pedigree cows, but this is an exaggeration, isn't it?'

'When David was working in his first job near Dereham,' I said, 'he was left in sole charge of the herd of ten pedigree Jersey cows for a week while his employer was away on holiday. During that time, two of the cows calved, and David dealt with that, as well as everything else that had to be done, single-handed. But he is now working with a show herd of seventy pedigree Jerseys, on a 3,000-acre farm in Cambridgeshire. His employers speak very highly of him.'

Here, Mr. North intervened again to say, 'But I daresay you can look after cows without education?'

'I think the time has passed,' I said, 'for the traditional picture of a farmer driving his cows home to milk. Farming is more complicated today, and looking after cows involves a good deal more than that. It requires mental ability and considerable knowledge and experience.'

'And is Robin also doing well?' asked Mr. Leach.

'Yes,' I said. 'Robin has always showed skill with his hands, combined with a certain creative ability. He is demonstrating both in his work as a plasterer—a highly skilled trade. His employer also speaks well of him.

'I think I have made a much better job of their education than the authorities would have done,' I added. 'My sons have shown that they can stand on their own feet. I am very proud of both of them.'

When Mr. Leach had finished his examination, I stayed in the witness box to be cross-examined by Mr. Ives.

'You are determined that your children should never go to school?' Mr. Ives asked.

'It would be nothing but the utmost cruelty to send them to school now,' I replied. 'I do not see how any competent education authority could think otherwise. It would destroy them.'

'But none of your children has ever gone to school?' asked Mr. Ives.

'No,' I said. 'I have not sent my children to school because I believe the harm it would do them would by far outweigh the good. They would become contaminated by the bad habits of speech and behaviour of the children who attend the secondary modern schools.'

'Do you think they can succeed in life without having gone to school?'

'I see no reason why not,' I said. 'There have been many successful people in this world who never went to school.'

'Mrs. Baker,' said Mr. Ives, 'with three younger children to look after, how can you find time to educate these children?'

'I have always found sufficient time,' I said. 'I have even had time to write a book. I usually get up in the morning at five, and I seldom go to bed before midnight.

'My children learn continuously, throughout their normal daily life. Education should be regular and consistent. It is ridiculous to stuff children's minds for a few months and then let them go entirely during the holidays, as they do in school.'

Mr. Ives looked at his notes.

'At a previous appeal to Quarter Sessions,' he said, 'Lord Evershed suggested that there was a danger of your children growing up cut off from the rest of the community?'

'That is utterly absurd,' I said, 'and my children have already proved that Lord Evershed was wrong. He suggested that my boys would be unable to support themselves when they grew up, but both David and Robin obtained good jobs on their own initiative. David, at sixteen, is now living away from home, has a life of his own, and is self-supporting. They have never been cut off from anything except the unnatural world of school, and they have never experienced any difficulties as they grew up, as a result of their home education.'

'You are opposed to state education, Mrs. Baker?' asked Mr. Ives.

'I think it is an excellent thing that education should be made available,' I said, 'but it should not be compulsory, and it should not be a criminal offence to keep children away from school.'

At the conclusion of my evidence, the court adjourned for lunch. I was granted bail until two o'clock—but I didn't want any lunch. When the court resumed, I was back in my place in the dock, with the prison officer by my side, and Mr. Leach addressed the Justices.

The principal requirement of the Education Act, he told the court, was that children should receive an education which would foster their spiritual, moral, mental, and physical development. On three of these—spiritual, moral, and physical—there was no dispute.

'On the fourth—mental development—can this be achieved only by sitting behind wooden desks in a secondary modern school?'

asked Mr. Leach. 'These schools do not even give a certificate of education comparable with other schools.

'This lady is not a crank,' he said, 'but someone who holds very strong views about the education of her children.'

He asked the court to say that these children were receiving education which would foster their spiritual, moral, physical, and mental development, as required by the Education Act, and allow the appeal.

The Justices left the court, and I sat and waited. Now that the effort of fighting was over, I felt tired and frightened, and the gleam of hope that had arisen in my heart when Mr. North started questioning me—he was the only judge, throughout all the years, who had shown any real interest in what I was saying—flickered out. I was back facing reality, with a warder by my side. Mr. Leach walked across the court to speak to me. He had done all he could, he said.

I nodded, not sure of my voice. Then I swallowed hard and leaned over the edge of the dock. Was there any further right of appeal? I asked. Mr. Leach said there was, but taking the matter any further wasn't covered by my Legal Aid Certificate. 'You can ask for it yourself,' he said and showed me the relevant passages in a law book. 'You refer to this section—and this,' he explained, quoting the appropriate numbers. I tried desperately to memorize them. He must have seen that by then my mind was beyond taking in any precise detail. 'All right, don't worry—I'll do it for you, and we'll deal with the legal aid after that,' he said. I gulped and said, 'Thank you.' And then the Justices came back.

Mr. Leach returned to his seat, and I listened, at first in agony.

'What we have got to decide,' said Mr. North, 'is whether the education these children are getting complies with the Education Act of 1944. We cannot see that it doesn't.'

Suddenly, I realized what he was saying.

'There has been little evidence,' continued Mr. North, 'apart from what Mrs. Baker has told us, of what education the children have acquired. An education official said he had visited the home in May 1960 but was not sure whether he saw the girls. It was impossible for him to say what degree of education they had attained.

'Mrs. Baker has told us a great deal about her views on education, and we cannot see that what she has described fails to satisfy the rather wide terms of the Education Act. The appeal therefore succeeds.'

After seven years, I had won.

It did not matter now that my eyes were full of tears. I stood up and said, 'Thank you!' At my side, apparently unable to believe what she had heard either, the prison officer grabbed my arm and tried to pull me down again. But it was really true. And this decision also wiped out the magistrates' order to bring the girls before the juvenile court. I left the dock victorious—and free. I had won outright at last.

I went to the dancing school, where Felicity, in the true tradition of the stage, was carrying on with her ballet lesson. 'It's all right!' I told her. 'We won!'

She and I were immediately pounced upon by Mr. Ted Chamberlain from the local B.B.C. office and rushed to their studios to appear in the news on television. When we got home, the other children had already heard it on the radio. The next day, the newspaper headlines announced, 'Mrs. Baker Wins Her Battle'—'Win for Rebel Mother.' The complete transition from defeat to victory was rather overwhelming.

Two weeks after the appeal, I wrote, as I had promised, to the Chief Education Officer:

'With reference to your letter of November 8th, following the hearing of my appeal, at which it was decided by the Court that my two daughters, Felicity and Wendy, were receiving a proper education in accordance with the requirements of the Education Act, there would appear to be no further point in arranging a visit by your inspectors to see my son Hugh, as the education which he is receiving is the same, with due regard for his age, ability, and aptitude, as that accepted by the Court.

'I assume that you agree with this?'

In reply, Dr. Lincoln Ralphs wrote on November 29th:

'Thank you for your letter of 28th November 1961.

'I have no reason to believe that the Authority would wish to vary the statement made in my letter of 25th September 1961, that they are not satisfied that Hugh is receiving efficient full-time education suitable to his age, ability, and aptitude and that it is expedient that he should attend school.

'In your letter of 7th October 1961, you expressed your willingness to accept the offer of the services of the Committee's inspectors to satisfy the Authority that he was receiving efficient and suitable education.

'This offer is still available, and I shall be pleased to know whether you wish to take advantage of it or whether you wish me to accept your letter of 28th November 1961 as indicating that you are not prepared for the inspectors to visit.'

I did not reply to this until after the schools' Christmas holidays. Then, on January 25th, 1962, I wrote again, saying that I could see no point in Hugh being visited by the Committee's inspectors when the education he was receiving had already received the approval of the court.

Dr. Lincoln Ralphs replied on January 30th:

'With reference to your letter of 25th January 1962, the decision of the Norfolk Quarter Sessions Appeal Committee on 15th November 1961 related to Felicity and Wendy and not to Hugh. Hugh's case must therefore be considered on its merits, and there is no information before any court as to the education he is receiving; the Education Authority's opinion is that expressed in the second Statutory Notice of 25th September 1961, to the effect that the Authority are not satisfied that Hugh is receiving efficient full-time education suitable to his age, ability, and aptitude and that it is expedient that he should attend school.

'I suggest, therefore, that you should accept the offer of the services of the Committee's inspectors to satisfy the Authority that Hugh is receiving efficient and suitable education.'

To this, I replied on February 17th:

'I am in receipt of your letter of January 30th and note your remarks. I would point out, however, that my evidence before the Quarter Sessions Appeals Committee did in fact constitute a comprehensive statement of my educational methods, and the Chairman, when giving his decision, stated: 'Mrs. Baker has told us a great deal about her views on education, and we cannot see that what she has described fails to satisfy the rather wide terms of the Education Act of 1944.'

'My son Hugh is being educated in accordance with these same methods and views.

'Perhaps, therefore, you would be good enough to inform me on what grounds the Education Authority has formed the opinion that they are not satisfied that Hugh is receiving efficient and suitable education, when all the evidence already before them concerning this has been accepted as satisfactory by the court?'

Dr. Lincoln Ralphs replied on February 22nd:

'Thank you for your letter of 17th February 1962.

'It is the duty of the Authority to be satisfied by the parent that a child is receiving efficient full-time education suitable to his age, ability, and aptitude, either by regular attendance at school or otherwise. The question the Authority must ask themselves, therefore, is on what grounds can they be satisfied.

'If you are not prepared to accept the offer which has repeatedly been made of the services of the Committee's inspectors, it seems to me that you have denied to the Authority the grounds on which they might be satisfied that Hugh is receiving a suitable education. 'The matters under consideration at the Norfolk Quarter Sessions Appeal Committee on 15th November 1961 related to Felicity and Wendy, and not to Hugh, and, as I stated in my letter of 30th January 1962, there is no information before any court as to the education he is receiving.'

This seemed so obviously absurd, in view of the fact that I had stated on three occasions that the education Hugh was receiving was the same, in all essentials, as that approved by the court, that I did not feel it was necessary to reply to this letter; and I heard nothing more from Dr. Lincoln Ralphs about Hugh. But by then, I had heard from Mr. Hipwell that the Education Committee was making a last bid to retrieve the whole situation. They were appealing, by way of a case stated, as I had done two years earlier, to the Divisional Court.

This appeal was not heard until July 1962, by which time Felicity had passed her fourth ballet examination with honors; David had completed his first year in Cambridgeshire; Robin had left his first job and taken an apprenticeship as a plasterer with a building firm in Dereham; Wendy was thirteen; Hugh had passed his sixth birthday; Martin, at five, had reached compulsory school age; and April was four.

On July 17th, I took my seat again in the Lord Chief Justice's court and, for the second time, heard Mr. Paul Wrightson conduct the Education Authority's case.

I knew from Mr. Hipwell that the first round of the battle had been won already, in the wording of the case stated by the Justices. This document set out very clearly the evidence given before the Appeals Committee and the terms of the Justices' decision. There had been considerable argument about this, as the Education Committee insisted that the Justices had, in fact, given their decision on the grounds that the prosecution had failed to prove their case, as opposed to a finding that I had succeeded in proving mine; and in education proceedings, unlike any other legal actions, it is the defendant who has to prove his case. But Mr. Hipwell finally succeeded in getting the case drawn as he wanted it, the Justices agreeing that the wording Mr. Leach had included was a true statement of the case:

'We were of the opinion that the appellant had proved that the education given to the said children complied with efficient full-time education as meant by the Education Act 1944 and that the appellant had not failed to cause the said children to receive efficient full-time education suitable to their age, ability, and aptitude otherwise than by regular attendance at school and accordingly allowed the appeals.'

Epic words, which brought to an end a struggle that, as Mr. Hipwell said, had been carried on through nearly every law court in the land.

There was, therefore, very little left for counsel for the Education Committee to say, other than to claim that the decision of the Quarter Sessions Appeals Committee was 'perverse.' As he opened his case, the Lord Chief Justice, Lord Parker, commented, 'But this case came before me two years ago. Have these children still not gone to school?'

Mr. Wrightson explained about the delay caused by the Chancery proceedings. He then read out extracts from my statements in the various court cases during the previous seven years, including that made in the Divisional Court two years before and my statement during the last Quarter Sessions appeal.

'You will see, my Lord,' he said almost plaintively, 'that in all these cases, Mrs. Baker has said exactly the same thing.'

I felt that it might perhaps reasonably be said that this at least showed integrity and consistency of mind on the part of Mrs. Baker.

Mr. Wrightson argued for nearly an hour. At the end of his submissions, the three judges—Lord Parker, Mr. Justice Widgery, and Mr. Justice Winn—conferred together. Then, Lord Parker indicated to Mr. Leach that it would not even be necessary for him to present my case.

'The Appeals Committee was satisfied that Mrs. Baker is giving the children efficient full-time education. A very strong case must be shown for this court to say that no reasonable bench of magistrates could come to that conclusion,' Lord Parker said.

On my much-disputed educational methods, Lord Parker commented, 'All children start learning by asking questions. It is a recognized method of education.' The appeal was dismissed.

So, after seven years, the brick wall crumbled and fell. I had won my victory in the final court.

18

Summing Up

AFTER ALL the smoke of the High Court battle had cleared and the sounds of the firing had died away, I surveyed the battlefield behind me, where, I was told, I had made legal history and where I had won my ten-year fight for the right of a mother to care for her own children—the most fundamental right on earth.

People had often said to me, 'Doesn't all this make you feel very important?' But, in fact, what impressed me most was the absurdity of its ever having been necessary; the incredible fuss the Education Authorities had made over just one mother who would not agree to sending her children to school. And it was not that the Authorities, as they had so often maintained, were so very anxious about the welfare of the children; indeed, the more my children achieved, the more obvious it became that they were not in need of 'rescue,' the harder the Education Committee tried to ensure that they did not get away.

In the course of all these proceedings, a great deal of nonsense was talked about my children, their upbringing and education, my methods, and my views.

In the London Appeal Court, Lord Justice Upjohn said that I was 'in clear breach of my duties as a parent under the Education Act and had disregarded my natural duty as a mother.' But as an individual capable of independent thought, I do not agree with what are termed my duties under the Act, and my natural duty as a mother is to do what is best for my children without regard for any other consideration whatever. No Act of Parliament is capable of deciding the upbringing and destiny of any individual child, and any Act that restricts the natural right of the parent to care for the child is in breach of a higher law than that of Parliament. Or perhaps the Fifth Commandment should now be altered to read, 'Honor your father and your mother, provided they comply with the Education Act'?

In the same court, Mr. Sparrow, counsel for the County Council, stated that the children were being 'used as servants.' If this is a fair description of children in their teens sharing in the domestic work of their home, then every wife and mother in this country is being used as a slave. Personally, I think that a good training in domestic work is one of the first essentials in the education of all girls and is useful to many boys, whether they marry or have to cope with a bachelor life on their own; and more people have suffered from knowing too little about domestic work than from having had to do too much.

There was also Mr. Sparrow's equally far-fetched suggestion that the children were 'like little hermits,' and Lord Evershed's insistence that they were 'cut off from the rest of the community,' although neither Lord Evershed nor Mr. Sparrow made it quite clear whether they were referring to our life in our 'isolated farmhouse' or only to the fact that the children did not go to school. Perhaps the idea of living in the middle of a field might seem appalling to the softened citizens of our present civilization; but as the field took only three minutes to cross on foot, and at the end of it was a road and the houses of our neighbors, we were no more isolated than many country families; and if these circumstances had made my children more self-reliant and practical than the average schoolchild, I counted this an advantage. If, on the other hand, the children were said to be 'like hermits' because they did not go to school, then it must follow that all adult people, not in the army or some similar organization, living independent lives in their own homes and meeting people when and where they need or wish to do so, are living 'like hermits' too.

I am well aware that what has annoyed many people most about my children's education is the idea of any child not being exactly 'like all the others'—although what there is about 'the others' to make this desirable I have never been able to see. (One woman to whom I had remarked on my children's record of good health responded crossly, 'They ought to have had a lot of infectious diseases—like other children!') One of my strongest reasons for keeping my children away from school has been to avoid their being influenced, at a very early age, by an assortment of other people's children, in whom I had no choice and over whom I had no control. It is easy to say that children must learn to 'mix with all sorts,' but the time to do it is not during their most impressionable years. No one would deny the folly of encouraging teenagers to associate with undesirable companions; it is utterly wrong that children of tender age should be forced to do so. And a shy child does not become sociable by being forced into the company of others; you do not get to like people by having their company thrust upon you. Can there be any greater isolation than that of an unhappy child alone in a crowd?

It is also noticeable that this objection to a child being 'different' is far stronger if the 'different' child appears to be happy and successful. It seems incredible to me that anyone should regard this cult of sameness, which is inflicted on schoolchildren, as being a part of any real education. Felicity and Wendy, in their turquoise and pale-green dresses, standing on the platform of the local station a little apart from a crowd of navy-blue-uniformed schoolgirls, looked like a bunch of flowers against a row of cabbages.

The contention of Lord Evershed, repeated afterwards by Mr. Brighton, that my children's education amounted to 'little more than a conscientious parent would give a child in any case,' is not, in fact, one with which I would disagree. It is indeed my contention that school teaching is virtually useless because all the basic education of any value to a child is, or should be, what is learned from the child's parents and close associates in the course of a good upbringing in a good home. And if the Education Authorities really do insist that most children do, and all children should, learn reading, writing, arithmetic, and a number of other subjects in their own homes out of school hours, it seems strange that so much time and money, and so many wasted child-hours, should be expended on teaching them the same things in schools.

No one, I think, would maintain that the whole period which

children spend in school is occupied with serious mental or physical training. It seems to be generally assumed that there is some benefit to a child implicit in the mere fact of being in a school, which is included in the hours allowed for in the term 'full-time' education. Yet too often the out-of-class periods in schools achieve only the acquisition of bad manners and behaviour; and for a great deal of the time in class, the teacher is filling the children's ears, and not their minds. It is a prerequisite of all learning that the mind should be receptive, interested, and absorbent; but the method of teaching employed in schools stultifies instead of encouraging this. When a child is interested in a subject, then, and only then, is the time to learn; and you cannot enforce by law that every child will take an interest in the same subject at the same time.

When I was at school, I was quite hopeless at geography and never acquired more than a vague idea of the geography even of my own country. I was equally hopeless at arithmetic, having no interest or ability whatever in handling figures. Five years after I left school, I was working in a publishing office where I had to handle a card index giving the names and addresses of subscribers to the magazine. After I had been doing this for two or three months, I realized that I had learned the counties and postal towns of several hundred villages all over England. Being the addresses of people with whom I corresponded, they had come to life for me, and I was able to visualize the country as a whole, which I had never been able to do while I was at school. At the same time, I had also to prepare the banking every week, including the listing and totaling of several hundred postal orders. At first, this terrified me, and I wondered what would happen if I made mistakes; but I soon found out that if I did, all that happened was that the bank sent a courteous little printed slip, pointing out, and stating that they had corrected, the error. I realized that school values were false; in adult life, reasonable mistakes were allowed for and dealt with. As my confidence increased, so did my skill in adding up, and soon the bank had no need to send out corrections. Both these were subjects in which, in themselves, I had no interest; they became comprehensible to me only when they were connected with the work that I wanted to do.

I do not suppose, if my interest had not been awakened in this way, I should ever have learned to add figures accurately, or acquired any realistic knowledge of English geography, any more than I have ever been able to learn algebra, geometry, Latin, or chemistry. But I am equally sure that if I had a need for any of these subjects in connection with something in which I was interested, I would be able to learn what was needed without difficulty. Or if I could not, it would indicate that the thing in question was beyond my capabilities anyway. Both children and adults are happiest—and most successful—doing those things which they know they can do and really want to do. Too much time is spent in schools trying to force children to study subjects for which they are not ready or in which they have no interest, at the expense of those for which they already have a natural ability.

One more recent comment on the result of my children's education I found peculiarly striking. Mr. Owen Leeming, interviewing us for the B.B.C. during our broadcast, 'The Children Who Stay at Home,' on September 9th, 1962, described them as appearing 'innocent.' This was not the first time I had heard them referred to in similar terms; a lady living in a nearby village, who had seen my daughters on the train to Norwich, remarked on their 'look of purity.' I had not previously considered the matter from quite that angle; but faced with these two concurring judgments, I did so, and I came to the conclusion that this was indeed what the Lord Chief Justice would call a finding of fact.

I had brought up my children on the assumption that children are, automatically, pure and innocent; but when I came to consider the point, I did realize that my older sons and daughters still had, in their teens, a look of purity and innocence that made them stand out from their fellows. Mr. Leeming appeared undecided whether, in teenage children, this was a good or a bad thing. But what struck me most forcibly was the fact that we live in a world where innocence and purity in children are sufficiently startling to provoke comment.

In any case, just what does this 'innocence' consist of? Not ignorance, certainly not ignorance of what are commonly known as the facts of life, since being brought up in the country and having observed the whole cycle of animal life, they had accepted these since infancy. David, at the age of five, did indeed provide me with a problem which none of the child experts I had read appeared to have thought of: having asked, and been told simply and factually, how babies were conceived and born, he considered for a little, and then said very matter-of-factly, yes, he saw—but could his father and I show him? It took a good deal of insight into the utterly innocent mind of the five-year-old child to reasonably answer that one.

In their early teens, therefore, having by then helped on the farms for several years, seen me through three pregnancies, and associated with many different—although mostly adult—types of people, they definitely knew the facts of life; they had also acquired a noticeable maturity of outlook; they were practical in their approach to events; they were self-possessed and self-reliant. And they stood out among contemporary school-children because they had a look of innocence. I could not avoid the rather disturbing conclusion that the explanation did in fact lie in their lack of contact with other children. Lacking continual contact with other young people also passing through the difficult stage of transition from childhood into adolescence, they had never had their cruder emotions prematurely or artificially aroused, or had to come into contact with depravity of mind and thought before they were old enough to deal with them. In protecting them from contamination by the bad manners and stupid behaviour of the majority of the local school-children, I had achieved something more: I had kept their minds free from the first adolescent smearings of dirt and depravity. And I see no reason why they should not continue through life with this same unsullied outlook, since with full maturity they will acquire the mental filter through which most intelligent adults are able to strain out the ugliness of physical existence and retain the good and worthwhile in their own lives.

At the same time, my children have not been sheltered in any way from any knowledge that could be of value to them; throughout their childhood the girls have understood the danger of accepting familiarity from strangers and have maintained an unassailed reserve in public; the boys have been warned of the existence of homosexuality and appreciate the unwisdom of casual sexual behaviour. In this respect, all of them have been brought up on a slight variation of the marriage service, which I believe should be made clear to all young people: the *purpose of sex is the procreation of children*; a wider understanding of which basic truth would clear up a lot of nastiness in the world today.

I am convinced that nothing which a child is told, factually and calmly, in its own home, disturbs its natural 'innocence,' but only widens its understanding. It is the constant association with other, immature, and not unmuddied minds during the 'mixing' process regarded by most people as so desirable a part of school education that destroys the natural and intelligent purity of the growing child. The lack of innocence in the average schoolgirl or schoolboy today is not approaching maturity; rather, it is a symptom of perpetual adolescence. It is true maturity to acquire knowledge and still to lack any evidence of depravity.

There has been one other notable comment on my children's outlook on life: their capacity, and indeed their liking, for work. Here at least are young people who do not think in terms of less work and more money; they have been brought up to regard work as a natural part of life, and they are happy in the work they have chosen to do.

A year after our final victory, David, at eighteen, is still working with his Jersey herd; competent, reliable, happy in his independence; dreaming of, and planning for, the day when he will have a farm of his own.

Robin, at seventeen, has completed his first year as an apprentice plasterer and has obtained a transfer to a larger firm in Norwich. In July 1963, he took his first exam at the Norwich Technical College—the first written examination ever to be taken by any of my children outside a court—and out of a class of twelve boys, he was one of the seven who passed.

Felicity, at fifteen, is still training for a career in ballet. In August 1962 she changed to the Russian method, finding this more satisfying because it is more difficult and the training is harder than the Cecchetti method she was studying before. She is now a student at the Norwich School of Dance and Drama, where she won the school's cup for ballet in July 1963, having taken her fifth examination a month previously and passed with Honours. Her examiner reported, 'She shows marked promise,' and a well-known teacher has said of her, 'When she dances, she lights up the room.'

Wendy, who has been in legal danger for most of her life, is now, at fourteen, learning to live without fear and spread her wings in the sun. She has decided to learn hairdressing, for which she shows considerable talent, as a career; but says that 'what she really wants is to be a mother,' and if this is the outcome of her education at home, I don't think I have anything to be ashamed of.

This, then, is the end of my long, lone, legal battle; and these the children, who all their lives will be the living witnesses for or against me. The four who won the ultimate victory—there is not a failure so far amongst them; and the three who are growing up into a new world—a world free from the shadow of the Education Committee.

Hugh, at seven, spends his days gardening, playing with his brothers and sisters, making things—from birthday cards to combines—and inventing toys and games of his own. He has built himself a playhouse in a corner of the garden out of old pieces of wood and sheets of corrugated iron, painted it red, turquoise blue, and yellow, and made a table and chairs, a sideboard, and a pretend oven inside, with space enough for us all to come to tea. A wooden path leads up to the door, with flower beds on each side where he grows cornflowers, nasturtiums, marigolds, and lettuces; and he is now starting to write a book about it. 'Mr. Milne wrote a book about the House at Pooh Corner,' he said to me thoughtfully, 'and you wrote a book about the House on the Hill, so I shall write a book about my house, and I shall call it *The House of Days*.'

Martin, at six, has the distinction of being the first member of our family who has never even had a School Attendance Order served on him. A willing lieutenant under Hugh's leadership, he is also a protective elder brother to April and takes her for walks to pick wildflowers and hogweed when Hugh wants to play on his own.

And April, fair, five, and free, has already seen all that she wants of law courts. She can write the alphabet and her own name, she can count up to fifty, and she has a mind of her own. April sits on

the lawn in the golden autumn sunlight, singing our own version
of the song from *Annie Get Your Gun*:

> 'Folks like us could never fuss
> With schools or books or learning.
> Still, we beat the N.C.C.—
> Doing what comes naturally!'

Thuxton
September 1963

EDUCATION ACT, 1944

Section 36

It shall be the duty of the parent of every child of compulsory school age to cause him to receive efficient full-time education suitable to his age, ability, and aptitude, either by regular attendance at school or otherwise.

Section 37

(1) If it appears to a local education authority that the parent of any child of compulsory school age in their area is failing to perform the duty imposed on him by the last foregoing section, it shall be the duty of the authority to serve upon the parent a notice requiring him, within such time as may be specified in the notice, not being less than fourteen days from the service thereof, to satisfy the authority that the child is receiving efficient full-time education suitable to his age, ability, and aptitude either by regular attendance at school or otherwise.

(2) If, after such a notice has been served upon a parent by a local education authority, the parent fails to satisfy the authority in accordance with the requirements of the notice that the child to whom the notice relates is receiving efficient full-time education suitable to his age, ability, and aptitude, then, if in the opinion of the authority it is expedient that he should attend school, the authority shall serve upon the parent an order in the prescribed form (hereinafter referred to as a 'school attendance order') requiring him to cause the child to become a registered pupil at a school named in the order:

Provided that before serving such an order upon a parent, the authority shall, where practicable, afford him an opportunity of selecting the school to be named in the order, and if a school is selected by him, that school shall, unless the Minister otherwise directs, be the school named in the order.

(3) If the local education authority are of opinion that the school selected by the parent as the school to be named in a school attendance order is unsuitable to the age, ability, or aptitude of the child with respect to whom the order is to be made, or that the attendance of the child at the school so selected would involve unreasonable expense to the authority, the authority may, after giving to the parent notice of their intention to do so, apply to the Minister for a direction determining what school is to be named in the order.

(4) If at any time while a school attendance order is in force with respect to any child, the parent of the child makes application to the local education authority by whom the order was made, requesting that another school be substituted for that named in the order, or requesting that the order be revoked on the ground that arrangements have been made for the child to receive efficient full-time education suitable to his age, ability, and aptitude otherwise than at school, the authority shall amend or revoke the order in compliance with the request unless they are of opinion that the proposed change of school is unreasonable or inexpedient in the interests of the child, or that no satisfactory arrangements have been made for the education of the child otherwise than at school, as the case may be; and if a parent is aggrieved by a refusal of the authority to comply with any such request, he may refer the question to the Minister, who shall give such direction thereon as he thinks fit.

(5) If any person upon whom a school attendance order is served fails to comply with the requirements of the order, he shall be guilty of an offence against this section unless he proves that he is causing the child to receive efficient full-time education suitable to his age, ability, and aptitude otherwise than at school.

(6) If in proceedings against any person for a failure to comply with a school attendance order that person is acquitted, the court may direct that the school attendance order shall cease to be in force, but without prejudice to the duty of the local education authority to take further action under this section if at any time the authority are of opinion that, having regard to any change of circumstances, it is expedient so to do.

(7) Save as provided by the last foregoing subsection, a school attendance order made with respect to any child shall, subject to any amendment thereof which may be made by the local education authority, continue in force so long as he is of compulsory school age unless revoked by that authority.

Section 76
In the exercise and performance of all powers and duties conferred and imposed on them by the Act, the Minister and local education authorities shall have regard to the general principle that, so far as is compatible with the provision of general instruction and training and the avoidance of unreasonable public expenditure, pupils are to be educated in accordance with the wishes of their parents.

Acknowledgements

The author wishes to express her appreciation of the invaluable help in her battles given by all her legal advisers who figure in this chronicle; and particularly by Mr. James Hipwell, whose unfailing patience, skill, and energy achieved so much.

Acknowledgements are due to the Bedfordshire Education Committee, the Acting Deputy Clerk of the Peace for Norfolk, and the Norfolk Education Committee, for permission to publish their letters. An extract from *Perseus in the Wind* by Freya Stark is quoted by kind permission of John Murray (Publishers) Ltd.

The author would also like to take this opportunity of thanking the many people to whom she has not been able to reply personally, who have written to her expressing their sympathy, encouragement, and support for her views.

www.ingramcontent.com/pod-product-compliance
Lightning Source LLC
Chambersburg PA
CBHW051259210726
48287CB00002B/572